Jim Harrison, an outdoorsman and man of letters, lives with his family in northern Michigan, USA. With six novels and seven collections of poetry to his name he is considered one of the finest American writers of his generation.

Fiction

Wolf
A Good Day to Die
Farmer
Warlock
Sundog
Dalva

Poetry

Plain Song
Locations
Outlyer
Letters to Yesenin
Returning to Earth
Selected & New Poems
The Theory and Practice of
    Rivers & Other Poems

Jim Harrison

LEGENDS
OF THE FALL

Paladin

An Imprint of Grafton Books
A Division of HarperCollinsPublishers

Paladin
An Imprint of GraftonBooks
A Division of HarperCollins*Publishers*
77–85 Fulham Palace Road,
Hammersmith, London W6 8JB

Published in Paladin Books1991
9 8 7 6 5 4 3 2 1

First published in Great Britain by
Collins Harvill 1980

The lines from 'Gacela of the Dark Death' (translated by Stephen Spender and J. L. Gili), 'Casida of the Reclining Woman' (translated by W. S. Merwin) and 'The Faithless Wife' (translated by Stephen Spender and J. L. Gili) are from *The Selected Poems of Federico Garcia Lorca*, translated by Stephen Spender, J. L. Gili and W. S. Merwin. Copyright 1955 by New Directions Publishing Corporation. Reprinted by permission of New Directions.

ISBN 0-586-09138-6

Printed and bound in Great Britain by
Collins, Glasgow

Set in Electra

TO GUY AND JACK

REVENGE

Revenge is a dish better served cold.
(Old Sicilian adage)

CHAPTER
I

You could not tell if you were a bird descending (and there was a bird descending, a vulture) if the naked man was dead or alive. The man didn't know himself and the bird was tentative when he reached the ground and made a croaking sideward approach, askance and looking off down the chaparral in the arroyo as if expecting company from the coyotes. Carrion was shared not by the sharer's design but by a pattern set before anyone knew there were patterns. The vulture had just eaten a rattler run over by a truck outside of Nacozari de García, a little town well off the tourist run about a hundred miles from Nogales. The coyotes would follow the vulture's descent out of curiosity whether or not they were hungry from the night's hunt. As the morning thermals developed more vultures would arrive until the man's dying would have an audience.

As the dawn deepened into midmorning and the heat dried and caked the blood on the man's face, the blood lost most of its fresh coppery odor. The man was dying fitfully now, more from the heat and dehydration than from his injuries: an arm twisted askew, chest a massive blue bruise, one cheekbone crushed in with a hematoma rising like a purple sun, his testicles inflated from a groining. And a head wound that darkened the sand and pebbles and drew him down into his near fatal sleep of coma. Still, he kept breathing, and the hot air whistled past a broken tooth and when the whistle was especially loud the vultures were disturbed. A female coyote and her recently weaned pups stopped by but only for a moment: she snapped at the pups saying this pitiful beast is normally dangerous. She nodded in passing to a very large, old male coyote who watched with intense curiosity from the shadow of a boulder. He watched, then dozed, even in sleep owning an alertness unknown to us. His belly was full of javelina and watching this dying man was simply the most interesting thing to happen his way in a long time. It was all curiosity though: when the man died the coyote would simply walk away and leave it to the vultures. And it had been a long vigil for him, having been close by when the naked man had been thrown from the car the night before.

In the first comparative coolness of the evening a Mexican peasant (*peóne* in Mexican slang) and his daughter walked along the road making short forays into the brush for stray pieces of mesquite firewood. Rather, the man walked doggedly under his light load of wood and the daughter pranced, hopping from one foot to another, skipping, running then waiting for her father. She was his only child and he wouldn't let her pick up firewood for fear she would be bitten by a scorpion, or a *corallo*, a coral snake which unlike the rattlesnake gave no warning though it was shy and retiring and meant no harm. It simply bit when cornered or provoked, then slid away and calmed its nerves under another log or stone. The daughter carried a bible. She helped in the kitchen of the Mennonite mission where her father had long been the custodian.

The daughter began to sing and that flushed the vultures still another hundred yards down the road. They were about to leave anyway for the safety of their mountain rookery before evening deepened. The coyote withdrew a little farther into the gathering shadows. He recognized the voices of the man and his daughter and knew from the seven years of his life that they weren't dangerous to him. He had watched them on their way to the mission countless times but they had never seen him. The great birds flushing in the evening sun aroused the curiosity of the father and he quickened his pace. He had a hunter's inquisitiveness, not unlike the coyote's, and he remembered the time when he had found a large deer freshly fallen from an escarpment by following a descending gyre of vultures. He told his daughter to wait at a distance and he cautiously entered the dense chaparral along the road. He heard a rush of breath and a faint whistle and quickly opened a long pearl-handled knife. He crept noiselessly toward the whistling, smelling a trace of blood amidst the vulture dung. Then he saw the man and whistled himself, kneeling to feel the pulse. At odd times he had accompanied the missionary who was also a doctor on his treks into the mountains and he had learned the elements of first aid.

Now he stood, whistled again in unison with the dying man, and looked at the sky. He was mostly Indian and his first thought was to simply walk away and avoid any contact with the Federales. But then the doctor was friends with the Federales and the man remembered the parable of the good Samaritan and looked back down at the body somewhat fatalistically, as if to say, I'll help but I think it's too late.

He came out of the brush and sent his daughter running to the mission a half mile down the valley. He squatted in the roadway and rolled pebbles back and forth with the blade of his knife. The sight of someone so gravely injured had quickened his heartbeat but he coolly rehearsed his story of finding the body. In his youth, in addition to being a hunter, he had been a small-time bandit and he understood that when speaking to authorities it was best to keep things simple.

At the mission Diller sat at his loin of pork roast with sauerkraut and potatoes. His VHF radio was tuned into a mariachi station in Chihuahua. Though he was a Mennonite and officially disapproved of radios, he felt he deserved certain concessions and had begun listening to such music ten years before when he came to the mission under the guise of speeding his learning of colloquial Spanish. Huge and rubicund, he was likely to bray along with the music to the amusement of the women in the kitchen. The church allowed neither alcohol nor tobacco but Diller owned an unproscribed vice: gluttony. He savored the pork loin that was prepared for him every Thursday night as the sole remnant of his life in the States. He much preferred

Mexican foods which he consumed in volumes that made him fabled throughout the area. Not that he wasn't profoundly devout, but he understood it was his doctoring, his medical skill, that made his particular brand of Jesus popular in the impoverished mountain country. He no longer returned to the States for his annual month's leave. It bored him to sit around for thirty days in North Dakota and pray for the heathen throughout the world. Diller rather preferred the heathen and the bleak beauty of their country, their long-suffering ironies and pre-Christian fatalism. He loved to eat the chickens, pigs, piglets, goats and lambs the people brought him as presents when he performed some medical miracle. He even loved his absurd pansy male nurse, Antonio, who was forever inventing reasons to drive off to Nogales or Hermosillo. The year before the Director of Missions had visited and questioned Diller, wondering if Antonio weren't a "bit peculiar." Diller played dumb, cherishing Antonio's knack for fancy dishes beyond the reach of the cooks, and his singing of ballads even though the gender in the ballads tended to get switched around.

Diller groaned when Mauro's daughter rushed in announcing the wounded man up the mountain. Mauro's daughter lugged his medicine bag out to the Dodge Powerwagon that served as an ambulance, with a canvas cover and cot in the back. Diller followed carrying the casserole with him. He liked best the sauerkraut in the bottom soaked with pork fat. He paused on the porch of the hacienda and breathed deeply the odor of the evening air: dung and sweet cloves, crushed and rotting flowers, the smell of overheated rocks and sand fading into night. He loved this valley that seemed somber and umbrous even in the brightest sunlight.

At the scene Mauro held the flashlight while Diller wiped pork grease from his hands onto his pants and stooped by the body, said a prayer and made his inspection and prognosis. He suspected the man would live but it would be chancy for the first twenty-four hours, so severe was his dehydration. The skull wasn't fractured but from the flittering eyeballs he saw the depth of the concussion. Diller took his penlight from the bag and bent close to the naked man's eyes seeing the bulge in the optical disc, papilledema, a severe concussion. Then he ran his big hands skillfully over the man's body determining the only fractures were in the ribs and left arm. Diller slipped his arms under the man and picked him up. Mauro took the bag and led the way with the flashlight.

Back at the clinic Diller worked through the night with Mauro in attendance. He wished that Antonio were there to help but Antonio had disappeared for the usual spurious reasons. Diller was more than a bit mystified by his patient. Under the flashlight he had assumed that he had yet another sorry, battered victim of the drug wars that raged beneath the border. Such refugees provided Diller with some of his most interesting cases, alternating the routine of the aged cancer victims whom he dosed with the potent Dilaudid to ease their way heavenward. The naked man proved to be pure gringo when the blood was washed off: his hair was finely barbered, expensive gold fillings in his teeth, trimmed nails, a strong tan demarcation, a well-conditioned body, all qualities that made him an unlikely smuggler.

Near dawn Diller smiled at the improved pulse rate, and the response to the intravenous liquids. He probed gingerly at the shattered jawbone that later would require plastic surgery if the man wished. Mauro bathed the sunburn with vinegar and applied hot compresses to the swollen testicles, joking in his fatigue that it was a much better job for Antonio. The doctor laughed in spite of himself—it was impossible to remain prissy in such matters. The doctor sang "La Paloma" as he wrapped the ribs with Mauro filling in on the difficult trilling bars of the wonderful song.

Mauro and the doctor moved the man to the only private room in the clinic and then went out to the porch where Mauro's daughter served them coffee in the first light of dawn. Diller winked at Mauro, gave him a Dexamyl and took one himself. Mauro smiled at this little secret they indulged in during emergencies when sleep was impossible, though he would have much preferred the bottle of mescal hidden under his bed, having publicly in the chapel sworn against alcohol. The doctor's thoughts were synchronous: only once in his adult life had he tasted alcohol. Long ago in his second year at the mission his wife had left forever, explaining in hysterics that she could not endure life in Mexico and that she no longer loved him. Diller had sat in the dirt of the courtyard all night and wept while the nervous help had watched from the porch and hacienda. In the middle of that pathetic night Mauro brought Diller a whole liter of mescal which Diller drank hungrily. Diller slept throughout the hot day in the dirt with everyone taking turns shading his face and keeping away the flies. Diller smiled at the remembrance of the pain.

Now the first rays of the sun were hitting in the fawn-colored side of the mountain top. The peculiar blurred brownness of scree always reminded him of the flank of a deer and this morning the flank of the deer reminded him of venison chops. The pork and sauerkraut had not set well, and he decided to give it up and go completely native. The rooster crowed and he thought of roast chicken. The cook called out and Mauro and Diller went into the kitchen where they ate huge bowls of *menudo* and corn tortillas. The doctor believed along with the Mexicans that this tripe stew was a restorative though he wouldn't have believed so had he not loved the dish. He was a man of certain tastes. And he was mindful that his tastes were killing him slowly as he eased up toward three-hundred pounds despite his huge frame and heavy musculature. The Dexamyl made the blood drum in his ears; adopting the doom that pervaded the countryside, he enjoyed his flirtation with death. After breakfast, he sang little ditties of love and death as he made his rounds. He remarked to himself that the patient would need a strong stomach to endure the pain when he emerged from the coma.

That evening Hector, the captain of the regional Federales, stopped by to make a report on the wounded man. When he received the radio report at midday he became happy and ordered his assistant to ready the jeep for an overnight trip. A visit to the doctor meant a fine dinner and a long evening of chess, discussions on gardening, politics, the raising of animals for food, and a chance to talk at length about his health, for Hector was somewhat of a hypochondriac in his mid-fifties and worried about his waning potency. He respected the doctor's deeply religious nature so he approached the medical aspects of potency very subtly, which amused the doctor who advised that he reduce his use of alcohol and tobacco and take plenty of exercise. As a final teasing thrust he suggested that Hector might forget his *conchitas* in favor of more spiritual concerns. The doctor had only recently felt the rare terror of lust when he had treated an attractive mountain girl for a scorpion bite on her upper thigh. He prayed mightily but it didn't seem to help much, casting his thoughts back to his first year of marriage in North Dakota when he and his young wife had exhausted themselves with lovemaking.

When Hector and the assistant arrived they went immediately to view the wounded man in order to rid themselves of the irksome detail so the evening could be enjoyed. The doctor forbade fingerprints at the time saying that he would send them along when the injuries mended somewhat. In this case he would merely send his own fingerprints, not wanting to cause problems for anyone. Mennonites never go to the law over each other and the doctor applied this principle to his practice. He cared for souls and bodies and believed that civil authorities had the equipment to conduct their business without his aid. Hector was happy enough to make a return trip for his interrogation at which point the doctor would advise the patient to feign amnesia if he so chose, anything to escape the red tape and the severity of the Mexican penal code. The assistant made out a perfunctory report with Mauro's scanty information and then went off to a country tavern down the valley to impress the locals. Hector and the doctor sat down to an elaborate dinner, Hector with the air of a man who had done a long day's work he has no intention of remembering.

On the third day after finding the wounded man Diller became a little doubtful. The man had a mild touch of pneumonia and did not respond quickly to penicillin and the doctor prayed he wasn't allergic. Diller didn't want to lose the man to the superior facility of Hermosillo via helicopter. Two more days and the fever passed but not the coma. Now Diller decided he would give the coma two more days before calling Hector on the radio. He liked the symmetry of working in twos and his curiosity about the wounded man was so great that he longed for excuses to keep him. The night before the morning of the deadline he noticed that Mauro had hung a necklace of coyote teeth over the post of the bed. The necklace was no doubt from Mauro's mother who fed the animals and who the other help tended to avoid for her reputation as a herbalist and witch. Diller lectured often on the dangers of these old superstitions but now he smiled at her good intentions which he recognized as a form of love. As Diller turned out the light and left he did not realize that the wounded man watched through the slit of his one unbruised eyelid.

* * *

It is not necessary to know too much about the wounded man squinting up at the darkness and the soft whirr of the oak-paddled ceiling fan. His name is Cochran and he hears the chugging of the diesel generator, the whine of a single mosquito in the room, and farther off and faintly, the music from the doctor's radio, so heartlessly sad and romantic it seems to make the night as bruised as his body. But all his tears were shed in the past few semiwakeful days when, as any animal that plays dead, he tried to learn the nature of his immediate threat. And now that he knew there was no immediate threat, rather than relief he felt a suspension, as if he were dangling in some private dark while outside the universe continued on rules he had no part in making.

He had been beaten far past any thought of vengeance. He saw his beating as a long thread that led back from the immediate present, from this room almost to his birth. Rather than the obvious balm of the amnesiac, his mind owned a new strangeness in which he could remember pointillistically everything along the thread up to the unbearable present. He couldn't avoid anything, anymore than his chest could escape of itself from the swathes of tape. He hurt too much to sleep and tomorrow he would have to let the doctor know he was conscious to get relief from the pain. He felt half-amused at his caginess, a will to live past anything he understood consciously. He was past regretting for the moment how he tracked mud from one part of his life into another. He was bored with his regrets and the sole energy left that night was to figure out how it all happened, a mechanical ambition at best.

It would be his longest night, and the energy that fueled it was akin to a hard, cold, clear wind blowing through the blackness of the room: first there was the doctor muttering some prayer, and before that an old lady hanging a necklace on the bedpost and placing her hands over his eyes, then a young man with the gestures of a dancer who pulled back the sheet to look at him. Then a long, black space of pure nothing interrupted by a shutter click in which he saw the vermilion wattles on a buzzard's neck and heard a guttural sound that came from the yellow eyes of a coyote as the buzzard flapped skyward and the coyote stared at him, both of them impenetrable beyond these simple gestures, and his breath whistling through a broken tooth. Before that the car exhaust and the jouncing when he lay bleeding in the trunk and kept coughing painfully to clear the blood from his throat and there was almost too much of it. Then being hurled through the air, falling through the brush, his chest striking one rock, then rolling and his head striking another.

It's not necessary to know too much about the man who was wounded so badly because he was wounded badly enough to alter his course of life radically, somewhat in the manner that conversion, the sacrament of baptism, not the less an upheaval for being commonplace, alters the Christian, satori the Buddhist. You could, though, jump over the incoherence of his suffering and look at what we like to call the simple facts, a notion we use quite happily when we want to delude ourselves out of whatever peculiar sump our lives have become.

* * *

The morning before Mauro and his daughter had found him by the roadside, excepting the following morning when he was nothing but a dying piece of meat rotting through the day into evening, he had awakened in an uncommon state of what he thought was love. He lived in a moderately expensive apartment complex on the outskirts of Tucson, the chief winning aspects of the place being a lime tree in his small private courtyard and three clay tennis courts. He subletted the quarters, which was a condominium owned by a New Yorker who had recovered sufficiently from his asthma to have another go at the money game back East.

He was in love and he called his lover the moment he awoke, a gesture usually associated with the young or dopey, or, jumping across two decades, to those who fall in love strongly in their late thirties or early forties. The lovers spoke hurriedly, lapsing back and forth between Spanish and English with ease. They would meet in a little while in public, conduct their public business, then drift casually away to a small cabin the man leased and used in the borderland south of Agua Prieta, Mexico, primarily for hunting quail.

He had really nothing to get away from, he thought in the shower. He had been at the end of his tether for two years in a time when the meaning of tether had long been forgotten. At forty-one, and in front of the mirror and shaving, he no longer paused to admire the good shape he was in, because the eyes were usually tired and showed signs of being dominated by barbiturates.

In the living room he toweled off, let his bird dog, an

[15]

English setter named Doll, out the sliding doors and began an elaborate series of semiyogic stretching exercises. He paused to put Debussy's *La Mer* on the stereo and to smile at a large poster he had made out of his daughter's fifth-grade class picture. He felt a pang behind his smile, a small electric current of loneliness, remembering when he was stationed at Torrejón outside of Madrid and he and his daughter would go to the market on Saturdays to do the shopping for their big Sunday dinner. She had her mother's golden hair and liked to ask for everything in Spanish, which charmed the clerks. Then they would go to a café where he would have a half bottle of white wine and she an orange juice that she would draw out slowly in her child's voice, *"jugo de naranja al natural."* The old Spanish men liked to watch her eat a plate of *tapas*, expostulating about her depth of "soul" for eating pickled squid, tentacles and all. Now she lived with her mother in San Diego. His tour in Laos among other things (alcohol, womanizing, an incapacity for sitting still) had broken their marriage. Over Laos he took a 75, ejected from his Phantom leaving a dead navigator, and spent two months with some friendly fishermen in a junk avoiding the Pathet Lao and the Cong. He was essentially antipolitical and now the war only reappeared in nightmares. He had been a twenty-year man from nineteen to thirty-nine, a fighter pilot, and now he could not bear the sight of a plane. He drove everywhere in a battered Mark IV bought on a drinking spree in California.

After he finished the exercises he drank a cup of coffee and examined his three C6 Trabert graphite tennis racquets. The day before he had placed second in a club tournament, only losing to a young man half his age who was considered the most promising pro prospect in Arizona. Today he and his partner were considered the favorite for the doubles that were easier on his legs. Yesterday the match had gone 7–5, 4–6 and 6–4 on a very hot day and even when he won the second set he knew his legs didn't have it for the third. Tibey had had his man put a case of Dom Perignon in the car with a single white rose taped to the card. Now he looked at the white rose that he couldn't figure out and thought of Miryea who was Tibey's wife.

Tibey's actual name was Baldassaro Mendez. Like many extremely wealthy Mexicans he kept a spare house in the States. They were a small community and traveled to each other's parties in Palm Beach, Dallas, Phoenix and San Antonio. They invested heavily in real estate, the simplest thing to keep a distant eye on, and entered social circles easily because of their great wealth and continental charm. Tibey used him as a ringer in matches at his home and Cochran admired the man for his sometimes coarse energy. He always refused money from Tibey though he accepted trips to Mexico City where as doubles partners they suckered two Texans in a rooftop match at the Camino Real. He pocketed three grand for that which was nearly the amount Tibey blew in a banquet for twenty at Forquet's.

Miryea. He put down the racquets deciding the strings were in good shape. He took the society page photo from his wallet and looked at her cold, slender figure mounted on a thoroughbred jumper. What patent nonsense. He had been through enough of the battles of love to regard love almost as a disease, a notion prevalent in former times when the world seemed younger and wiser.

He lay on the floor and breathed deeply, trying to forestall the knot forming in his head. He had always laughed when other pilots had presentiments of doom, as if the void were already forming under their breastbones and beginning to spread. But then it happened the day of his near-fatal mission; a nondirectional chokiness, a kind of free-floating dread. Doll scratched at the sliding doors and he let her in, refreshed her water, and then petted her in her nest on the couch. She was always so slight, feminine, coy at times, and he marveled that when he got her into the field she became an utterly serious hunting machine.

Everyone wishes a measure of mystery in their life that they have done nothing in particular to deserve. Before he met Miryea he had a short love affair with a girl from Corpus Christi who had just graduated from Wellesley, but the mystery soon dissolved into bitching and he recognized he had "willed" himself into the affair out of unrecognized boredom. He had spent two years trying to get the handle on civilian life, realizing that he had never exactly had a handle on the Navy which had been some sort of quarrelsome mother and he an adopted orphan whom she treated as well as he performed his job. The Texas girl was lovely, long-limbed, intelligent but far too young and daffy: she was a house that wanted to be haunted while Miryea, only a few years older, was haunted. He had played tennis at Tibey's house for more than three months before she did anything more than casually recognize him. Then after a dinner at Tibey's, during which far too much wine had been consumed, she had caught him looking at the books in her library while the other men had begun a high stakes billiards game and the women were talking about the new Givenchys and how corny Halston had become.

After tours at Guantánamo when he first entered the service and his later tour at Torrejón he spoke fluent Spanish. He could not bear to be stupid—as a boy in Indiana he had disassembled a Ford V-8 to see how it worked, and only entered the Navy to work on jet engines. He was always amazed how civilians underestimated the intelligence it took to fly a jet fighter. His incursions into Spanish had been as thorough and methodical. The Midwest specializes in a certain lonely farmboy type who wants to know everything and he began at Guantánamo by simply wondering why people spoke different languages, not the less fascinating for being such a simple question. But these farmboys own a visionary energy and he loved the idea of the artificiality of language and learned Spanish as a test case, studying like an idiot savant who is familiar with the Chinese calendar and keeping up through novels and poetry. None of his friends and bunkmates had the temerity to question him because he was a natural leader and the best at everything he chose to do whether pool, snorkeling and gradually tennis—the native ability to monopolize the bullshit and be enviably crazier and bolder than anyone else.

Now this lovely creature approached him as he held one

of her books, a collected Lorca he was familiar with, printed on onionskin and bound in leather in Barcelona. He had been totally confused by her inattention in the past three months. The situation had gone way beyond the idea of making a "move" into an area of reserved tension so that when he saw her he seemed to lose his easy grace and mastery. He felt thrown off stroke at her merest glance and the day before while swimming he needed a drink to watch her take one bite of a club sandwich before she decided on a nap and Tibey shrugged in that universal gesture of incomprehension. He felt that as a friend of Tibey's she assumed he was a business moron and he did everything he could to subtly disabuse her of the idea. When she approached him at the bookcase it was the first moment he had found to speak to her alone. She tipped the book in his hands reading its title upside down. She smiled and quoted from Lorca, *"Quiero dormir el sueño de las manzanas, alejarme tumulto de los cementerios . . ."* ("I want to sleep the dream of apples, far from the tumult of cemeteries.") He thought he had never heard anything more beautiful and stared at the ceiling in an unaffected schoolboy blush and quoted back from the same poet: *"Tu vientre es una lucha de raices / y tus labios una alba sin contorno. / Bajo las rosas tibias de la cama/ los muertos gimen esperando turno."* ("Your belly is a battle of roots,/ your lips are a blurred dawn./ Under the tepid roses of the bed/ the dead moan, waiting their turn.")

She stared at him a moment and his temples pounded witlessly. She flushed and looked away and he wished to say something stupid to ease the tension but could find no words. She tilted her chin upward as if looking at some faraway object and he looked at her throat thinking he could detect an odor somewhere between clover and an orange. He dropped the book to the floor and she laughed and walked away. He swallowed a gobletful of brandy that rose in his throat and brought tears to his eyes.

When he got home that night he found himself pacing and sleepless despite pills and alcohol. At dawn he took Doll out in the desert and let her work some quail but she lost interest because it was August and the season wasn't open yet so he didn't carry a gun. She pointed a small owl in a mesquite then ran in circles over the joke she had played on him. He decided a long trip was in order. Not since he was eighteen had there been a relationship with a woman in which he wasn't in complete control. She reminded him clearly of those Modiglianis he had seen in a museum in Paris. He remembered saying when he looked at one painting that there is a woman I could love. It was absurd. Doll pawed and whined at his feet as he stared sightlessly at the landscape of yucca and mesquite.

Driving back he had a splitting headache and changed the tapes in the tapedeck a half-dozen times. He listened to Jimmy Buffett's "The Pirate Turns Forty" and was filled with self-disgust. He invited Doll into the front seat, a rare event, and petted her head thinking he would return happily to waitresses and stewardesses. He had always disliked rich ladies. A few months earlier he had gone swimming with the girl from Corpus Christi who had forgotten to take off her Tiffany watch and he had reflected that the watch would have supported his family for a year when he was growing up in Indiana. They had owned a small farm and an auto-and-tractor repair shop. When pressed his father might trade a used battery for three chickens for Sunday dinner. He wondered what he was doing so desperately in love with the wife of a Mexican millionaire, or a great deal more as Tibey owned a Lear jet and a twin Piper Comanche for smaller airports. He decided to call Vonetta when he got home. She worked as a hostess in a steak house, was his age and a great lay, twice a divorcée. She had gone with him on several hunting and fishing trips, and could cook quail over a bed of mesquite coals beautifully. Of course she told hopelessly banal jokes all the time and the walls of her apartment featured paintings on black velvet, including a fiery-eyed bull and a Tahitian sunset. He had become angry with her one morning when he awoke to find her out on the driveway washing his car.

When he got home he took two sleeping pills, a hot shower and barely struggled to bed, covering the phone with pillows. He smiled as he fell asleep thinking of a note he got from his father. He had sent his daughter a photo of himself holding a trophy from a tennis tournament. His wife had married his oldest brother who worked with his father on the family tuna boat out of San Diego. They had left Indiana in his early teens, an event that still aroused sadness in him, but his father thrived in California. In the note he had said: "I saw the picture, big shot. When you get tired of running around in short pants there will be room for you on the boat. Love, Dad."

But when he awoke in midafternoon to a knocking on

the door the nightmare began again. Miryea sent a messenger with an elaborately wrapped box of books from her library, all leatherbound with many of her notes in the margin. There were some Barója novels, also *The Family of Pascual Duarte* by Camilo J. Cela, *Nina Huanca* by Faustino Gonzalez-Aller, and books of poems by Machado, Guillén, Octavio Paz, Neruda and Nicanor Parra. The note only said, "These are some of my favorites. I hope you'll like them. Miryea." She added a postscript: *"La luz del entendimiento/ me hace ser muy comedido."* ("The light of understanding/ has made me most discreet.")

He drank three cups of coffee, adding brandy to the third, looking for the source of the quotation which he assumed to be from Lorca. He finally found it in *La Casada Infiel (The Faithless Wife)*. He poured another drink and picked up the phone but only got a servant saying that Señor Mendez was in Mérida. He didn't dare ask for Miryea directly. He walked around the living room, light-headed and cursing. Now he couldn't simply drop by under the pretense of seeing Tibey. Tibey's servants seemed to be bodyguards too, having none of the comatose air of the usual domestic. For the first time he allowed himself to imagine her naked. He swore and hurled his glass against the wall above the couch. Doll barked hysterically and he gave her a hamburger patty to quiet her down. He dialed Tibey's house again hoping that she might answer but the same servant was there as if perched over the phone. He took a shotgun from the gun cabinet thinking he would go shoot skeet then put it back knowing he had neither the taste nor the concentration. He put on his hiking boots thinking a long evening walk in the desert might calm him down.

He was getting into his car when she pulled into the empty space beside him. He was dumbfounded enough that when she said she didn't want to interrupt his evening he had no answer. She smoothed back her hair and adjusted the scarf around her neck, then laughed at his speechlessness. He took her hand and kissed it in a parody of a courtly fool. She kissed his hand, then bit it and laughed again. "I've been thinking about being with you a long time."

They made love throughout the evening but at nine she said she had to go home to avoid suspicion. He said but Tibey is in Mérida, and she said but I have a half-dozen husbands who would kill anyone who harmed me. Then she told him to leave the room because she wanted to write him a note that he must not open until the morning. She left while he stood waiting in the bathroom mugging at himself happily in the mirror. He heard the door close and raced out of the bathroom and out the door only to see her ducking into her white BMW. She waved and sped away. Doll met him at the door. Whenever a woman visited him she either slept or pretended to sleep all the time in some shy form of jealousy. He ripped open the note that only said she hated good-byes and repeated "I love you" seven times. He cooked himself a huge steak singing giddily at the stove but only ate half of it handing the plate down to Doll. He slept well that night for the first time in months.

It was as if his soul had gotten over some prolonged and terrible wisdom toothache.

That had all been only three weeks before. The dread that pervaded him as he packed his tennis bag was not unfounded. One evening she had spilled hot coffee on her bare breasts and wept. He ran to get some ointment but she waved him away saying that she was not burned, only so sad because there was nowhere to go. He tried to kiss the pink splotch the coffee had made on her white breasts and she became frantic asking him not to touch her. He stood there a half hour as she sat rigidly staring at him. He had never looked upon so profoundly beautiful a body and he finally knelt and kissed her knee and she drew him to her. He told her in a rush that he had it all planned and he would take his savings and they would run away to Seville which was his favorite city on earth and no one would find them there. But she said that if he mentioned it again she would never see him again. She was oddly cold to him when she left that night.

Neither of them knew when they kissed at her car that a "servant" watched leaning against a palm tree a hundred yards away.

The real warning and break in their secrecy came when he happily confessed his affair over drinks with his doubles partner who immediately turned white. His partner was his only friend and confidant in Tucson and a pilot for Aeromexico. And he said you shithead, you fool why do you think Tibey is called Tibey and he didn't know and was shocked at the reaction and his partner said, "Tibey is for *tiburón tiburón tiburón* which is shark. Get out of here tomorrow and never come back. That bitch in heat has killed you if you don't go. You'll be buried so deep in the desert." He hit his friend and the friend seemed not to notice pouring them both a huge drink and saying he had connections and could secure a false passport for secrecy and besides could give him money if he needed it.

It was an ugly and frightening evening that seemed benign when he awoke the next day. He mentioned it, though, in passing to Miryea and she laughed her high-trilling laugh and said don't be silly he won't kill you he'll kill me and refused to speak of it again. That was only a few days before. Now after the tournament they would have three full days together because Tibey was in Caracas. The ruse was that she was going to visit her sister who was the wife of a UN diplomat in New York. The chauffeur would take her to the airport after the tournament and he would pick her up there; then off to Douglas, a border town across from Agua Prieta, and they would reach the cabin the next morning.

All went well except the tennis match that dragged unmercifully on a blistering afternoon. He couldn't see Miryea in the crowd and after winning the first set by the grace of his partner they lost the second 6–2 and got off to a bad start in the third. His partner glowered at him and his legs felt leaden. He yelled at a woman in the crowd who stood up during his serve. Then Miryea came in and she winked shyly at him and he remembered how happy he was supposed to be and finished the third set electrically. When he was showering, Tibey's chauffeur came into the locker room and blithely handed him an envelope announcing that Señor Tibey wanted to make him a present. After toweling off he opened the envelope and found a one-way first-class ticket to Paris and then Madrid and several thousand dollars in one-hundred-dollar bills, with a note saying I knew you would win days ago my friend. He examined the ticket several times thinking the return might have been left out by mistake. He decided not to mention it to Miryea. Why ruin the weekend? he thought, trying to calm the palpable discomfort he felt deep in his stomach.

On the way to the airport he stopped to pick up Doll and his bag at the apartment. He had a quick glass of wine to try to dispel the butterflies that came in intermittent surges. He laughed at himself, thinking of all those years spent, often at Mach II, twisting and turning high above Vietnam, Laos and Cambodia, occasionally peeing in his pants while avoiding a rocket. Or even ejecting over the gulf off Eglin when the electrical fire started consuming the Phantom, or those near misses on night carrier landings. One of his closest friends had eaten it at Boca Chica, near Key West, after surviving a hundred missions over Southeast Asia. He tended to regard civilian life as utterly benign and this new danger alternately nagged and excited him with the adrenal rush that any mammal feels.

Nearing the airport the sky over Tucson looked bloated and filthy with a yellowish-pale cast by rush hour auto exhaust. A tape stuck in the deck and when he pulled it out it unwound like spaghetti all over the seat. Despite the air-conditioning the car stunk of ozone and he longed for the trip through the mountains with Miryea. He had decided to skip the hotel stop and Douglas. They would have dinner in a fine restaurant he knew in Agua Prieta, then make the small cabin near Colonia Marelas by nightfall. Perhaps Tibey had friends in Douglas and the discomfort of traveling farther on was mitigated by the thought of getting caught red-handed in a hotel. His friend, the pilot from Aeromexico, had insisted that Tibey was involved in every form of financial chicanery, legal and illegal, right up to and including the vast border heroin traffic. When he got home on Monday he would call an old friend in Naval Intelligence who could run a check on Tibey for him through Washington. Not that it would have mattered though; he liked Tibey very much and in three months they had gone from being casual acquaintances to something close to friendship. The last three weeks with Miryea had caused him some pain on this count but he was unbearably in love and held on to it as the first totally grand thing in his life in years. In fact he was as lovesick as a high schooler of an especially sensitive sort who wonders if he dare share a poem with his beloved or whether she will laugh at him. He does read her the poem and her feminine capacity for romanticism for a moment approaches his own and they are suffused in a love trance, a state that so ineluctably peels back the senses making them fresh again whatever ages the lovers might be. You see it happening from grade schools to retirement communities: the certainly accidental cohesion of two souls and bodies, often resulting in terror and unhappiness because so much previously unknown energy is released. It had been so long since he had felt anything remotely similar; he had had a half-dozen solid infatuations with women ranging from a Madrid television actress to the recent Texas girl, not counting his marriage which added up more to an affectionate companionship than anything else. She had been a nurse at the base in Guam, a farm girl from Indiana, and they became married almost by the force of nostalgia alone.

At the Braniff entrance he slipped a porter ten bucks to keep an eye on the car and went directly to the V.I.P. lounge where Miryea sat sipping a drink, breathtakingly tailored and cool. He had a Stolichnaya martini and she told him she went so far in her deception as to check a bag through to New York which was full of gift clothes to her sister. The two attracted far more attention than they would have thought possible: he was impeccably tanned and fit, looking a half-dozen years younger than his forty-one if you didn't look closely around the eyes, dressed casually but expensively with a Rolex on his wrist. And she was the vortex of attention nearly anywhere, especially when the audience was sophisticated, say in Rome or London or Paris. She was born in Mexico City with a Guatemalan-Barcelona background and educated in Lausanne and Paris. She had spent much of her young life (she was twenty-seven) in being cold, neutral and tasteful, under which patina burned a passionate and knowledgeable young woman. She was a little shorter than he was, about five eight, and owned an almost alarming grace so that when she did something so simple as to sit down in the Braniff lounge, light a cigarette and look at a magazine, many eyes were on her. Even now a thickset older man with a calf-bound briefcase watched occasionally from behind the pages of *Forbes*. He was a lieutenant of Tibey's out of Mexico City that she did not recognize. When they left he casually followed making a CB call and turning away from them at the first freeway exit ramp.

In the car she was happy and in a girlish mood, rewinding the splayed tape and singing him some Guadalajaran folksongs he liked. Outside the city limits she took her bag from the backseat and changed her formal Balenciaga suit for a light summer dress. He said he couldn't bear to see her sitting there at seventy miles an hour in her underthings and she said my love no one asked you to bear it so he drove off a desert two-track-rutted road and they made love in the late afternoon bent over the hood of the car. Some four hundred yards away on a knoll a man watched them with Zeiss-Ikon binoculars. He leaned against an anonymous pickup and sighed to himself as Miryea's legs raised, fell and clutched at the man. He took a Tres Equis from a cooler on the seat, feeling as feverish as the hot air that wavered and distorted the view through the binoculars.

He thinks to himself that if Tiburón were there he would take the rifle from under the seat and shoot them as one would a deer or mountain goat. Meanwhile he watches them complete their love and her mouth open in laughter that he barely hears. She dances in a circle and the viewer swears as the man slumps to the ground and yells something. He lowers the binoculars a moment and thinks he can't fault the gringo on his taste and that she is a vision, and he had only seen her once from a distance when Tiburón visited his old mother in Durango for a week.

Back in the car she said she felt like a wonderful whore what with her sweating and her damp hair sticking to her temples. And how grand it was to go for a trip in a car and how it had been years since she had done anything but fly. He had begun to wonder paranoiacally about the pickup a quarter-mile back, thinking he had noticed it before they stopped. But the pickup had turned off in Benson and he left off worrying until they passed through Tombstone and she had shut her eyes thinking it was a terrible name for a town. He remembered making a tombstone when he was ten for his horse who had entangled herself in barbed wire so badly his father had to shoot her. He had painted on a large rock: SUSY BORN IN 1943 DEAD IN 46 HERE LIES A GOOD MORGAN MARE OWNED AND LOVED BY J. COCHRAN WHO MOURNS HER PASSING. He got the last part out of the newspaper in the county seat that printed commemoratives in the personals column.

They were in Douglas by seven, bought some supplies and drove over the border into Agua Prieta where he bought her a purse from a saddlemaker and they had a dinner of shrimp soup and roasted *cabrito*, a young haunch of goat that the cook dressed with oil and garlic and fresh thyme. He loved Mexico and asked her about Durango, Tibey's hometown down in the Sierra Madres. She said Durango was hopelessly vulgar, a ranching and mining center that went unmentioned in the tourist books and that was why she liked it so much. Tibey had a ranch there and he had been invited for the shooting in a few months. Miryea said it looked like Montana or parts of Catalonia or Castile and that there were a lot of quail and wild turkey on the ranch where she kept her horses. Tibey had built a clay tennis court and drove her crazy with it to the point that she refused to play, whereupon he had trained several of his henchmen with the help of a tennis pro imported from Mexico City.

They neared the cabin in the last of the twilight, carefully moving up the mountain two-track. Twice he stopped and left the car to remove rocks washed down in flash floods from the arroyos. He wished that he could get a hold of good topographical maps of the area but there were none. In his usual methodical way he already knew more about Mexico and Mexicans than all but a few visiting Americans. He read Wolmack's *Zapata and the Mexican Revolution* and a half-dozen other available texts on recent Mexican history. He was still somewhat of a professional warrior and like the Japanese samurai it was an instinctual part of his code to be mindful, to know and understand as completely as possible where he was and why. He was just as instinctually a nonspectator and could not bear to have his immediate energies directed by anyone else. In the service this had made him unpopular with senior officers, and somewhat of a natural hero to everyone else. In the vacuum of his first two years of civilian life he was competent to no particular purpose. Here in Mexico, after only a few visits, he was known and warmly welcomed in a little mountain village cantina. The locals teased him about his

Castilian pronunciation, doing elaborately humorous imitations.

When they got to the cabin he could tell immediately that she liked it. Doll went berserk snuffing around her hunting grounds but wary as she was trained of the scorpion and rattlesnake. He unloaded the car and started a fire in the small fireplace in the last light. He unrolled the double sleeping bag on the bed as she stared at the fire, listening to a brief shower beat off the tin roof. The dry wood smelled almost of perfume and she asked him to bring the foam rubber cushion and the sleeping bag to the hearth. He turned the kerosene lamp down low and thought of the morning walk he would take her on to where a small mountain creek made a clear green pool in the rock. They made love slowly and he marveled at the way the flickering light of the fire ran moving shadows up and down her body. They were mildly tipsy and he moved a large log away from the fire as the room seemed dense and overheated. She dozed for a while and he made another drink trying to remember when he felt so full and at the same time so alive and totally released.

Now we must back away from the lovers and let them rest but only for the shortest of moments. Let us perch on the log mantel, an impassive stone-eyed griffon, for it is best to have stone eyes for what we are going to see. The room is turning cool and the lovers hug themselves for warmth, then move, still in sleep, to each other. The light of the lamp is low and the shadow of the fire has become cold and weak. Outside the wind has picked up and hums under the eaves like the keening of a warlock. Doll is restless by the door and growls and whines, then barks frantically as the door bursts open. The room is flame-blue as a shotgun blasts the life from the dog. Three men rush into the cabin, one of them grotesquely huge. They pounce upon the lovers and Cochran howls as the wind is crushed from him and he is caught in a choke-hold by the huge man who is shouting in Spanish. Miryea is caught by her arms and she faints, held tightly by the man we saw watching with the binoculars. Tibey stands back and turns up the oil lamp. He revives the lovers with a pitcher of water from the table. His eyes look even wider apart than usual and his mouth hangs open though he is wordless. The huge man holds Cochran close so that he may watch as Tibey takes a razor from his pocket and deftly cuts an incision across Miryea's lips, the pimp's ancient revenge for a wayward girl. Lips may never be sewn back up perfectly especially when there is a long delay, which there will be. Tibey nods. It is Cochran's turn. The big man begins beating on him with long powerful punches, propping him up against the fireplace. Miryea faints again but Tibey, holding her by the ear, forces the lids of her eyes open with his other hand. As Cochran passes out he thinks he sees her ear come off in Tibey's hand. Tibey groins Cochran with a boot then washes his hands. The smaller man gives Miryea an injection and they are loaded into the trunk of a limousine down the trail. Tibey sits in the limousine breathing deeply, saying out loud to himself that perhaps they are making love in the trunk. The big man and the smaller man busy themselves spreading kerosene throughout the cabin. They back Cochran's car up against the door. The smaller man throws a match in the cabin and as they walk down the road they are silhouetted by the burning cabin. It is a long drive to Durango and Tibey lays back drinking from a bottle of Scotch as they jounce down the trail toward the road. He sees the explosion of the car dimly in the rearview mirror. About thirty miles down the road, still far from the main highway, they stop and pitch a body into the brush.

CHAPTER
II

The change was akin to dreaming that you were on another planet only vaguely similar to our own, then waking in a state of vertigo to find that you were on that planet. It was as strange as permanent *déjà vu*, so that what he thought of as his own reality drifted farther away from him every moment, dwindled until only an occasional picture floated from his mind—his daughter, the road in front of an Indiana farm, his bird dog. In the month in the room he had systematically exhumed and exhausted his memory so that when he was finally ready to leave the room he somehow did not recognize the world as the one he left behind. The resemblances simply weren't strong enough to draw him back and at night when the pictures came he felt no attachment so the pictures hurriedly left. At first he thought the concussion in its severity had scrambled his brains, but he quickly lost interest in medical explanations. There was an impenetrable ache that he localized and insulated, and would protect to keep him alive. When the image arose he saw it again through the reddish tinge of the blood that had blurred his eyes, the dog flung across the room and high shrill white screams that still burned against his eardrums and that he could recapture as clearly as putting a record on a phonograph. He only remembered idly how his arm had given way in a sharp crack, the jaw and cheekbone and ribs caving. They were of no interest to him, only the voice of the other he could recreate so that it would eerily sing or whisper to him.

After that long night he let Diller know he was fully conscious in the morning and Diller began with Demerol without trying to draw him out. Diller only asked if there were someone who should be notified, adding that he was out of danger: the arm and the ribs had set okay but one side of his face was a mess and he should seek surgery back home wherever that was. Diller took a small mirror from the wall and showed him the swelling had subsided but the injury drew his eye down until he squinted to compensate. Then the doctor added that a captain of the Federales would be coming by in a few days but he need say nothing, with the concussion he had as an excuse to the law.

Later a young man came into shave him but he refused. He said his name was Antonio and then proceeded to bathe Cochran in an irritatingly familiar way. Antonio said that if he needed cigarettes or anything he would advance him the money and get the cigarettes until money came from the States. Antonio laughed and whirled to the door saying that they never had a patient arrive so strangely nude as if he had been born battered and flayed in the bushes. Cochran decided that Antonio was crazy enough

[37]

to be appealing. Then he was disturbed because he couldn't remember if he smoked. "I don't remember if I smoke," he said.

"Then don't. It makes your mouth taste terrible. For me, I like to drink but only off duty. I can sneak you booze but it's forbidden here." He winked and left.

When Antonio left, Cochran struggled out of bed and shuffled gingerly to the window. His chest ached and the cast on his left arm threw him off balance. He became dizzy at the window and held on tightly to the sill, focusing his eyes on his bare feet. He liked what he saw behind the hacienda: it was a green world, a huge vegetable garden with the rows raised between small trenches for irrigation, and beyond that, some sheds and corrals holding a big Percheron and three sorry-looking quarter horses, a few sheep, a large pen of pigs and some milking goats. The oldest woman in the world slid from behind a bush and stared through the window at him, not a foot away. He was utterly impassive and so was she, then she broke into a smile and he smiled back and she disappeared.

Back in bed he felt hungry and examined the large needle wound in his right arm that told him he had been fed intravenously. He felt hollow as an Easter egg that had been emptied by a pinprick. He slept deeply but awoke with a start when he dreamt of sitting in the sand laughing next to his car looking up at a lovely nude woman whose mouth was bleeding horribly. He yelled then until his eyes bulged and came fully awake in the twilit room. Diller, Mauro and Antonio came running, Diller still chewing on some food and holding his bag.

Cochran found himself saying, "I'm sorry I disturbed you. It was a dream." Diller approached him with a hypodermic and Cochran said, "I want something to eat." Antonio left and Diller smiled. The man is polite, he thought, and went back to his dinner. Mauro stared at him in his faded-green work clothes and drooping moustache and eyelids.

"I found you and thought you were dead," he said, then paused. "I wish you safety from your enemies and vengeance if that's what you wish."

Antonio, carrying a tray, passed Mauro going out the door. The tray held a bowl of soup, a glass of goat's milk and some corn tortillas.

"You must begin gently with food. I am sure you are an intelligent man by your appearance and will not listen to any Injun hocus-pocus of Mauro. Sometimes I think he and his daughter are ghosts though they are kind. When you get your money you might give them a few dollars for finding you. God knows I'm only a poor lonely boy dedicated to the science of medicine and you needn't listen to me, but if you wish to borrow my radio, have me take a letter because my English is perfect, or just read to you let me know. I hope to move to Los Angeles someday. Where is it that you come from?"

"Indiana. I come from Indiana."

Antonio was stymied for a moment then announced with conviction, "I know its reputation well. It is close to Georgia and full of strife. You would be better off in Los Angeles. Now you should eat and sleep and tomorrow begin walking or your fine body will lose its shapeliness."

Antonio arranged the pillows behind him and left. Cochran ate a few bites then fell deeply asleep, tipping over the soup. Mauro's daughter came to pick up the tray and cleaned up the mess, replacing the bed clothing. Cochran awoke terrified, thinking he saw Miryea as an adolescent.

He sat on the porch for two weeks watching the brown dust of August arise in clouds around walking feet. His beard grew and at the end of the month Diller took a chisel and mallet and broke the cast on his arm which looked bleak and pale. When it was damp his ribs still hurt. He was polite and extremely distant. The Federale captain came and went, issuing a tourist card to him for want of anything else to do with his bleary and distant silence. Finally he wrote a note to his daughter, something he ordinarily did once a week. Then one day he explained that the timing gear on Diller's Powerwagon was off and he would fix it, which he did with Mauro assisting. Diller kept a polite distance and during dinner he included Cochran in his blessing. They spoke obliquely about Mexican history and about Cozumel, which they had both visited. Diller was not disturbed, preferring the present to any knowledge of men's tortured histories with which he was all too familiar. After all, the man had begun to make himself useful, attended the services in the crude cement-block chapel, and most of all was intelligent and conversant on all matter of things as long as it remained impersonal.

Early in September Cochran began working hard in the garden. He cleaned the manure out of the sheds and rode the broad back of the Percheron around the valley, a better mount by far than the barely broken horses that Mauro rode. When the Percheron had arrived several years before at the mission as a pointless gift from Diller's hometown, Mauro decided to break the horse for riding as they had no harness or fields to work him. But when he mounted the horse it merely walked around at his bidding and now the great bulk of Diller rode it on calls into the mountains inaccessible to the truck. Mauro liked Cochran who even helped deftly with the slaughter of a steer, two sheep and a small goat that they roasted when the Federale arrived again with a gentleman who was a friend of Cochran's.

It was the Aeromexico pilot who laughed in relief when he saw him. Cochran was polite but saw his old friend as a possible interruption in his plans that had begun forming when he was running and climbing in the mountains. His running amused everyone for September was still hot, though an old man dying of cancer who had mescal smuggled into him told Cochran that running might turn him into a mountain lion. Life was better if you were no one's victim. The old man said he had been a *Maderista* in his youth, then changed his fidelity to Zapata. It had been a just and proper pleasure to shoot his enemies.

Cochran and his friend from Aeromexico sat in the dining room drinking coffee in strained silence. Antonio peeked in to check out so important a visitor. The visitor intended to wait out the silence of his friend.

"You don't look like you've been playing much tennis." He smiled, then was baffled by Cochran's look of incomprehension. He took another tack. "Is she dead?"

"I don't know. Maybe. I want to find out."

"You'll probably die. The doctor said you almost did. Perhaps I understand what you want to do. But I wish you would come back to Tucson."

"Not for a while."

The pilot sighed and looked around the room in embarrassment. He was somewhat of a romantic himself and recognized his friend's affliction with doom. He suspected that Tibey had not been kind to Miryea and that there was a matter of unavoidable vengeance.

"Okay. You must work it out. But please accept some advice. You look like a *peóne* now, a hippie *peóne*. Stay that way and you will not be conspicuous. Take this money I brought along in case it is needed to soften the way."

Antonio interrupted by bringing in more coffee and they fell silent. When Antonio left the pilot went on to say that his older brother was high in the government in Mexico City and could be trusted. That was how he found Cochran. It would be best not to stay at the mission longer as Tibey might change his mind and could easily trace him there. The pilot added some of his own identification to the envelope of money and wrote down the name and number of his brother. Then he pulled up a pant leg and took his boot halfway off, revealing a small .22-caliber Beretta in a half-holster. He handed it to Cochran.

"This is for when someone gets as close as they have already been. If you live through this you must get your face fixed." He stood and they embraced. Cochran walked him out to a jeep but his throat was choked and he found nothing to say.

[42]

That afternoon he made up two envelopes, each containing five hundred dollars in pesos for Diller and Mauro, keeping a thousand for himself, the better share of it stuffed behind the pistol against his calf. Diller was overcome and prepared a carpetbag of secondhand *peóne* clothes, a Spanish bible and a bottle of pain pills. He apologized for the poor clothing that actually was leftover from those who died. They joked about the fact and Diller said he would be sadly missed and prayers would be said. He did not pry into Cochran's plans. In a booming voice he ordered up an elaborate meal in honor of his patient's recovery and departure and his own insatiable appetite.

Before dinner Cochran and Mauro sat on the porch watching the evening shadows slide down the mountains. It had been very difficult to get Mauro to accept the money which was an immense amount for him. Mauro gave him his pearl-handled knife saying that it was a lucky knife, razor sharp, and perfect for cutting off the balls of those who had beaten him and left him for dead. Cochran said that if anyone came in search of him he should leave a phone message in care of a certain gentleman in Mexico City. Mauro wanted to go along and it took Cochran a while to convince him that he could not.

At dinner Cochran chose to sit with Mauro, his daughter and mother and felt a strong rush of sentiment over his new life that made the old seem a light-year away, flat and stale as a bad magazine article except for his daughter. He was wary to the point that when he wrote his daughter he included no return address. Now he was at a table groaning with food with a dozen people chattering in Spanish, inter-

[43]

mittently singing along to the radio which Diller decided to allow. Under the table Cochran and Mauro poured glasses of mescal, the first alcohol for Cochran in two months. Diller ordered everyone to sing a song and there was an eerie silence after Mauro's mother did a hypnotic Indian chant in a language no one recognized. But after that Antonio sang a buffoonish ditty, and the old cancer patient did a powerful rendition of a song welcoming spring, a spring six months away that everyone at the table knew he wouldn't see. The old man nearly passed out from the effort and Mauro snuck him a glass of mescal that revived him wonderfully. Mauro refused to sing and instead recited a version of "The Star-Spangled Banner" he had learned somewhere that turned out very comic. When it was Cochran's turn he stood and sang the Guadalajaran folk song that Miryea did so beautifully: but halfway through the song he was overcome, tears came to his eyes and he rushed from the room.

It was fortunate for him that he did not know, in the unique state of drunkenness that mescal offers, the precise condition of his beloved, the search for whom would begin at dawn. There is an impulse for vengeance among certain men south of the border that leaves even the sturdiest Sicilian gasping for fresh air.

Tibey Baldassaro Mendez was born in Culiacán of grotesquely impoverished parents. His mother was half Mescalero Apache, a tribe not noted for humility or gentleness. By the time he was fourteen he was a full-sized man, quick of mind, improbably arrogant and a pimp in Mazatlán. He gradually left pimpdom for a large part of the drug traffic in Culiacán. Now he was only peripherally involved in the drug traffic as a majordomo, but it had been the axis of his holdings in Mexico City real estate, resort hotels in Venezuela and Rio and Mérida, a huge, internationally flavored stock portfolio. One of his sons was a doctor and the other a lawyer. His first two marriages were local and had been shed as he rose in the world. Miryea was an implausible showpiece, a woman striven for over a period of years, and finally an access to Mexican social life that had been totally denied him. With the socially impeccable Miryea his great fortune was bathed overnight, not an uncommon event anywhere in the world.

The betrayal by Cochran whom he hoped had become a friend was a great blow to him. He even forgave the first few clandestine meetings that Cochran and Miryea had naively assumed were secret. Tibey knew and understood the vagaries of a woman's emotional life and Cochran was a thoroughly attractive character. He had made a veiled warning to the man's friend, the Aeromexico pilot, and there was a white rose on the case of champagne, the money and the ticket to Paris. How much warning did the fool need? The taps on her phone were outrageous and filled him with shame. He became desperate when he heard of a tape of Miryea telling her sister in New York about the new and final great love of her life who asked her to run away to Seville and perhaps she would. Tibey broke down then and put the muscle of his full operation into following the lovers to their surprise in the cabin. He hated to do it because he would be known in his own world as a cuckold and the word would spread to Culiacán to Mexico City and back to Tucson. That thought fueled his rage and rekindled his pimp's essential disgust for women. He would let no one know that he suddenly felt old and that losing her meant everything to him. He would teach her a lesson that would accompany and mitigate any gossip about his cuckoldry. He made love to her the final time on the day before she left and then went to his own bedroom and wept. He suddenly envied his simple *contrabandistas* with their whoring, drinking life and the way they happily shot down the government planes that came to spy on their marijuana and poppy crops. Tibey could easily call the infamous, albeit intelligent and dignified, assassin, El Cociloco, but it was necessary in the crime of cuckoldry to do your own revenging. He drank incessantly to work up a rage, because he, in fact, was so tired of it all that he wished to go to Paris, say to the Plaza Athénée, eat and drink and forget. But that would mean the end of his pride and he would have nothing left except money.

When the limousine had left the brutal scene at the cabin Tibey tried to expunge his near regret and horror until four hours later and halfway to Durango he was nearly incoherent. He had the chauffeur stop a little while later and in the bare dawn light he examined the sedated Miryea and slapped her bloodied face. Partly for histrionics—the men in the car would spread the story of his vengeance—he screamed and ranted: "O my love whom I wanted to bear sons, you fucking faithless whore, you thankless evil bitch, you want to fuck you shall be fucked fifty times a day before you die."

[46]

And that was what happened for Tibey was a master of revenge: for three days in a bare white room Miryea sat on a high stool dosed with amphetamines while a half-dozen rattlesnakes crawled around the floor. When she was on the verge of slipping to the floor she was administered ever-increasing doses of heroin over a period of two weeks, then prettified by a hairdresser and taken to the crudest of whorehouses in Durango, patronized by the poorest cowboys and miners and riffraff. Her lips and torn ear which had been sewn up by a veterinarian had begun to heal but the blotched-up job was heartbreaking on her otherwise flawlessly beautiful features. Despite this she was the most popular girl in the house, mostly because everyone knew the story and the men were conscious of feminine infidelities, real and imagined, and the slight pale figure of Miryea on the soiled sheets aroused their lust to previously unknown levels. Toward the end of the month, though, the madam erred out of greediness and cut Miryea's heroin dosage to the point that she recaptured her consciousness and sank a knife into a man's neck, drawing it secretively from his pocket as he was punishing her. The man was a foremen on a big ranch and the incident created a scandal. Tibey relented and had Miryea placed in an asylum run by an order of nuns for terminally insane women and girls. A heavy donation was made and would be repeated every year as long as she was kept there. During this period Tibey returned to a small ranch he owned near Tepehuanes, north of Durango. He was in mourning in his soul and deflowered a number of *peóne* girls in manic fits which alternated with periods of despondency so severe he wished to go to the whorehouse, and after that, the nunnery and try to claim back the happiness that had been so briefly his.

Mauro woke before dawn, dressed and then jogged the mile down the mountainside to the mission. He would drive his mysterious friend and benefactor, for no one knew his name, except the Federales, to Hermosillo to catch a bus or plane, he didn't know which. When he got to Cochran's room which was attached to the sheep-shed, Cochran was fully dressed and packed and sat as if in a trance on the edge of his bed. Mauro sat down in a chair and folded his hands in thought; he realized the gravity of the man's mission, and wished to go along and protect him as his new friend seemed to be too much of a dreamer to deal with the hard facts of killing. Then the door began to open and Cochran was up in a flash with the gift knife extended but it was only Mauro's mother bringing them coffee and *pan dulce*. Cochran apologized at his welcome saying that he didn't recognize her footsteps which made Mauro happy—a man who memorized footsteps can't be that much of a dreamer.

It took half the day in the old Powerwagon to get to Hermosillo. When they reached the main road Cochran had been shocked to see his first cars in two months, and recoiled when he saw a new car with an Indiana license plate drift past at a high speed. The truck made too much noise for talk and Cochran thought idly that he wouldn't like to be on the wrong side of Mauro who, like a Mala-mute, would never bark before he bit. Mauro was at the same time sleepy and lethal. Cochran was bright enough to realize that such simplicity and decisiveness were out of any truly civilized man's reach. At least he had never met such a man out in the world and doubted whether there were any. One Sunday when he had ridden the Percheron up to Mauro's small adobe cabin he felt he had begun to understand the man; on a dresser there had been a small shrine to his dead wife, and beneath the garishly tinted wedding picture, lying on a mountain lion pelt with a silver cross between a bleached mountain lion skull and a coyote skull, there was a fresh vase of votive flowers his daughter replaced daily though she barely remembered her mother. The vase sat on an unused Spanish bible that Diller had given them. Mauro couldn't read.

Now in the truck Cochran had the wit to recognize he was in the right frame of mind for what he had set out to do: he had few thoughts, only a purpose; the thoughts were so few that they would not interfere with his mission which clearly to him was to kill Tibey and to get Miryea back if she was alive. He had been so empty of thought that the world had begun, in an odd way, to delight him again because there was nothing in his mind to interfere with the beauty of the valley or, for that matter, the energetic ugliness of the contemporary world he was entering.

When they came to the outskirts of Hermosillo he told Mauro he wished to eat something then go to a place to catch a bus, but not inside the city because there was no point in taking a chance on being recognized. Mauro's uneasy confidence in his friend was further fortified.

On the far side of Hermosillo they found a roadhouse cantina with a full parking lot that also served as a stop for buses heading south. In a field beside the cantina parking lot they helped a Texan who was walking an unruly quarterhorse stud. Cochran realized the Texan was a first-rate horseman but he was coughing hard and seemed weakened by illness and had been knocked flat. Mauro picked up the Texan while Cochran calmed the horse and put him back in the trailer. The Texan began cursing in Spanish as he staggered, then leaned against his pickup.

"That sonofabitch has got me about buffaloed but boys I tell you I'm not quite myself or I'd throw him and put the goddamn boot to that cocksucker expensive as he is because he's bought and sold or I would sure as shit put a bullet between his fuckin' eyes but I want to deliver him in good shape so I'm going to dope the fucker so they think they got a good calm stud, then I'm getting the fuck out of this country which gives me the shits the minute I cross the fucking border."

Then the Texan offered his hand to Mauro and Cochran and they spoke about the problems of hauling stud horses. Cochran oddly took his cue from Mauro who saw the man as guileless. The Texan was caught awry when Cochran spoke perfect English.

"Hey buddy I thought you was a fucking *campesino*, you know a *peóne*. You get the shits in this place too? Let's eat on me. Have a few drinks."

They went into the cantina. Mauro had a beer and said it was time for him to leave for the long drive back. The Texan insisted he stay but it was a bad thing to leave the mission without its ambulance overnight. Cochran walked out to say good-bye in private—the noisy cantina put him on edge—and Mauro seemed embarrassed. He handed him a small package.

"My mother asks that you wear this. She says it will help you destroy your enemies. I know that you are an intelligent man but it can't hurt to wear it under your shirt."

Cochran unwrapped the package. It was the necklace of coyote teeth. He had not a trace of superstition in his bones but appreciated the gesture.

"Tell her I'll wear it gladly. I'm sure it will help."

Back in the cantina the Texan was drinking shots with beer chasers. The food had arrived but the Texan only picked at it. He rambled on about picking up the stud horse in Arizona for delivery in Torreón. He got a ten percent cut for engineering the deal between two wealthy breeders and delivering the horse.

"Tell you the truth *pardo*, I'm plumb fucking tired of this racket. Had a good string of mares myself on a little ranch over by Van Horn but my wife left and I just pissed away these good mares on booze and ladies. You oughta stop and visit someday because there's always two deer in the freezer and a few good old girls stopping by. You ain't a dope addict behind that beard are you?"

"Nope. I'm on the run from the IRS, you know." Cochran liked his invention.

"Fuck'em. Don't pay a cent. I work on cash and they don't know I'm alive, friend. If they come in your yard just shoot the cocksuckers." He paused and drank deeply. "You give up and go to prison and the crazies are liable to booger you. Never let them take you alive. Where you going anyhow?"

"Down toward Durango, I think . . ."

"Shit, why didn't you say so. Got to go to near there myself. You got a free ride. You don't want to ride on no bus where everyone pisses on the seat."

The Texan ordered a drink and it occurred to Cochran that he was being shimmied pleasantly into a driver's job which was fine by him. The Texan looked to be in his early fifties but it was hard to tell, he had obviously lived so hard. He was an arrogant old peacock with a concho belt and Tony Lama python skin boots. The Texan winked and lifted back the lapel of his denim coat revealing a cold blue ·44·

"Anybody goes for that horse he's liable to get his nuts shot off. I can shoot the pecker off a running buck at one hundred yards. Maybe more."

Cochran ate with relish but limited himself to two beers thinking of the bleak wave of sentiment drinking with Mauro had caused. He looked up hearing a booming voice at the door and his heart raced, he shivered and his body turned cold and clammy. It was the huge man from the night at the cabin, elegantly dressed and with two scruffy bodyguards. Cochran watched as the man's eyes swept over the cantina passing him without noticing anything.

"You seen a goddamn ghost or something?" The Texan looked at Cochran, then watched the huge man walk back toward the men's room while his guards sat at a table and began flirting with a waitress.

"Big sonofabitch."

"Please go start the truck. I'll be with you in a moment." Cochran's voice was so cold and level the Texan nodded soberly, stood up and threw a hundred peso note on the table.

"Be waiting for you kiddo. Be careful."

Cochran moved swiftly to the men's room keeping his eyes down and walking slightly atilt like a drunken *peóne*. At the men's room door he palmed Mauro's knife and exhaled his breath. The big man was standing at the mirror combing his hair and barely glanced at Cochran, who owned the invisibility of the poor. Cochran splashed water messily on his own face and on the huge man who turned in instant rage and raised his arm to club the idiot *peóne*. Cochran stooped as if to take the blow and brought the knife upward, holding the handle in both hands, ripping upward with all his strength starting at the huge man's balls, upward to his sternum where he pivoted and swiped the knife across the man's neck laying it open to the neckbone. As the big man teetered he kicked open a toilet stall and pushed him in where he crashed against the stool. Cochran glanced in the mirror checking himself for blood, grinned and left unhurriedly.

The Texan had pulled the truck and horse trailer up to the front of the cantina and smiled as Cochran came out diffidently swinging Diller's carpetbag. "Always liked a winner," the Texan said as Cochran got in the truck.

"That one wasn't even close." He leaned back in the seat and sorted through the tapes as the Texan pulled onto the highway. The Texan wanted to make Culiacán by dark but then Ciudad Obregón had the best whorehouse in the world and maybe he had one more hard-on left in his system.

By midafternoon Cochran took over the driving while the Texan slept off his lunch with a three-hour nap. He stopped in Los Mochis for gas and the Texan awoke coughing violently and gasping for breath. He tore open his kit and shook out a half-dozen pills which he swallowed with a beer from the cooler. The Texan held his head in his hands for a long while and Cochran was alarmed as he pulled back on the highway. He was oddly unworried about pursuit, knowing the local police would interpret the killing as a dope revenge number and a Texas-licensed truck hauling a stud horse was an unlikely prospect. The Texan slumped back in the seat and tried to breathe deeply, and smiled.

"Jesus, you drove right through Ciudad Obregón and I was thinking of stopping for a piece of ass. You never know when it's your last and it appears I'm hanging on a short string." He paused, listening to a Willie Nelson tape on the deck. "I heard him sing years ago over in San Antonio and he sure looks like a pisshead hippie but he sings good."

"I hope you feel okay."

"Boy, if I could give you a list of what's wrong but it'd bore the piss out of anyone. At the VA Hospital because I'm a bonafide veteran they said to me now we don't know why you're alive and I said I been too sick to die for years. I'm just going to disappear, right. They wanted my body and I said piss on you I'm going to be buried in Van Horn next to my mother."

They stayed that night at a coastal hotel outside of Mazatlán. It was moderately expensive and the Texan loaned Cochran some clothes saying he was far enough

[54]

south not to need that bean-picker costume. In the room the Texan swallowed a big glass of tequila and said he was ready for a woman and when he asked for his expenses from a rich horse breeder they had to throw in an extra five hundred bucks for what he explained as "whores, booze, tattoos and shit medicine."

After dinner the Texan invited Cochran to accompany him to a whorehouse but he declined saying he'd feed, walk and water the horse.

"Strikes me you had a big day and some poontang might ease your mind."

"Nope. Killed a man I hated today and I don't want to mix my pleasures. I want to lay in bed and think how good it felt."

The Texan nodded and lit a cigar. He was no man's fool. "I expect you had your reasons. I blew the foot off a man years ago who screwed my wife. Did a year for it but I smiled thinking of that bastard's empty boot."

The Texan made an arrangement with a waiter who called a cab. Cochran went back to the room, looked in the mirror and barely recognized himself. He rinsed the dried blood off Mauro's knife in the sink, then fingered the strange necklace. He whistled that folk song and one bar soared tremulously against the back of his brain. He knew he had barely begun and couldn't care less if he died in the trying. In a curious way he was one of those pilots to whom the distance from the ground never removed the threat of death: his imagination was too great for that. He went out to walk the horse thinking morosely that the Texan was

[55]

tottering precariously on the edge of death, knew it, and was stepping on the gas.

He awoke just after dawn and was alarmed to see the Texan hadn't returned. He found him in the pickup, gray-faced with his shirtfront caked with blood and vomit. He examined him for wounds and found none, then took his pulse which was irregular. He walked the horse a few minutes wondering what to do. Back in the truck the Texan squinted at him and asked feebly for a beer. He drew a beer from the tepid water of the cooler and watched the Texan swallow his pills.

"You got to see a doctor, friend."

The Texan nodded and fell asleep. Cochran found Route 40 to Durango and Torreón, then stopped for coffee to think things over. He knew the wise blood would say to abandon the man and get on with his business. But he hadn't the heart to do it and it should be anyway just another day. He walked back to the truck and now the Texan's eyes were open.

"I can see what you're thinking. Is this old fucker going to die on my hands? What will I do with him for Jesus's sake and what will I do with the fucking horse? So don't worry, just help me deliver the horse and I'll make it worth your while. I says to this lady last night, make it good it might be my last and she made it pretty good." He mumbled all of this and Cochran stared out the window embarrassed, driving intensely along the twisting mountain road to Durango, as the Texan fell into a deep sleep.

The Texan perked up somewhat after lunch in Durango and they had started on the road for Torreón. The air-conditioning had given out and it was nightmarishly hot. He talked giddily about the horse business while Cochran brooded about Durango. He thought that once you got off the tourist tract Mexico became a lot less comprehensible, almost feudal and difficult to move in without notice. He needed desperately to devise some sort of cover and horse trader wouldn't do. He might have to use his friend's Mexico City government connection though he wished not to. He had to be smart enough to reach Miryea without getting murdered in the process. He was startled halfway to Torreón to find the Texan grasping his arm.

"Was that the big man that shoved in your face? Maybe more?" Now the man was flushed and clenched his hands repeatedly. "You don't have to say nothing. Tell you the truth I think I'm shitcanned but this is good-looking country and I never wanted to die where it was ugly. I dreamed I'd die in Big Timber, Montana. Just put me under a fucking rock as I don't want buzzards to get me."

A little later they reached a resplendent hacienda with two sets of gates with guards, concentration camp barbed wire, formal gardens, swimming pool, a clay tennis court, jumping ring for horses, a lavish home and stables. They drank sherry waiting for the *baróne* to arrive. The Texan accepted the open cigar box of money and closed the box without counting the money.

"I assume I'll be able to reach my home without being relieved of this money," the Texan said in surprisingly formal Spanish.

The *baróne* laughed and said in Oxford English, "I sympathize with your worries." He handed the Texan his card. "Just repeat the name to anyone who would bother you. They will shit down their legs and run like rabbits."

They were shown to a guesthouse next to the stables where they were served a meal and a bottle of Scotch. During the night the Texan began talking to his mother and walked around alternately laughing and weeping and drinking. He died just after three A.M. and Cochran adjusted him in a sitting position so rigor mortis would cooperate with the seat of the pickup. At first light he loaded the Texan into the pickup and drew his Stetson over his eyes. He waved to the guards on the way out through the double gates and buried the Texan a few miles down the road under the rocks as he had desired. Three cows watched with momentary curiosity. Cochran drove straight through to Mexico City with occasional brief naps. On the way back through Durango he whistled Miryea's little song which gave him strength. He was a hard man to beat now; he was on his way. Somebody had stolen his soul and he meant to have it back. He made Mexico City in twenty-four hours and abandoned the truck and trailer in the parking lot of the airport. In the trailer he dressed in the Texan's best clothes and caught a cab for the Camino Real with a cigar box under his arm.

The nunnery in which Miryea was held as a prisoner was seven miles or so from Durango in the country house of an eighteenth-century nobleman, now fallen a bit over the edge of decay but pleasant to look at from a distance where it reminded you of Normandy. After a detoxification process to cure her of her month's forced addiction in the

brothel, she was let out of her room and left to wander in
the courtyard with the other patients who were considered
well mannered enough to be given this minimal freedom.
She was watched closely by a homely mean-minded nun
with a trace of a moustache. No chances would be taken
with so profitable a prisoner. Miryea especially disgusted
the mother superior; how could a woman of such noble
birth and good education become a drug addict and a
crazed prostitute in the cheapest brothel and have her
features severely marred by some pimp. The letter given
her by Señor Mendez's chauffeur was a heartbreaking plea
to save the poor woman's soul. But the mother superior was
essentially kind, if a trifle venal, and after a month she
allowed Miryea to order some books from Mexico City
though she inspected the letter carefully. The young girls,
barely more than children and schizoid, received a great
deal of mothering attention from other inmates, but there
were three little autistic girls who were left totally alone in
their mute darkness because they responded to no one.
Miryea decided to make them her own special charge and
sought books on the subject. She sat for days on end in the
sunny courtyard with the three children, helped dress and
feed them, sang them to sleep and used her considerable
wit to try to get any conceivable response. She nervously
rubbed the scar on her lips which had healed into a thin
cord of hardened tissue. She was traumatized to a degree
that her thoughts turned mostly to her childhood summers
on Cozumel. She and her sister would swim all day, pick
flowers, collect seashells, and when their household held no
other guests, accompany their father out into the Gulf on

his big sportfishing boat. Her father had died years before or he would have surely come to her aid. One of the boatmates had made love to her sister when she was only thirteen and her father had had the man conveniently drowned on a long trip looking for sailfish. She dared not believe her lover would come for her though she refused to believe him dead. Someday she would leave this place and find out the great harm she had done him, and perhaps, if he were not repelled by the scars, they would be lovers again, if only on the moon. Often she would lose contact totally in her dreaming and on becoming conscious again, would be surprised she was alive, would touch her hands together and look around the room or courtyard with truly appalled curiosity. When her dread became especially great she subtly looked for ways to escape but there were none and then she would find a place to weep until she had sufficient composure to return to her charges, who looked at her with no signs of seeing or hearing, like blind and deaf puppies.

Back on his ranch outside of Tepehuanes, Baldassaro Tibey brooded the autumn away. From his breakfast room he could see the *cordillera* of the Sierra Madres but the mountains brought him bad thoughts of his father whom he considered far nobler than himself. His father had been a close friend of Eufemio Zapata, the brother of Emiliano, and a lieutenant in the Revolution. He died when Tibey was ten from the remnants of wounds and years of hard riding, drinking and fighting. Many old men in Culiacán still spoke of his father and despite Tibey's great wealth they did not give him remotely equal honor. Tibey, shrewd as he was, owned an idealistic streak and dreamed in his youth of leading some preposterous insurrection. He lived as a victim, albeit prosperous, of those dreams he built at age nineteen when all of us reach our zenith of idealistic nonsense. Nineteen is the age of the perfect foot soldier who will die without a murmur, his heart aflame with patriotism. Nineteen is the age at which the brain of a nascent poet in his rented room soars the highest, suffering gladly the assault of what he thinks is the god in him. Nineteen is the last year that a young woman will marry purely for love. And so on. Dreams are soul chasers, and forty years later Tibey was feeling cornered. He slept badly and became careless and haggard. He went out with his ranch foreman in the helicopter and shot three dozen coyotes who were bothering the sheep, knowing full well it was likely one decrepit coyote doing the damage. Miryea had made him promise not to shoot coyotes and showed him a book on the subject that he read with curiosity. He made the promise. He was often a baby in her arms. She was the only release he owned from what he was on earth. She had drawn him back to nineteen. Now, both in night-mares and in waking moments, he felt the tick in his hand when the razor went through her lips and struck against her teeth.

At the Camino Real Cochran was told there was noth-ing available except a suite which he signed up for with an affected Texas accent to accompany his clothing. He wanted to get out of this lobby suddenly, remembering the feast after the tennis match win with Tibey. He ordered up dinner and a bottle of wine, feeling bone-tired and jittery. He had a quick shower, taking the cigar box with the money paid for the stud horse packed inside. Over dinner he would count the money for no reason he could think of, and someday trace the Texan's heirs in Van Horn, perhaps pay the horse breeder though he doubted it. He called the brother of his friend, the Aeromexico pilot. The man welcomed him cordially to Mexico City, told him that it was not good to speak on the phone, not to leave the room, and that he would be there at midmorning to offer any help he could. Cochran slept well with the Texan's cold blue .44 under his pillow.

At dawn he ordered up coffee and sat on his balcony looking down at the gardens in a reverie until the first human, a gardener, arrived, at which point he went back into the suite to meditate on his plans for both vengeance and survival, two instincts which are rarely married with any security.

When the man arrived Cochran at first didn't like the suavity contained in the pale-gray pin-striped suit, the outward shell painted so deftly on the surface of the politician. Then the man became nervous, ordered a drink on the room service, and asked Cochran to speak in Castilian as well as he could. Satisfied, the man said he could do nothing to help Cochran with Tibey other than offer him an identity and the aid of the only man he could trust, a lifelong friend of honor who lived in Durango. The man explained that they made many movies in Durango, usually American and Mexican westerns and Cochran would be able to move freely under an identity as a textile mill owner from Barcelona who was interested both in real estate and the movie business. He opened his briefcase and gave Cochran some convincing letters of introduction, and money which Cochran refused saying he had plenty. And a .38 Police Special that his brother passed along. Cochran laughed and said he was already overarmed. The man turned grave and handed him a folder on Tibey which he refused saying that he knew enough.

"You understand that Señor Mendez is what you call laundered; I mean he is powerful politically and his money is clean now. You will surely die and my brother whom I love cares for you. But even in this absurd suit I know it's probably better to die than to live with it. My friend in Durango has found no trace of the woman but is working hard on the search."

Now Cochran liked the man and tried to reassure him but the man swallowed his drink in a single gulp and looked away. He said he had received a message from a Mauro at the mission, the man who had taken Cochran to Hermosillo, and soon after they had left that dawn a huge man and two henchmen had come looking with murder in their eyes.

"I gutted that fucker like a big fat pig," Cochran said with a wry smile.

The man nodded, acting reassured. Before he left he asked Cochran to destroy his phone numbers after memorizing them. He had a brother, but he also had a wife and children and hopefully a future.

He spent the afternoon getting himself tailored to look like a wealthy businessman from Barcelona. He took out a few thousand dollars and packed the cigar box inside the television set. He bought several suits and accoutrements, and had his hair styled and his beard trimmed, had a manicure and made his reservations for Durango for the next morning on an early plane. He practiced the sort of good foreigner's English where a stray indefinite article is left out. He posted a long ruminating letter to his daughter saying that he hoped to be home soon, and that he had been a little sad lately because his bird dog Doll had been hit by a car. Early in the evening he packed in a new, expensive piece of luggage. He ate lightly and lay naked in the dark on his bed listening to a Bach concerto on the radio.

He lay there sleeplessly remembering a minor quarrel he had one evening with Miryea in the apartment. It was over some silly literary matter about who killed whom in *Pascual Duarte*, that murderous book, and a certain coolness entered into the evening as he blathered on. He knew he was arguing on hormones, stirring his brain with his dick, as it were. He was a beautiful talker but she pursued his wrongheadedness without mercy, reminding him that language was a convenience of the heart, not something to bludgeon people with. He slapped a pillow over his face in embarrassment and yelled for Christ's sake forgive my big mouth. He heard her laugh and under the darkness of the pillow he felt her mouth caressing him. He slid the pillow back above his eyes and saw her knee and had an awakening of sorts, a prolonged and lucid sense that he had never looked at a woman's knee. His eyes moved upward until he saw all of Miryea and for a moment it seemed he was looking at her incomprehensibly and for the first time. He repeated this newness of vision, sweeping his eyes from her curled toes to her falling black shiny hair over his belly. His love for her became at the same time complete, fearsome and unbearable. Afterward he spoke to her about it and she seemed to understand perfectly. There was a lightness to the mood as if for the first time he comprehended the reality of life on earth outside himself; it calmed him in a strange way so that he slept easily because he no longer cared if he slept. He gave up quickly trying to attune the experience to a language construct, as if life were an especially filthy mirror and speechless love cleansed this mirror and made life not only bearable but something lived with eagerness, energy, an expectancy whose pleasure didn't depend on fatality.

In the morning he slept calmly through his departure time, but just as calmly chartered a Beechcraft, ate breakfast and took a taxi to the airport. It was a clear sunny morning and a brief rain in the night plus a wind from the north had swept the normally filthy air of Mexico City clean and clear. Standing on the tarmac he looked to the mountains in the south out of which a religion lost to the present had been born. The pilot was deferential and they flew into a brisk headwind and low to look at the country.

They flew over Celaya, Aguascalientes, over the Quemada ruins and Fresnillo, over the Zacatecas border and into the province of Durango and its capital of the same name. They beat the airline which had a layover in Guadalajara by a few minutes. A man named Amador was waiting for him.

CHAPTER

III

The appearance of Amador confused Cochran momentarily. He wished to be a great deal more anonymous than is possible in Mexico. They exchanged pleasantries in Spanish, then turned in alarm to watch a woman who was screaming. Cochran recognized her as an American actress-model.

"*Dónde esta* my fucking *gato vivo*," she screamed over and over while the baggage man flipped through the suitcases in alarm. "Oh, you fuckers probably eat cats." Others at the baggage counter stepped back shocked, then·began smiling. Cochran approached and attempted to calm her down, but she was inconsolable. Then another baggage wagon arrived and the cat was found. She opened the small cage sobbing, "Oh my dear Pooky, my lover, I won't let them eat you." She looked up at Cochran and smiled but Amador drew him away gripping his arm tightly.

In the car Amador admonished him, speaking English in a southern drawl, explaining he had once been on the

Dallas police force. It was unthinkable of Cochran to speak in public the way he had when his cover had been so carefully prepared. "In this town it isn't a game."

Cochran felt a little depressed and apologized and Amador laughed. "My friend, I don't want us to get our asses shot off." Then he fell silent and Cochran looked at him sensing the badness of the news and not wanting to ask. On the floor by the seat was an ugly looking sawed-off shotgun with a scarred and worn stock. The statue of Saint Christopher on the dashboard seemed to stare down at the gun with a pastel stare, the silly pink lips open in benediction. Amador was of only medium height but thickset, with a massive neck and arms. He slowed down for a cow ambling across the road.

"I am sorry to say that the woman you are looking for was kept in a whorehouse for a month, shot up with smack. Now Señor Mendez has removed her from the whorehouse and taken her God knows where. I've not found out yet."

Cochran was suddenly wet from head to toe. He gazed at the green fertile valley and brown mountains beyond. He forgot to breathe and felt vertigo to the point that the car seemed to float.

"I must tell you that you'll be shot like a dog unless you are careful and probably shot like a dog anyway."

In the hotel suite at the El Presidente Amador ordered up some food and drink. He told Cochran that he had found a house because a hotel was too public to be suitable. Señor Mendez, or Tiburón as he was known locally, was at his mountain ranch but there were a dozen men in Durango in his employ. Cochran should move to the house in a few days when it became available, meanwhile there were necessary meetings with *políticos* under his guise as a film and land investor. They both relaxed a little over the meal and Amador spoke of the Aeromexico pilot and his brother in Mexico City, for whom his mother had served as a nursemaid in their youth. Then Amador lapsed into silence, drew inward and his face became impassive.

"The truth is she stabbed a man while he made love to her. This man has announced he will strangle her. So she is in double danger. I would think Tiburón would put her in a place where no one could reach her but I have no idea where. I know you must do nothing without me."

Amador left early in the evening after elaborating on possible plans and accepting a large amount of money to be used as bribes for information. Cochran lay on the bed feeling waves of nausea roll through his soul, shaking him until the bed rattled, clenching his fists and his legs cramping in a rage far past weeping. He had been foolish enough to believe that as he recovered over the past few months the world might be recovering with him, that in the back of his mind Miryea might be found in reasonably good health and he could convince Tibey how hopeless it was and he and Miryea would fly off happily as if in some tragic but pleasant-ending movie. But now he felt murderous and at the same time without hope. He touched the small pistol strapped to his calf, then got up and put on the shoulder holster with the .44. He put on his suit coat and checked himself in the mirror. He had visibly aged a half-dozen years in a few months. He poured a glass of tequila and sat down out on the balcony sipping at the bittersweet liquid and watching the full moon of late September cast sweeping shadows through the scudding clouds. The shadows swept intermittently across the courtyard of the hotel which was an elegantly remodeled prison. The moon shone white on the back wall where prisoners had no doubt once been lined up and shot for reasons too simple to be worth remembering. He thought of Tibey in the distant mountains in the direction of the moon, then wondered if Miryea could see the moon. All three of them were, in fact, watching the moon in their separate agonies, all of them envious of the moon in its aerial distance floating so far above earthbound agonies. He remembered a hot summer night in Tucson when they turned out the lights and took an air mattress out to the balcony and made love under the full moon. Both the moon and their entwined bodies had been hot and still, and the sheen of Miryea's damp neck had caught the moonlight. There had been people below them in the distance drinking wine on a blanket on the lawn and listening to classical music on a radio.

He grew restless and went downstairs to the hotel lobby and bar. The actress-model was sitting with two producer types parodically dressed in pressed denim and lavish Indian jewelry. Cochran pretended not to notice her but she jumped to her feet and approached holding her cat. She thanked him profusely for helping her recover the cat. Cochran glanced around at the dozen pairs of watching eyes, bowed and said something polite in Spanish and walked away. She stood there puzzled for a moment and shrugged. He had a drink and thought about the woman whose photo he had seen so often in magazines. In person she glistened with her cold, hard classical features becoming more angular and rough at the same time. She had glittery cocaine eyes and the low husky voice of a pissed off barmaid.

After a sleepless night Amador picked him up for a meeting with the local governor and a member of the film commission. The provincial government was headquartered in a huge palace once owned by an eighteenth-century duke. Cochran paused to look at some splendid imitation of Diego Rivera murals, a colorful agitprop display rendering rather honestly the torments of the *peónes* and *campesinos*. The head of the film commission met them in the hall and seemed very nervous about Amador, which pleased Cochran who knew it was best to have a badass on your side. Amador waited in the hall as he and the film man had a polite cup of coffee with the governor who made him nervous with his florid reminiscences of Barcelona.

Cochran and Amador were escorted to a limousine for a trip to an active movie set on the property owned by John Wayne, who had made a number of westerns in the area. At the last moment the film man was called to the phone and he asked Amador why he made the man so nervous. Amador told the chauffeur to stand outside and laughingly said that the film man was a gentleman while he, poor Amador, was responsible for the security of a number of big American-owned ranches and mines and his methods were occasionally a bit crude.

Out at the movie set, which had absurdly tight security, Cochran noted the huge size of the crew. It never occurred to him that it took so many people beyond those you saw on the screen. He had been distracted on the way up the valley because the corn crop looked so rich and green that if you squinted to block the mountains you could have been in Indiana. He remembered the boredom of cultivating corn on the rickety old Ford tractor. His brother had been much better at farming though he had been glad to move to San Diego. Indiana farmers made good Navy men and good fishermen. In his youth his father and uncles had gone on fishing expeditions up in Michigan returning severely hung over but with coolers full of bluegills, bass and trout. He had been taken on the last trip before the move and had been allowed to drink cut-rate A&P beer and play poker, though in recognition of his low status he cleaned fish far into the night.

He ordered the car stopped when the chauffeur said *corallo*. Amador wanted to kill the snake but Cochran said no, and followed it off the road and into the dry grass where it wriggled under a rock. Once when he was at Torrejón he had taken a hop on a C5A down to Nairobi. They only had a twenty-four-hour layover which had limited his view of Africa, other than from the air, to a long night of gambling, and later, the company of a Galla woman from Ethiopia, a tribe legendary for the beauty of their women. But he had a few hours to kill the next morning and had taken a taxi to the Nairobi Herpetarium where he wandered slowly among the tourists looking at the snakes in the glass cages. His favorite had been the green mamba—long, thin, a translucent green resembling a green buggy whip with motions so abrupt and quick one backed away from the cage. He reflected on the beauty of threat: the fatal equipment of the mamba owning a beauty shared by the grizzly, rattler, hammerhead shark, perhaps even the black Phantom he flew—an utterly malign black death instrument.

Two guards at the cattle gate had waved them on. The guards stooped in the hot dust watching a scorpion they had dropped on an anthill. Beyond the fence a mare watched with her ears tilted back while her foal pranced sideways, then was still in the shimmering heat. He turned to watch the brown cloud of dust from the passing car float over them. This idiotic charade increased his taste for the kill.

Cochran was introduced to the producer who happened to be down from Hollywood for a few days. The man was very short, wore a French denim suit and smoked a big stogie. He attached himself to Cochran with a string of inane patter, smelling the obvious money and circling Cochran in the heat of the canyon like a rabid ferret. The director was a noncommittal, stylish Englishman who spoke halting Spanish and Cochran asked him questions to the exclusion of the producer. The actress-model was brought forward, dripping wet, wearing a towel around her head, and a lightweight white cotton robe. He bowed and kissed her hand, catching a glance in a part of the robe of her pubic mound behind wet flesh-colored panties. She called out for a translator and the director offered his services.

"These yo-yos have had me in the river through seven takes. I look so awful but it's the obligatory piece of skin, you know." She primped while the director translated.

"On the contrary, you look edible."

[73]

She laughed raucously hearing the translation. "Tell him I would love to be part of such a dinner."

Some hundred yards away beneath an immense cottonwood tree a pickup was parked next to a semi holding the gaffer's equipment. In the pickup a man watched the scene through binoculars. He wondered what Amador was doing with the elegant gentleman who walked to the fine piece of ass he had just watched swimming through the binoculars. He focused on the gentleman, stared for a long moment and sharply drew in his breath. It was the man who made love in the desert and whom his dead friend had beaten in the cabin, the lover of Tiburón's wife. He exhaled as he started the truck in confusion, knowing he should report to Tibey immediately.

At that moment Tibey was sitting at the desk of his study, far up in the mountains in the ranch house near Tepehuanes. He was sweating profusely from quail hunting and his hunting companions from Mexico City were eating lunch in the dining room. He would join them when he finished his business which offered itself in the form of a supplicating ranch foreman, the one whom Miryea had stabbed. Tibey was twirling a .357 in whirling circles with a pen through the trigger guard on the inkblotter.

"I've known you since you were a child. Now your big mouth says that you will strangle my wife for stabbing you. I don't blame you but you have forgotten whose wife she is. I could kill you . . ." Tibey paused and aimed the pistol, pulling the trigger and the hammer clacked against the

[74]

empty chamber and the man shrieked, falling to his knees. "But I won't kill you. Leave for Mérida by tomorrow. Never return. Here is the name of a man who will give you a job." Tibey scrawled a name on a slip of paper and held up his hand to silence the man who tried to speak. "Take this pistol as a gift. It will help you remember your mouth." The man scurried off with a dark ring in his crotch where he had pissed his pants. Tibey joined his friends at lunch with a smile. "I have learned my cattle are doing especially well this fall."

Miryea had lapsed after her comparatively pleasant hiatus. The autistic children did not respond; she could not penetrate their brains to the extent of even a minimal response. They sat next to her on the bench uttering the moans of the damned and she imagined that she looked to them as a photo would to an animal, that is, an incomprehensible shadow to which neither the memory nor the senses brought an offering. She ate very little and had become painfully thin and sallow. The mother superior fretted over her profitable charge, not understanding that Miryea was what a previous century had called "pining away," drawing inward in her own peculiar autism caused by love and the aching vacuum of the loss of love, so that her nights had become insomniac and barren of hope; nights of extreme consciousness shared by those on the edge of severe breakdown, terminal patients in the cancer ward whom drugs have assuaged into a state of nonlocalized dread. A flowering tree they had looked at when they were ten years old and spending a lonely afternoon will come back to them with lucid poignancy so they may once again smell a magnolia blossom they picked up idly from the grass.

Tibey was having a nightcap in bed reading a week-old *Wall Street Journal* when his man drove up in the courtyard. Late arrivals always meant bad news and he threw the paper in disgust.

The man entered the bedroom accompanied by Tibey's bull mastiff who had, not incidentally, bitten a hand off a young *peóne* the week before. The young *peóne* had hoped to snatch a mallard from a flock Tibey raised for the table. In the not so distant past Tibey would have regarded the event as just, but he had spent a day considering destroying the old dog, rejected the idea; then that evening he rode his prize Arab mare over to the *peóne's* hut. While the wife prepared an herbal tea Tibey dangled the frightened man's two children on his knees, giving the little boy an expensive jackknife and the girl a small gold cross he wore around his neck. He told the man to appear at the bank in Tepehuanes the first day of every month where one hundred dollars would be waiting for him, and that the following day some men would arrive to move the family to much better quarters with those who worked his ranch. The man, who was a good horseman, would be expected to keep an eye on the foals. Tibey had begun to do oblique penance for what he had done to his wife, no matter her sins.

The man who stood by the bed remembered the night he had held the arms of Tibey's wife and his hands had come away flecked with her blood as she slipped to the floor. It was good that Tiburón didn't know that he had visited the brothel repeatedly and had given the woman a taste of his own private sexual tortures so that even in her heroin narcosis she dreaded his appearance.

He gave Tibey the news as simply as possible and was surprised at Tiburón's impassiveness. He added that perhaps it was the gringo who had killed the huge man whom they lovingly referred to as The Elephant.

"Doubtless. Watch him carefully. He'll never find her and if he comes close to me we'll kill him."

After the man left Tibey poured another nightcap and was distracted by memories of what a fine time they had had playing tennis and skeet shooting. Under Cochran's tutelage he had been on the verge of developing a fine backhand. He felt foolish standing there in a silk robe thinking of an absurdity like tennis when he should be thinking of killing the betrayer. Of course he would have to kill Cochran unless he went back to the States, or maybe he would anyway, and have Miryea poisoned to wipe the slate clean and have something that resembled a fresh start, which he recognized as an equally absurd idea. The die was cast so deeply in blood that none of them would be forgiven by their memories. Meanwhile he would let his former friend eat his heart away in the fruitless search for his beloved.

At the southern outskirts of Durango Amador had taken the temporary lease of a sprawling, elegant villa for Cochran. There was a pool, a lovely statuary, and the rooms were a cool-vaulted brick with many fireplaces and a well-equipped kitchen where Amador's sister prepared the meals. Amador had taken on another relative, a tall, thin man from the mountains as an additional guard so he could sleep with comfort, and do some snooping in town.

But the dog days had begun and Cochran found it difficult not to crack under the strain: days dense with heat and windless evenings when he did nothing but sit on the patio, drink Carta Blanca, and watch the insects fluttering against the backdrop of clouds beneath which in lazy gyres the vultures seemed to sleep in the air. The clouds were the most wonderful clouds on earth. Amador told him that scientists came all the way to Durango to study the clouds and he readily believed it. He stared at the clouds until they entered his dream life where they accelerated and rolled, hurtled past, as they had done at extreme speeds from his jet fighter.

Amador was plainly stymied and hated to admit it, though he knew Cochran understood. Amador had a passing acquaintance with Tiburón for a decade and considered him a master criminal of superlative wit and taste. He never admired Tiburón's wealth—there were many wealthy fools among the Americans whose property he protected—but he was a little envious of the man's consummate skills at engineering big deals to the extent that he no longer had to trifle with the filth of his past. To Amador, finding Miryea was another instance of Tiburón's wit: the woman had apparently disappeared from earth in a less than immaculate ascension. Wiped out. Erased. And not among all of Amador's reliable connections was there a whisper or shred of evidence to trace her whereabouts. Amador would not have been surprised if she had been dropped down some fathomless, abandoned mine shaft, or lay bound in a bag of rocks at the bottom of a mountain lake. He said so to Cochran who merely nodded in stony agreement one late evening when they had had a great deal to drink.

The cover for Cochran's visit was quickly becoming exhausted. They had visited every available ranch for sale in the area, heard every imaginable spiel from the film commission people on the advantages of the Durango area, visited every antiqued and genuinely bedraggled movie set from the past—at best a haunting procedure where movies from the past were recognized and the past that went along with the movies emerged from its peculiar tunnel. They had gone to a daffy cocktail party given by the movie people on one of the sets, with a lavish buffet table set up, and a mariachi band. The liquor flowed and the *campesinos* watched with curiosity from a polite distance. The actress-model had become angry with Cochran's indifference which she believed had to be feigned. On the drive home with Amador after the party Cochran suggested morosely that they go to Tepehuanes and blow Tibey out of his socks with the Ruger 30.06 that Amador kept in the truck. It would be fun, Cochran said, to watch the motherfucker buck and somersault through the air with half his head disintegrating into separate pieces of meat.

"Then you would never find her," Amador said.

"You're right, friend. I am only exercising my fantasy life. I see him in the crosshairs of a scope when I don't even want to shoot him. I want to take her away. That's it. Plain and simple."

"If she's alive."

"I'll have to ask you not to mention that possibility."

"I'm sorry, friend." Then Amador smiled at how he had put a roast piglet left untouched at the buffet under his arm and had given it to an old man beyond the fence. The old man would have a happy night of indigestion.

A few days later Amador said that there was gossip about his continuing presence in Durango. They sat drinking coffee by the pool trying to concoct additional plans: the last of the bribes had been paid fruitlessly to the former madam who had been traced to Mazatlán. She had invented a tale that had sent them eagerly all the way to Zacatecas to the frowsiest pigsty of an address. The trip kept reemerging in pieces; a half-comic nightmare, a costume mission of terror on a side street in a slum.

When they finally had found the whorehouse Cochran became uncontainable. Amador held the madam and two pimps at bay in a dimly lit hallway while Cochran methodically kicked in a half-dozen doors in a state of whirling whiteness, so that the gun he held on the occupants held a terror beyond a simple gun: its owner had become red-eyed, utterly berserk. When he reached the last door he somehow believed Miryea had to be there and when the whore was found facedown beneath a shocked fat man, the man was uprooted from his perch and flung into a corner. Cochran turned the head of the comatose whore revealing the blunt face of an Indian woman in her forties and he howled then, running from the room. He set upon the pimps until Amador restrained him. Amador knew by then they had been duped and on the way back home he was wordless in his anger and drank deeply, a rarity for him. Cochran sat massaging his foot and ankle against the dashboard in his private agonies which included a sense of defeat, however momentary, that had taken over the marrow in his bones. In this state he had decided to sneak away from Amador, drive to Tepehuanes and shoot Tibey. (That very evening Tibey had dressed a peasant girl in a dress of Miryea's and then hurled her out of the house in disgust. His drunken regret made him sleepless and he wandered around his property in the waning moon until he wrapped himself in a horse blanket and slept with his bird dogs.) In private, Amador was planning the capture of Tiburón's headman, the man who had replaced The Elephant after his death. But that would be a last-ditch effort, a gesture of panic. Amador owned a Latin patience not possessed in any degree by Cochran. He let grudges pass for years until the appropriate time came to relieve himself of their burden. But now he needed to buy more time.

"You must have that beautiful actress over for dinner. Then everyone in town will think you are just another rich Spanish nitwit trying to relieve the pressure in his balls." Amador was pleased with his idea.

Cochran looked up at the elongated cirrus clouds that reminded him of what it must be like to be inside the skeleton of a whale. He agreed with Amador though he felt curiously sexless. A half hour after he gutted the big man and was driving down the road in the Texan's pickup he had felt an immediate lust for a girl standing under a tree by the side of the road but had been mildly embarrassed. In Da Nang after washing off the reeking sweat of a mission he had enjoyed whores who fixed a meal before he bedded them. Without at least a glimmer of the illusion of the romantic he felt dead sexually, and had since the age of thirty when in a state of depression he vowed not to sleep with a woman he did not want to talk to, eye to eye, at breakfast. He was so much more sophisticated in human-sexual terms than he had ever, until Miryea, had an opportunity to show. Without really thinking about it he had traveled unreturnably far from the glandular collisions of popular culture. He was immersed in love distant from the technical strenuosities of what had become a belabored map of sexual ecology where the proper steps yielded everything and nothing. A man who had been ineluctably married to fatality on a basis far surpassing that of ordinary domesticity did not want to piss away his life on nonsense.

And he felt the generalized fearfulness of his approaching age: Miryea seemed transparently his first, last and only shot at filling his life to a fullness that everything else could only dimly suggest. If you added it up, without her there was nothing—but with her even the simplest gestures of walking a bird dog in the desert, or selecting the ingredients for a meal for two rather than one took on an ineffable charm. One evening she had brought over a half-dozen types of fish and shellfish to make a Málaga seafood stew, not forgetting a pound of fresh ground beef for Doll who had been charmed away from her usual indifference to women. Cochran sat there through the afternoon staring at the clouds, letting the sun burn him while Amador's mother brought him a succession of cold drinks and snacks which he left for the appetites of the flies.

Amador had gone off rather happily to invite the actress-model for dinner, stopping at a florist's for a dozen roses, also at an amused drug wholesaler to shop for what he was sure was included in an actress's pharmacopoeia: some spectacular marijuana and at least serviceable to strong cocaine. He needed to arrange this repast to buy time. His friend had shown him the cigar box and had given him five thousand dollars as a gift for starters. Amador wished to add to his small ranch in the foothills where he raised a few cattle and knew the ease and sweetness that had only been occasional since his youth.

At the set the actress had been a bit haughty accepting the flowers, but immediately relented into a state of eager cooperation. She was fascinated by this man who lapsed in and out of her past few weeks, so unlike anyone she had met in her profession. She would be there at the stated time and during the rest of the day's shooting, on the uncomfortable back of a quarterhorse, she thought about what she would wear and how she would act.

After Amador presented the bouquet he glanced around, fixing for a moment on a particular pickup which he almost subliminally recognized—he had seen it too often of late. He walked a bit closer looking askance as if interested in the nonsense of making movies. He put on his sunglasses and took a cup of water from the back of the food truck letting his eyes sweep past the pickup. He recognized Tiburón's headman leaning against the tailgate affecting interest in the mountains.

That evening the actress-model arrived for dinner and stayed under uncommon circumstances. She brought her cat which was amusing except to Amador's mother. Amador slid off leaving his tall cousin to stand watchfully in the shadows of the portico. Cochran began the drinks and dinner bored as if flipping the pages of a magazine while wanting or waiting to do something else. But he was hospitable across the table until the attempt at communications became silly in their separate languages. She nervously gulped her wine, sitting there brittle but radiant in a white satin sheath dress.

"I have to skip this horseshit. I have confidential business here and if you blow my cover your throat will be cut back to the neckbone," he said in a flat Indiana accent.

He was surprised when she laughed, saying that she remembered his first words at the airport. They became friends in an odd way, and she moved in though no mention was made of her utilitarian purposes. It was pleasant enough for her not to bother asking. It had been years since a straight man had been around her without trying to paw. She gave her most preposterously seductive shot and he obliged only as a robot obliged. He listened attentively to her griefs and told her to sit quietly on off days and simply watch the clouds. On one occasion, he prevented her from taking delivery of a canary from the marketplace to let her cat chase in her bedroom. She became hysterical, perhaps from the cocaine that Amador had supplied, until he took her for a walk in the field behind the villa and her cat caught his first mouse. The cat bit off the head of the mouse and lay purring in the grass; she was delighted announcing Pooky to be decidedly natural and not at all a Hollywood cat.

Cochran realized that she was trying the patience of all of them, him less than Amador or his relatives from the mountains or mother because he was cold and tight and believed however ignorantly that it was coming to an end. He fingered the necklace that Mauro's mother had given him as if it were not a rosary at all, but a powerful talisman, in that peculiar way that a soldier on a night mission can feel invincible uttering a prayer from childhood. The heart wants life so much and the brain is shocked at the approach of death. The soldier always thinks it will be someone else, the man before or behind him, or hopefully no one he knows will ever die.

Amador's mother had come running with a robe when she saw that the actress-model was speaking to her son while wearing only her bikini bottoms. Amador laughed but was secretly irritated that the woman didn't show his mother more respect. And one late night under the portico when Cochran had refused her company she seduced Amador's nephew while he stood guard. She became angry when he covered her quickly, refusing to take off his gun. His kind uncle was paying him more than he made in a year for a week's work. In rebellion the next day she sent the propman for three more canaries which she snuck into the house after the day's shooting. She sat in her room smoking in her underthings watching Pooky chase the birds. She removed the drapes to deny the birds a vantage point beyond the cat's reach. She began weeping then and wept for hours until Cochran heard her, entered the room and held her, speaking the necessary soothing words until she slept. He dusted yellow feathers off his pant leg, petted the cat and left. He understood his cruelty toward her but was helpless, as self-sunken as he was in his own somnambulistic torment.

One morning Miryea did not awake. When she was found missing at breakfast her guardian nun discovered her charge so deep in fever that she had lost consciousness. The mother superior drove off with her handyman to Durango to seek permission from Señor Mendez's man for a doctor to visit. She was told cynically to go back to wait. Not only had the man lost his dear friend The Elephant but his boss had become so distracted and drunkenly sentimental that he had begun to lose his manhood. Tiburón had become so suddenly older that the man feared for the future of his job. It was all this nonsense over his faithless wife whose throat should have been cut the night in the cabin. He would have been glad to do it though he admitted the delight he had taken in her body. The conversation took place in a small fish restaurant called the Playa Azul. He did not know that the dozing *peóne* leaning on the building across the street was Amador's nephew.

The report was received by Cochran and Amador with only momentary puzzlement and then it became obvious. Amador said there were only three nunneries in the area. Cochran was electrified and ran to the bedroom where he

strapped on the .44 in its shoulder holster. He kissed his
private rosary and hung it around his neck. Amador followed him pinning him to the door.

Cochran struggled, but Amador held him firmly. He said
that they had to plan carefully or neither the woman nor
he who had become close to him would leave the country
alive. Tiburón had to be confronted or they would be
hunted down instantly. Now that they knew of the nun any
fool could find Miryea but the point was to find her and
not die. Amador led him down the hall and into the
kitchen where he poured drinks and told his mother to
prepare a pot of strong coffee. He called in his nephew and
told him to give Cochran a change of clothes and not to
leave his mother's side. Amador rehearsed plans while
cleaning their weapons laid out upon the table. He put
ham and bread and beer in a canvas bag. They left as the
actress pulled up after her day's work. She began to com-
ment on Cochran's costume, then looked at their eyes and
stopped talking. Cochran kissed her on the forehead and
they left.

Up in the mountains at Tepehuanes Tibey had dispatched
a plane for Mexico City to pick up a society doctor who
owed him a fortune in gambling debts. He had become
sickened with his revenge to the extent that he planned to
move to the top floor of his hotel in Cozumel. He had
given up his notion, held for three days, of going into
Durango and shooting Cochran. He was tired of love and
death and wanted a particular Mayan girl he knew in
Valladolid. She was a schoolteacher and not an inappropri-

ate woman to take to Paris when the weather became bad in Cozumel. Now he wanted Miryea to live or he would surely go to hell, or at the very least, continue to live in hell. He seriously considered shooting his man as he talked to him, freeing everyone from the psychopath's threat. He knew that this wave of generosity might pass when he became drunk again so he avoided liquor and went hunting until it became dark. He roasted the quail in the fireplace as he had as a young man. And ate them with his hands squatting before the fireplace.

The ride up to Tepehuanes took several hours. They pulled up behind a small cantina around midnight and went into a tin shed kitchen lit by an oil lamp. They ate some supper and spoke to the cook, an old man, who was Amador's contact and mostly Indian. Tiburón had been going hunting every morning early. Surely Amador remembered the valley. His henchman, referred to as The Crazy One, had arrived and would probably be with him. Tiburón had become crazy himself and even had got drunk in this same cantina with the *campesinos* who feared him. The old man laughed saying that Tiburón was so deranged that he was trying to find out if "who he is understands who he is," at which point a man becomes what he remembers as best. The old man said he had become a cook after a lifetime as a *caballero* because he remembered how he enjoyed cooking for his brothers and sisters when their mother died. Amador nodded saying that in between those times the man had been a wonderful bandit and whoremonger. The old man laughed and jumped around, then offered them a drink from his bottle of mescal. Amador refused saying they were on business of a very grave nature.

Amador drove up a mountain two-track, stopping when the trail became too treacherous for the car. They sat in silence for an hour with Cochran lighting one cigarette with another, listening to the ticking of the heat fading from the motor. Amador turned on the car radio and they were amused to pick up in the high altitude a New Orleans country music station aimed at truckers. It made Cochran homesick until he realized he had no home. Next to Miryea he missed his daughter terribly and he doubted his emergence from the gaps, the holes that he tore, or had been torn in the fabric of his life. But then his heart lifted as he thought of Miryea hidden in some country nunnery patiently waiting for him to take her away to Seville. His mind fixed on seeing the old Roman aqueduct in the moonlight with her. Maybe his daughter could come spend the weeks around Christmas with them.

Amador interrupted his thoughts by saying that they had to make a long walk a few hours before dawn. There was a good position to intercept Tiburón in a place where the valley narrowed into a gorge and the trail ran along a creek. They had to assume that Tibey would make no variance in his recent habits. It was up to Cochran to make what peace he could with the man, a long shot at best. He, Amador, would be hiding with his 30.06. The negotiations should be far easier when they had the drop on the enemy. Amador jerked his head around and Cochran flicked off the radio thinking that he too had heard something. They rolled the windows down and heard the sharp barks, yelps

and short quavering howls of the coyotes talking to one
another. Amador told a story of how, when he was young,
he had found an old, dying coyote lying by a stream. He
raised his gun to shoot it out of pity then lowered the gun
not wanting to interrupt the coyote's last hours of life.

"It's sad that you can't simply shoot the man. It would
be so simple. And get us all killed."

"I figure it's far past killing him unless it's necessary. I'd
like to think he knows when he's beat."

"Neither of us knows when we are beat. How can we
expect it of him? Losing a woman isn't being beat, it's
losing a woman. It happens to everyone." Amador paused.
"I lost my wife when I was a young man but I was a fool.
She was less a fool than me and walked away."

"Same thing with me. The business of killing doesn't
make good husbands. I miss my daughter but my wife is
now married to my brother. I was her father by accident
and now he's her true father." Cochran paused to listen to
the coyotes, then fingered the teeth around his neck. He
felt the ache of a man who had followed his passion far into
the nether reaches of human activity with the full understanding that a return was improbable. Any number of
men would go to the moon on a rocket designed for a
one-way trip. It was stupidly enough in the genes, either
as a molecular mishap or a simple throwback to a time
when a knight would go off to the Thirty Years War and
be surprised when no one recognized him when he walked
back in the door. That was why he revered the year at
Torrejón though he had seemed anxious and hearth-bound

teaching young pilots. But as the year receded into the past it provided the single total grace note of his adult life: his wife as a country person loved walking too, and they covered the old districts of Madrid, and Barcelona and Seville too when he had taken a few days' leave. Once they had gone to Málaga for a week and lived in a seaside *pensióne,* spending the days watching their daughter swim and their nights talking about the future, deciding to invest all their substantial savings in his father's tuna boat that badly needed new engines. Then he would have a full share in the business when he left the service. The debt had long been repaid but he had let it lie fallow in the bank in San Diego.

Amador shook him awake and offered a cup of coffee from a Thermos. Music full of night laments and broken hearts and busted guts came from the radio and for a moment he thought himself back at Diller's mission with the grand fat man checking his pulse through the night, muttering his prayers and humming to the first shrill birdsong of dawn.

"It's a long walk in the dark but I know the way. Too cold for snakes and we have a three-quarter moon."

They got out of the car and he shivered and the coffee steamed upward from his cup in the moonlight. He smelled the strange animal smell of the oil Amador had put on his rifle. In the distance a mountain wall cast a huge shadow beyond which the tips of the pines picked up the shimmering moonlight. He traced his fingers on the frost on the car hood, blew on his hands and felt for the .44

behind the warm goatskin vest borrowed from Amador's nephew. He walked around the car and touched Amador's shoulder.

"Look, friend. If this gets messy your first thought must be to save yourself. It makes sense for me to die. But not for you."

"Don't worry." Amador breathed deeply watching the vapor turn cold and visible. "I had a dream last week that I'd die an old man, you know, in a rocking chair on the porch of my little ranch. I trust my dreams." Then he laughed, "And my skills. This is the only thing I was ever good at."

They made the long hike in total silence following a winding shepherds' path. Once they paused on an escarpment to watch a creek glittering silver far below. They were startled by a mule deer crashing through the brush but the sound of the coyotes grew farther and farther distant.

They reached the spot early and stood by the creek smoking cigarettes. Then the first light came from the east as a faint gray smear on the horizon through the neck of the canyon. The birds started then, and Amador walked to a cottonwood tree ten yards off the trail.

"You sit here under the tree. I'll be hidden on the hillside. Tiburón will think you are a ghost. Have your hands out-turned and empty to show you aren't armed. And trust me."

"Of course. What else?" They shook hands and Cochran watched Amador scramble easily up the hillside with the rifle swaying from the strap on his back. He waved when Amador stopped and turned around, then he sat under the tree and stared at the small meadow beside the creek. He sat so still and long that the birds came close and a doe and her fawn drank from the creek. He sat through his miseries until he had no more thoughts by the time the dawn warmed and he no longer could see his breath. A crow passed giving him a sideward glance and a puzzled squawking. The first vulture appeared catching sun on his wings far above the canyon's cool shadows. He was watching the vulture when he first heard the horses in the distance. Then Tibey's bird dogs, a male and a female English pointer, trotted past, swiveling suddenly at his scent. The male approached growling while the female stayed on the trail, curious and wiggling with excitement. He shushed the male and it sat wagging its tail in a thump against the ground. He petted the dog and pointed with his hand and the dogs, obedient to hand signal, rushed off looking for quail.

The Crazy One was riding lead but Tiburón had come into view behind when the lead horse neighed and twisted, his neck catching the scent of the man under the tree. They both saw him at once staring blankly through them. The Crazy One raised his shotgun and Tiburón raised his hand to say no when Amador's first shot tore through The Crazy One's head, catapulting him from the saddle. Two more shots sent him sprawling on the grass. Tiburón reined his rearing horse while the riderless horse galloped off. Then Tiburón dismounted without turning around to look at the dead man. He tethered his horse on a bush and sighed deeply. Tiburón stopped in front of him and then suddenly between his thighs and out of the sight of Amador there was a gun in his hand and Cochran was staring down the small black hole of the barrel.

"Perhaps we should both die now," Tibey whispered.

"Maybe so," Cochran nodded coldly. Tibey was red-eyed and haggard, smelling of last night's whiskey. Tibey shrugged and looked up at the bows of the trees catching the first rays of the sun to enter the canyon. He flicked the gun away into a clump of grass.

"I ask you as a gentleman and a former friend to ask my forgiveness for taking my wife away from me."

"I ask your forgiveness for taking your wife away from you."

Both men stood then and Amador scrambled down the hillside shaking his head at the pistol in the grass. They walked off following the same path Amador and Cochran had taken in the night. At the car they drank a lukewarm beer thirstily and Amador and Tibey spoke about the mountains.

They reached the nunnery by noon and the mother superior was shocked at the sudden appearance of Señor Mendez and the two sweating ruffians with so noble a gentleman. She apologized to Tibey for the condition of his wife and said the doctor was with her. Tibey put his arm on her shoulder and smiled.

"What kind of gossip have you listened to? It is the wife of my friend here. You take care of him."

The woman led them to Miryea's room where Cochran sat on the edge of the bed, then leaned kissing her wounded and fevered lips. The doctor came to the door where Amador and Tibey stood looking at their feet.

"I doubt that anything may be done for her. She is too weak to move."

Tibey's face contorted and he hissed. "Make her well or I'll put your heart in your mouth, you fucking pig." Amador led Tibey and the startled doctor away. The mother superior stood there for a moment then followed them down the corridor sighing and offering prayers.

Cochran sat there for an afternoon and a night—drinking coffee, holding Miryea's hands, caressing her brow, pacing the room when the doctor entered. At first light she regained consciousness and they embraced wordlessly. She slept for a while and he dozed off sitting in the chair until the afternoon heat awakened him. Then he had to be restrained as the doctor gave her a tracheotomy to ease her breathing and then she was near death for another night and day. He lay on the floor in the night refusing all thought, listening to her rasping breathing through the oxygen unit Amador had brought from town. The pauses in her breathing at times became agonizing in their length and then short and staccato. When he no longer could bear it he ran down into the courtyard and screamed. The lights were turned on and the patients returned his screams hearing his particular voice for the first time. Amador, Tibey and the doctor came running from their temporary quarters in the kitchen. He fought them until Amador subdued him with a choke-hold. Tibey helped hold him down and the doctor gave him a shot to allow him to sleep.

Hours later when he awoke on his pallet in a strange room he stood and glanced at the hot sun through the barred window. He found the kitchen and poured a cup of coffee while Amador, Tibey and the doctor sat at the table. The doctor nervously averted his glance.

Later on the afternoon of the third day Miryea regained consciousness. He spoke eagerly and in a rush of nearly incoherent words. She whispered that she wanted to go out in the garden. He ran for the doctor who shrugged in defeat and followed him back to the room and bandaged Miryea's throat. Cochran carried her down into the garden where the patients were being herded in for dinner. The autistic children passed them without seeing, keening their private dirges like hoarse earthbound birds whose sufferings would never be answered on earth. He held her tightly in his arms remembering how light a dead bird felt when he picked it out of a thicket in the Indiana woods. He spoke again in a rush trying to keep her alive by the power in the energy of his words: it was as if his brain had split open and he plunged, raked, dug, mining any secret he might hold to bring her to health. He put the necklace from Mauro's mother around her neck remembering with horror that she had said he would only take vengeance on his enemies. He invented a universe of words but they were only words. He invented a child for them to walk with in Seville and she smiled and nodded yes. Twilight passed into near dark and Amador watched impassively, partly hid by a column. He stopped the doctor from approaching them. The half-moon came up windblown but shrunken and a gust whipped the flowers from a flowering almond. Cochran whispered on and then as full dark descended she sang the song he knew so well in a throaty voice that only faintly surpassed the summer droning of a cicada. It was her death song and she passed from life seeing him sitting there as her soul billowed softly outward like a cloud parting. It began to rain and a bird in the tree above them crooned as if he were the soul of some Mayan trying to struggle his way back earthward.

EPILOGUE

There was one man digging under the tree and two men watching. The man dug with a mechanical intentness, using an ax for the tree roots, a pick for the rocks, and a shovel for the heavy soil. He noted the marbling and striations of soil as he descended into the earth on a hot afternoon. The man named Amador sat on a bench and drew down his sombrero and sang in a hushed voice. The man named Tiburón, Tibey, Señor Baldassaro Mendez sat on the bench and held his face in his hands as the man dug with terrible energy, methodical, inevitable. The mother superior watched with a mildly bored priest from beneath the portico. A number of patients idled back and forth, distracted by the activity. A pine casket lay on top of two sawhorses. On the casket a large bouquet of wild flowers sat wilting in the sun. When the hole was dug the man paused, sweating, then pulled himself up and over the edge. He knelt by the side of a pile of soil and the two men on the bench slid forward and knelt beside him. The priest and the nun moved forward with the insane crowding behind them. The priest said a short service and the two men in front of the bench lowered the casket into the hole. The man who had dug the hole lowered himself into the earth, knelt and kissed the flowers. He lifted himself from the hole, picked up the shovel and threw in some earth with a thump he would hear on his own deathbed.

BUSINESS REPLY MAIL

FIRST CLASS   PERMIT NO. 673   MARION, OHIO

POSTAGE WILL BE PAID BY ADDRESSEE

P O BOX 2073
MARION OH 43306-2173

THE MAN
WHO GAVE UP
HIS NAME

CHAPTER
I

Nordstrom had taken to dancing alone. He considered his sanity to be unblemished and his nightly dances an alternative to the torpor of calisthenics. He had chided himself of late for so perfectly living out all of his mediocre assumptions about life. The dancing was something new and owned an almost metaphysical edginess to it. At forty-three he was in fine but not spectacular shape, though of late he felt a certain softness, a blurring in the perimeters of his body. After cleaning up the dishes from a late dinner he would dim the lights in the den and put an hour's worth of music on the stereo though recently he often increased it to two hours; the selection was eclectic depending on his mood and might on any evening include music as varied as Merle Haggard, Joplin's *Pearl*, the Beach Boys, Stravinsky's *The Rite of Spring*, Otis Redding and The Grateful Dead. The point was to keep moving, to work up a dense sweat and to feel the reluctant body become fluid and graceful.

The fact of the matter is that Nordstrom wasn't a very good dancer but when you're dancing alone, who cares?

Beginning with his childhood in Wisconsin he had been an excellent swimmer, a fair fly-caster and bird hunter, a fair basketball player, a fair linebacker, a fair golfer and a fair tennis player. Only the swimming haunted his dreams, all other sports had been discarded. Perhaps swimming was dancing in the water, he thought. To swim under lily pads seeing their green slender stalks wavering as you passed, to swim under upraised logs past schools of sunfish and blue-gills, to swim through reed beds past wriggling water snakes and miniature turtles, to swim in small lakes, big lakes, Lake Michigan, to swim in small farm ponds, creeks, rivers, giant rivers where one was swept along easefully by the current, to swim naked alone at night when you were nineteen and so alone you felt like you were choking every waking moment, having left home for reasons more hormonal than rational; reasons having to do with the abstraction of the future and one's questionable place in the world of the future, an absurdity not the less harsh for being so widespread.

The first indication of dancing in his life had begun quite by accident. As a sophomore scholarship student at the University of Wisconsin he had noted that he couldn't possibly reach the men's gym from a classroom in the allotted ten minutes. Yet in 1956 four semesters of physical education were an absolute requirement. At registration he approached his track coach who remembered Nordstrom from fall term for having won the half mile and the shotput in his section, an oddity that removed Nordstrom if only momentarily from the anonymous pile of sophomores. The track coach suggested he run between classes, a bit unrealistic in view of all the unshoveled snow on the campus sidewalks. A muscular middle-aged woman sitting next to the track coach behind the registration desk recommended that Nordstrom take modern dance, which was held in the women's gym and only a short walk away from the classroom buildings. Nordstrom signed up and walked away with scattered imaginings of competence at the waltz, fox-trot, samba and rumba. As an economics major working thirty hours a week in the statistics library he had no social life and rather thought this enforced dancing would open up some new vista of romance.

The shock that neared paralysis in effect was that the class taught truly modern dance à la Martha Graham. He was the sole man among thirty young women in leotards and his ears rang and his mouth dried in embarrassment. It was the nature of his upbringing to stick things out and this, in addition to not wanting to admit his stupidity, kept him in the class. But the paralysis remained with him and other than the perfunctory warming up exercises he could not move. He feared that the girls who were strikingly midwestern, largely dumpy and ill formed, thought him a "homo," the commonest word in the dorm. After a few weeks he had the minimal wit to change his position in the back row until he was directly behind the loveliest girl in the class. Her name was Laura and Nordstrom often saw her in the library studying with her boyfriend, a gaunt and lanky basketball star. Her grace at the exercises threw Nordstrom into a trance of lust that gave the class a dream-like atmosphere. He wore an especially tight jockstrap to conceal the results of her postures, the especially taut flex of her high buttocks and how she knelt and stretched like the most beautiful dog on earth with his nose not more than a few feet behind. He only spoke once to her to tell her she shouldn't chew her knuckles one day after class. She simply stared at him as if preoccupied and walked away.

As winter semester slid into spring the class became more painful because the new warmth allowed the girls to wear leotards without leggings. Nordstrom thought Laura's legs far surpassed any he had seen in bathing suit ads in magazines. It enraged him that the basketball player might have gone "all the way" with her as they said at the time. She never turned around to meet the eyes burning into her backside. And Nordstrom was pathetically flunking the class which meant an additional semester of physical education. He was desperate. On the hot late May afternoon in which the final exam was held—a four-to-six–minute solo dance of one's own devising—Nordstrom drank deeply from a pint of schnapps his father had given him at Easter vacation for his nerves. He had been up all night studying for an economics exam with the aid of a green and white time-released Dexedrine spansule. He felt he had done well in the exam and there remained only the dance before he could carry his suitcase to the station and take the bus from Madison to Rhinelander in northern Wisconsin for the summer. By the time he reached the gym he felt like the damp and rotting lilac blooms he had noted along the path beside the river. The blooms reminded him of the odor of the gym and the schnapps tingled in his brain which seemed to be sweating like his body. He wondered why he could dance in his imagination while his body remained stiff, almost frozen in the self-consciousness of its unruly lack of grace.

In the gym there were only four girls left who hadn't completed the solo test. Laura leaned against a window casement in the shadow of a long stream of sunlight waiting her turn. Nordstrom picked the next window and glanced at her somewhat furtively but turned away when he found her staring at him. He watched a plump girl thump and twist around to a Modern Jazz Quartet number and smiled idiotically with tension. The teacher approached him with a smile and said that she wanted him to watch the next performance closely and then merely react to it in his own dance. He swallowed with difficulty and nodded as Laura put on a Debussy record and began to dance with an inconsolable grace. He felt a lump arise beneath his breastbone and swim toward his throat, then the emergence of the inevitable hard-on at which point he put a hand in his pocket and squeezed it painfully to make it go away. By the time she finished he was a moon walker with feet of tingling fluff.

In fact he scarcely noticed when the teacher wrapped a blindfold around his eyes. Laura had gotten up slowly from the floor where she had lain on her stomach limply in imitation of death, with the soft, damp leotard drawn up tightly between her legs dividing the buttocks which owned a sheen of sweat. Then he was blinded and the teacher said that would relax him. He heard Bartók's *The*

Miraculous Mandarin above his breathing and went berserk with the berserk music.

Twenty-three years later in a large apartment in Brookline, Massachusetts, the event still seemed the most extraordinary of his life. It had taken that long to dance alone again. The teacher had removed the blindfold, laughed and kissed his forehead. He saw Laura standing by the door then abruptly leave. He buried his face in the towel, returning freely to his native embarrassment. He got drunk with some acquaintances in the dorm and missed his bus, barely awakening to make the bus the next day. Throughout the summer he brooded while working for his father's small company that specialized in building cabins for the cottagers that came to northern Wisconsin from the cities each summer. His family were provident Scandinavians and Nordstrom had worked summers since his twelfth year, saving for college he had thought, but really simply "saving" as is the want of the stern, mostly snowbound Lutherans of the north. While others were playing baseball he learned rough carpentry, how to mix mortar, and finally how to lay blocks and bricks. And that particular summer he volunteered for all the roughest jobs: digging well-pits, the foundation work, unloading cement blocks and mortar and carrying the squares of roofing up the ladders. He was trying to exhaust his infatuation with the girl in manual labor but secretly fantasized a run-in where he would thrash her basketball player. He had been embarrassed when his grades had arrived and the "A" in Modern Dance had amused his father into saying, "You must cut a rug."

To abbreviate our tale, Nordstrom spent nearly another year before he made contact with Laura again. Frankly, he lacked imagination. He would stare at her name and number in the student directory, sigh and occasionally go out with a girl from his hometown who had at least a fashionable promiscuity in her favor. But she was a cheerleader type and often when he hovered above her punching away, Nordstrom thought of this act of love as only a tolerable form of masturbation. His mind was elsewhere. Once he saw Laura across the floor at a basketball game and he had to leave, so deep did his heart plummet. Then in mid-May, in a tavern habituated by the sorority and fraternity sorts where he only stepped in one Friday afternoon to get out of the rain he felt, of all things, a wet finger in his ear as he stood at the bar.

"You never called me. I thought you would call me," Laura said.

He was stunned and they drank for a while with two of her "sisters," Nordstrom very quickly to overcome shyness; then even more quickly when a group of athletes joined them. The athletes arm-wrestled to see who would buy pitchers of beer and to their surprise Nordstrom beat them having been raised on the sport and the labor it takes to be good at it. Then the athletes bet on Nordstrom against all comers until he was tied by a Polish football tackle and Laura stood and said she had to go back to the house to get ready for her date. Nordstrom was stunned and followed her to the door. She put an arm around him and said she was tied up for the weekend except perhaps Sunday afternoon and to stop by at three.

Years later Nordstrom pondered the degree of accident in human affection as do all intelligent mortals. What if it hadn't rained that Friday? How tentative and restless an idea: he ended up marrying Laura because it rained one Friday afternoon in May in Madison, Wisconsin. The rain led directly in specific steps to the Sunday afternoon which began in a light rain and a drive in her car into the country with a half-gallon of red Cribari wine. Then the rain lightened and it became warm and muggy and they walked through a woodlot into a field of green knee-high winter wheat. At the far edge of the field he spread his trench coat at her insistence and they sat down and drank the wine. She wore penny loafers, no stockings, a brown poplin skirt and a white sleeveless blouse. Sitting there while she laughed and talked he felt totally lucky for the first time in his life. Her legs were brown because she had gone to Florida for spring vacation. She stared upward at the marsh hawk. He stared downward at her legs and the skirt slipping upward a bit while she leaned back to gaze at the hawk skirting the field in quadrants. He was transfixed and wanted to lay there until the green wheat grew through him.

"You're looking up my legs," she said.

"No I wasn't."

"If you're honest you can kiss them."

"I was."

He kissed her legs until neither of them wore anything. And the hawk now perched in a tree in the woodlot could see an imprecise circle of flattened green wheat and two bodies entwined until late in the afternoon when it began to rain again. The man tried to cover the girl with the coat but she stood up, did a dance and drank more wine.

Such simple events last lovers a long time. Scarcely anyone can turn their backs on the best thing that has happened to them. So she went to California for the summer and he retrieved her for the last year of school in the fall after a hundred letters both ways. He bloomed as much as perhaps he ever would and they were married to the mild disgust of her ambitious parents and the delight of his own the week after graduation. They moved to California where she worked for a small company that made documentary movies for corporations and he worked for a large oil company. They lived in a duplex out in Westwood and after one year Laura gave birth to a daughter, returning to her career a year later. It was the sexual mystery that made their marriage last eighteen years. The word "mystery" is still appropriate despite the implacable vulgarizing of the media, so total in attempt that it must express our desire to smash this last grace note in our lives. (On the way back from California after the summer before their senior year they had made love in the car in the daylight, standing up for novelty in gas station bathrooms, like dogs back in the roadside evergreens with pine needles sticking to knees and palms, on a picnic table in North Dakota, on motel room floors, in a sleeping bag in a cold fog near Brainerd, Minnesota, in a movie theatre *(East of Eden)* in La Crosse, Wisconsin:

Do you want to screw Julie Harris?

I don't know. Never thought about it.
Do you want to screw James Dean?

Of course. Don't be silly. But he
just died.

The marriage had been unhappy for years before it ended rather amicably. He suspected that she had a lover and the lover had turned out to be a good friend of the family, Martin Gold. Both Nordstrom and Laura had been successful but never together. She traveled a great deal as a line producer and he made a great deal of money with the oil company. The sole meeting point had been their daughter Sonia, a rather fragile child until the summer of her twelfth year when it seemed she gained health and vitality overnight. But this seemed to remove their only mutual concern and they faded into their careers. Laura became more important to her company which gradually had entered the television market with feature specials and made-for-TV movies, most of them shot on location. Nordstrom owned a nagging jealousy over the glamor of her business compared to the boardroom composure of his own. Businessmen are by and large hapless wretches like anyone else and Nordstrom had that rare particular strength of the well disciplined, intelligent, good-looking man who never shoots off his mouth; terribly solid, never slick with the "sticktoitiveness" that Nordstrom's father-in-law so admired when he saw the fruits of the labor—a fine home in Beverly Glen.

They may have gone on indefinitely in this stasis but one night at dinner their daughter, with the terrifying intensity of a sixteen-year-old, told them they were both cold fish. Laura only laughed but Nordstrom was deeply hurt: to have worked so hard for sixteen years only to be called a cold fish by your own daughter. But then he was bright enough to know he *was* a bit of a cold fish, what is known in the business world as a hatchet man. Until this particular moment the idea had never bothered him.

That night after the unpleasantness of dinner Nordstrom broke with the rigidity of his drinking habits that confined him to two highballs after work and a little wine with dinner. He drank a lot of brandy and tried to talk on more intimate terms with his daughter. She was receptive though it later occurred to him that she was being kind. He had been so much what is thought of as a "model father" that he didn't really know his daughter and she, like any child, played the same formal though skittish game. After their talk he noted that he had smoked a half-dozen cigarettes in succession and promised his daughter a BMW when she graduated from college if she wouldn't smoke.

Then he talked with Laura about getting a less demanding job, or anyway something different. But she was preoccupied readying herself for the driver. She was taking the "red-eye" to New York for two days on business. They stood in the kitchen talking and he asked if they could quickly make love. She said no it'll mess up clothes, then offered a blow-job. So Nordstrom sat back in the breakfast nook getting what turned out to be half a blow-job because

the driver rang the doorbell. Laura kissed him on the forehead and left, the job barely half done as it were, though
Nordstrom didn't mind, being a good enough lover to
prefer the process to the conclusion. Now he felt totally
alone and an edge of panic crept into his soul that would
stay with him for years. He thought, "What if what I've
been doing all my life has been totally wrong?" He sat in
the den the entire night thinking it all over. By dawn he
decided he wanted to escape into the world rather than
from it: there was nothing particularly undesirable or repel-
lent in his life, only a certain lack of volume and intensity;
he feared dreaming himself to death, say as a modest brook
in a meadow eases along sleepily to a great river just beyond
the border of trees.

The most vexing thing in the life of a man who wishes
to change is the improbability of change. Unless he is an
essentially sound creature this can drive him frantic, perhaps insane. Nordstrom knew that at base business was a
process of buying or manufacturing cheap and selling dear.
Long before he took Economics 101 at the University of
Wisconsin he had been attracted by the simple grace of
capitalism: his father would build three cabins for five
thousand and sell them for eight thousand; years later the
cabins would be built for fifteen thousand and sold for
twenty-two thousand, but despite this variation in price
over the years to account for the increase in materials and
labor—and inflation—it amounted not oddly to the same
amount. His father was without greed and despite the
urging of Nordstrom would not expand the business, say

to ten cabins a year. In the oil business it was a trifle more complicated in that the big profits came from outsmarting the regulatory and tax structures and swindling the Arabs (he was amused when the situation reversed itself). It was pretty much a gentleman's game within the infrastructure.

But it was all ruined during that long night in the den, no matter that the poison, like the changes Nordstrom wished to make in his life, was slow in coming. Between his thirty-seventh and fortieth year he began going to a number of plays and screening parties with his wife and was filled with a curious envy over the easy familiarity show business people had with each other, no matter that the lust for profit was the same as the oil business. There was at least a sense of play involved and Nordstrom had forgotten how to play, in fact had never learned. So he bought a sailboat but it turned out that there wasn't any particular place to go from Newport Beach. He played tennis with his daughter feverishly and built an expensive court behind their home, but she broke her ankle at Sun Valley and they never played tennis again. He tried skiing in Aspen; he went skeet shooting; he quail hunted with oil friends on an island near Corpus Christi and was nearly bitten by a rattlesnake. The rattlesnake incident was so actual that it secretly thrilled him for months; he reached under a mesquite bush to retrieve a dead quail, heard the strange sound but reacted slowly because he had never heard it before, and the snake's open mouth hurtled forward barely grazing his shirt cuff. He changed his hairstyle. He bought himself a silver ring in Cabo San Lucas where he went marlin

fishing. He bought a camera. He began reading biographies
and a few novels. One silly evening when Laura was away
his daughter rolled a joint for him and he laughed until his
stomach hurt, then became tight and mildly frightened.
He screwed his secretary and felt sad. He bought a sports
car which only his daughter and wife drove. He bought an
expensive painting of a pretty girl washing her feet. He
took up cooking when he resigned his arduous job in the
oil business for a simpler one as a vice-president for a large
book wholesaler. He learned to cook Chinese, French,
Italian and Mexican food. He rented a van and drove north
to the wine country around San Francisco, tasted the wines
of many vineyards and returned with as much as the van
would hold. He had visited, by referral, a high-priced,
exotic whorehouse in San Francisco to fulfill a fantasy of
being in bed with two women at once. It cost him three
hundred dollars not to get a hard-on, his first experience
at unsuccessful love. He brooded all the way back to Los
Angeles. He brooded about his cock, he brooded about the
young filmmaker friend of Laura's whom he had backed on
an unsuccessful venture. It wasn't the money so much (the
loss would be absorbed in the tax advantage) but the suspicion that Laura might have made love to the young man
on an air mattress in the shrubbery near the Jacuzzi in the
backyard. He brooded about his boredom with money because everything had been provided for by his own wit and
the death of Laura's father. He brooded about his daughter's departure for Sarah Lawrence only three months distant. Suddenly he was terribly lonely for the greenery, the
cold lakes, the thunderstorms and snow of his childhood.

He brooded about whether or not his wife had fucked an African when she had visited Kenya for a film the month before. Had she ever been in bed with two men, in an effort similar to his own abortive attempt? Nordstrom was appalled when his member rose up under his belt at the thought. It was time to pull things together.

That evening after a late dinner where they both drank too much wine Laura did a mock dance to the same Debussy song she had danced to in the gym nineteen years before. He watched with his mind frozen in dread because he knew their marriage was over and she knew it and was perhaps unwittingly dancing a swan song. Her body had changed very little but the grace had somehow been tainted with an almost undetectable hint of vulgarity. He went into the bathroom and wept for the first time in twenty-seven years, the last incident being when his beloved dog bit a deputy sheriff ice fishing on the lake in front of their home and was blown into a snowy eternity with six shots from a service .38. He dried his eyes with a towel that smelled of Laura's body, returned to the bedroom where they made love nearly as passionately as they had in the green knee-high winter wheat with the hawk circling above, but it was the terrible energy of permanent loss that wound them together and made them repeat every sexual gesture of their lives together.

That night was the final grace note of the marriage. It was three months before the divorce papers were filed (on the afternoon of the morning their daughter left for college). She had more money than he did, though not all that much more, and as an ardent feminist who took care of herself wonderfully she wanted nothing from him. He insisted for selfish reasons on paying the college bills (a fear of losing contact with his daughter) and they agreed to split the sale of the house down the middle. Certain necessary tortures were performed to insure the permanence of the divorce. Nordstrom was the simpleminded victim of these emotional barrages that accompany separation, the hacking of all the knots and threads that held the lovers together. He was told he was selfish, cold, calculating, intoxicated with his business success, with the toys that later decorated his life. During many wine-soaked summer evenings he heard ruminations about his midwestern infantilism, his self-satisfied ignorance of the real world, his insensitivity to the arts. Sometimes the ardor of the spleen was tempered by laughter or her ready admission that on a comparative basis it hadn't been all that bad a marriage. Unfortunately his potency waned as she drew away from him. He sought out wrongs, even imagined ones that he could present, but came up with nothing of substance. He loved her and had always been utterly uncritical of her often sloppy nature. He only felt anger when she told him about her lovers, and not that he was a bad lover, only that she saw life as too exasperatingly short to know only one man. He felt flashes of the cuckold's rage but his spirit had become too fatigued with sorrow to express himself. He invented a few infidelities but sensed she didn't believe him and was being kind to his inventions. It was their daughter who kept them totally civil: she loved them both for childlike reasons but questioned their sanity when they proposed only a tentative separation. She understood her father's nature, how while he could be lovable, he was also an introverted ignoramus, lacking even a touch of ease and spontaneity. She had known of her mother's lovers since fourteen and was only mildly embarrassed, owning a woman's matter-of-factness in sexual matters.

So a nearly twenty-year period of Nordstrom's life was over. After Christmas that year when he had tied up what he thought of as loose ends he moved to Boston where he had arranged a vice-presidency for another large book wholesaler. He was so dead to himself that the move actually constituted a way to keep at least cautiously near his daughter two hundred miles to the south. She even stayed with him for two months one year when she attended Harvard summer school. And that prolonged visit was what led to Nordstrom dancing alone. She had spent the two previous summers in Europe and now had a boyfriend at Harvard. They shared a mutually intense interest in art history and contemporary music, two subjects that seemed pleasantly impractical to Nordstrom. The young man was Jewish and this distressed him a little too until he spent an evening brooding about it and came up with nothing decisive one way or another. Laura had remarried and to a Jew; she was apparently quite happy, so perhaps it wasn't surprising that her daughter picked a Jew. Brookline was full of Jews and though Nordstrom didn't know any on a personal basis he rather liked them from a distance. He didn't know that he was somewhat an object of comedy in the delicatessen where he took his morning breakfast. He mentioned one morning to the owner that his Formosa oolong tea had said on the packet "this rare brown leaf tea from the island of Formosa has the exquisite odor of ripe peaches" but he hadn't smelled any peaches. This laconic form of midwestern humor escaped the delicatessen owner who sniffed the tea and said "so whadda I'm supposed to do." Then several weeks later the short-order cook didn't show up and Nordstrom called his office telling the secretary he'd be late. He looked a little absurd in the white apron with a J. Press shirt peeking out the top with a silk tie in a Windsor knot tightly in place. He cooked through the two-hour breakfast rush preparing basically simple orders—scrambled eggs with lox and onions, toasted bagels with cream cheese, a variety of omelettes, fried potatoes. When it was over and Nordstrom took off the apron and the owner wondered aloud what Nordstrom might like in return he said jauntily "just put something on a horse for me," having seen the owner study the Racing Form. Later when his daughter had been in the delicatessen with him the owner had complimented him on the "beautiful piece of ass." Nordstrom hadn't had the heart to admit it was his daughter.

Nor would Nordstrom admit that he was lonely. If the idea had arisen, which it didn't, he would have insisted to himself that he was alone most of the time only so he could figure things out. At work he was cold and efficient, only perfunctorily social. In the three years in Boston he had quickly renewed his reputation as a hatchet man by firing ten percent of the firm's two hundred employees and increasing efficiency and volume by more than twenty percent. There was a lot of muttering among the shanty Irish and the lower level Italian workers but never in Nordstrom's presence. The fact of it was that Nordstrom was powerful to no particular purpose. If he were to walk into a bar and say "it's raining" all the drinkers would nod attentively even though they could clearly see the sun shining through the windows. Perhaps, though, his preparations for his daughter's summer arrival painted his solitary life accurately. The gestures weren't at all conscious but more like an animal preparing for spring or winter, not really knowing which. He had the large master bedroom repainted a pale blue, bookshelves installed and filled with art books; he shopped for a stereo set and ended up buying two combination stereos that included tape decks. Her frugality at college had always depressed him, reminding him of his own bleak years. When he first met her young man in New York they were both wearing blue jeans, not even particularly clean ones, so Nordstrom had to cancel reservations at La Caravelle and they had ended up in the Village. He had noted to himself to return there at a future date because a particular waitress had caught his eye.

At the beginning of the summer of 1977 Nordstrom wanted sex to go away. In the three years since the divorce he had proven himself in a few encounters to be utterly without versatility. Desire went away for a long while and he was relieved but recently it had surfaced again at odd moments: a photo in a magazine, the rare movie (the nurse in *Cuckoo's Nest*, Louise Fletcher, gave him a momentary hard-on), an overweight waitress at the delicatessen, and most reprehensibly in his view, a girl across the courtyard from his apartment. She had just moved in and was in the habit of turning out all the lights and watching TV in the dark presuming herself invisible. But the blue light on her body was startlingly sexual and one evening her hand had moved down as if to massage herself and Nordstrom rushed from the apartment to find a prostitute. There were none to be had in the neighborhood bars and he ended up watching a Red Sox game on television, baseball being an effective nationwide soporific. But he brooded about his sexual failures, the dead feeling in his body as he watched the future disappear in nightly units full of odd dreams; dreams that brought the strange glandular rapacity of his marriage back so strongly that he half-expected Laura to be beside him when he awoke exhausted in the morning. He read widely on the subject but the reading was like trying to translate a foreign language after one year's study: his sexuality had been wonderful for eighteen years and then vanished. The books weren't any good on the vanishing act as if it were an example of antimagic and too subtle to describe. Nordstrom didn't know that he longed to fall in love. In his rage for order he began to keep a diary and the simple act of writing calmed him a great deal.

May 77: Sold some stock today to cover an August rental of a house on the water in Marblehead. It was extravagant but it has occurred to me this will be the last chance I have to spend much time with Sonia. Also noticed that when the decorator and painters finished with the room I had made it look like a huge room we had at the Lotti on the Rue de Castiglione

in 1967 when she was eleven. Sid from the deli asked
me to go to the Red Sox–Tigers game tonight, then
to a stag party for his brother's fiftieth birthday out
on Revere Beach. He said there would be plenty of
"bimbos, floozies and coochy-coos" in addition to
food and movies. When Sid is dressed up he behaves
like Kojak on TV right down to the slightly vulgar
tailoring. Wondered why I said no? I might have been
able to let off some steam though I doubt it. After
twenty years of studying them I am no longer able to
read newspapers. Why? It's because they no longer
reflect the world I perceive. I will have to go along
with the way I see it even if wrong. And if they are
right, it lacks interest. Broke up a fight between two
stockboys in the alley slugging it out over a rather
attractive filing girl. Whole shipping department
watching and the girl crying rather too dramatically.
Good punchers but I got an old-fashioned wristlock
on one. Everyone thought they would be fired but I
hadn't the heart for it. In high school I thought it
grand to fight over a girl and these emotions swept
over me. Perhaps I am becoming juvenile. Anyway
the workers talked excitedly about the fight all afternoon. One said the boys were "pussy struck" which
is an odd term from years ago, a dormitory kind of
colloquialism as young men talk all sorts of filth and
then when they're with girls they quote snippets of
popular songs and become utterly dopey. Girl they
were fighting over caught me looking at her, wet her
lips and smiled. A stringy tart. Wangled lobster
mousse recipe from Locke-Ober's to fix for Sonia on
Sunday with asparagus vinaigrette and that Fetzer

fumé blanc she likes. Know she's coming Saturday but spending evening with her young man. Must make her understand that it's fine if he stays with her on occasion or I won't see much of her. She's twenty. It's usual to ask where the years went but I know very well where they went and sloppy sentimentality never did anyone any good. Dad wrote to say because of his bad heart and cholesterol he had to give up herring, fried salt pork, cheese, bacon and eggs, fried pork and onion sandwiches—his favorite. This is a sad thing. On Thursday we would go to the basement together and clean the salt herring and pickle them for Saturday night supper. Mother did not like to reach into the barrel. She saw a snake in the root cellar and screamed. He can still eat *lukefist*. Certain older men at work are always telling moronic jokes which must mean something. Read a Knut Hamsun novel to see what Norwegians could do (not much). The book made me quite unhappy and reminded me of certain dreams of Laura: once when she returned from one of her movie parties that I left early and she was very drugged up on cocaine and wanted me to make love to her which I did for a long time. Once in front of the mirror but in the dream the man in the mirror wasn't me. A bit scatterbrained of late. For instance I looked up earth, fire, water, and air in the Brittanica. Also radio as I had quite forgotten the principles on which they work. Certain other disturbing things are: why am I continuing to work? My wife is gone who ironically never needed what I made and my daughter is going and my parents well cared for. I am no longer torn to pieces by the collapse of my life but I have no idea what should come next. Perhaps nothing. My mother always closed her letters by saying "you are in my prayers" but I've never put much stock in religion, believing that prayer is trying to make a special case for yourself.

CHAPTER
II

Nordstrom's summer with his daughter went splendidly, so happily in a bittersweet sense in fact that he thought that it might mean that he was going to die. He was breathing more deeply and took to laughing at odd times. He thought that one ought to die when things were going particularly well rather than badly, then the deathbed would be without the usual accumulation of terror that Nordstrom thought was anyway fraudulent. He fashioned himself without superstition or imagination, though mostly because people always told him he was without either. Laura was his chief and most convincing accuser. During the lengthy and expensive period when she visited a psychiatrist on a daily basis Nordstrom asked her what on earth did she find to talk about so extensively, adding that she must be making a lot of it up whole cloth. This had caused a great deal of anger wherein Nordstrom had been told that he didn't have enough imagination to have valid mental problems. This hurt a bit so he had been delighted years

later when Laura's psychiatrist had been arrested for jack-
ing off in public on Rodeo Drive. But then the psychiatrist
had spent a year in Colorado getting his "head straight"
and it was business as usual with his old clientele including
Laura returning to have their griefs further exhumed.

Actually it was a matter of what is faddishly known as
"communication": Nordstrom's nature was deeply private
and there never was an occasion to express what he believed on certain matters. For his seventh birthday he had
been given the twelve volume Book House, edited by Olive
Beaupre Miller, who had assured her young readers that
"the world is so full of a number of things, I'm sure we
should all be happy as kings." Approaching age forty-three,
it would still be difficult to convince him that a Norse girl
didn't ride a polar bear on a long journey, or that Odin
didn't exist on some rainy northern taiga, dressed in rein-
deer skins and warmed by a huge fire fed on human marrow
with the music of the cries of the dying floating across a
misty lake. Merlin was real and so was Arthur; in twelfth-
century Japan there was a madman who painted pictures
of mountains and rivers by dipping his hair in ink and
whipping his head over the paper. Sometimes he painted
with live chickens. Why wouldn't certain ghosts live at the
bottoms of lakes and express themselves through the voice
of a loon? In his eleventh year Nordstrom shot a crow and
Henry, an Ojibway Indian who worked as a carpenter for
Nordstrom's father when he wasn't drunk, wouldn't speak
to him for months, after telling Nordstrom that any fool
"knows that a crow is not a crow." By fall Henry had
become pacified and that early winter for a Christmas

present he built Nordstrom a small rowboat out of white pine. Late the next spring Nordstrom found a baby crow in the woods fallen from its nest and nursed it to health with earthworms. The crow learned to fly and he left his bedroom window open so the crow could visit when it wished. He asked his father if it was a boy or girl crow and his father said it didn't matter to the crow, just as it doesn't matter to a dog. Nordstrom pondered this mystery. He surprised and delighted Henry though when he appeared at a building site with a crow perched noisily on his shoulder. The crow would sit on the backseat of the rowboat as Nordstrom rowed on summer mornings, squawking at his curious brethren in the sky who would circle at a distance and sometimes the crow would join them. Typically Nordstrom named his crow "Crow." The bird disappeared late in the fall and returned for three springs in a row. Then he didn't return and Nordstrom dug a small grave, then paused before returning the earth to the empty hole. He always remembered how excited the crow had been when they had watched a watersnake swallow a small frog. For two days he imagined himself turning from solid flesh into liquid in the belly of a snake.

But perhaps it was this largely secret imagination that gave Nordstrom his self-possession, hence his success in business which only recently he had come to consider valueless. Businessmen who are so good at passing off bung-fodder as a necessity can scarcely be thought of as witless, or unimaginative, he thought. Laura had been raised in Evanston, a suburb of Chicago some three hundred miles south of Rhinelander, but really another part of the country as far as humor or imagination. Nordstrom would laugh at the cat sleeping on the diving board above the pool in the backyard. He also thought it extremely funny when show people took to wearing Indian jewelry and French denims; other objects of humor were traffic jams (even when he was trapped in them), homosexuality (something to be given up by fourteen), politics and the evening news, including the fact that a great number of people still didn't believe we had reached the moon. The French were truly funny, except the food was wonderful: Nordstrom's repertory of jokes included only one, and that was about two Frenchmen meeting on the street: First Frenchman: "My mother died this morning at ten o'clock." Second Frenchman: "At ten o'clock?" The general unpopularity of this subtle joke led Nordstrom to reflect on the nontransference of ethnic humor. Duck feet looked funny to some but to the Chinese they were a delicacy. When he and his father fished on summer evenings and were overtaken by a thunderstorm they would continue fishing in the rain because they hadn't wanted it to rain. This made them laugh as did ice fishing on a twenty-below day with a thirty-knot wind, where after interminable hours of cold his father would decide it was a "bit chilly." When he shot his first deer at thirteen, a doe, his father and uncles while cleaning the deer had plastered the bloody cunt to Nordstrom's forehead. It stuck there for a few moments then fell to his lap as he sat there mournfully on a snow-covered stump. They assured him it was a blooding ritual, then laughed for days at his gullibility.

Sonia's boyfriend was a bit too smart for Nordstrom's

taste, very glib with a tendency to talk incessantly in paragraphs with subordinate clauses and divagations wandering off waiflike through history and the arts. As a Harvard boy he also owned the aura of fungoid self-congratulation that Nordstrom identified with Ivy League types. Back in Los Angeles he had noted that graduates of Yale and Dartmouth and so on had automatic purchase even though they were swine, fools or plain stupid as was often the case, looking as they did at the rest of the country with careless indulgence as if it were an imposition on their lives. But then the boy was very kind to Sonia, almost feminine with her and it was plain to see that a permanent bond was formed. Nordstrom had wondered about the young man's nervousness and Sonia had said that her lover had found Nordstrom a bit frightening at first. Nordstrom did have the peculiar habit of staring into anyone's eyes for a minute or so before forming a sentence and this was unnerving to employees, lovers, waiters, even acquaintances and superiors.

Despite this mutual anxiousness the summer went very well, especially with the arrival of August and Nordstrom's month of vacation when they moved to the house in Marblehead. The sea took over then and Nordstrom was incredibly pleased that he had had the sense to take this huge stone house on the water with its tangled hedge of sea-rose, the days of warm blustery winds and the harbor dotted with sailboats. There was a modest swimming pool, a tennis court in a state of mild decay. Best of all Nordstrom liked to take his morning coffee on a veranda and stare at the sea, leaving newspapers, magazines and business correspondence unopened in favor of the sea, watching the surface of the sea with the same intensity whether stormy or becalmed. The other truly fine feature was an antique cast-iron grill from an earlier time when people prepared feasts rather than meals. Nordstrom spent all the first morning horsing its bulk from the backyard near the kitchen door around to the front so that he could cook and watch the sea at the same time. Then he puttered across the harbor in an old Chris-Craft runabout to shop for dinner.

It was while cooking dinner that a strange feeling came over him that gradually forced a radical change in his life. It was an ache just above his heart between his breastbone and throat; at first it alarmed him and he placed a hand on his breast and stared out past the sea-rose to where the ocean buried itself in the haze of dusk. The sharpness of low tide mixed with the roasting meat and he looked down at the meat and sighed "Oh, fuck it." He was rather suddenly not much interested in past or future, or even his breaking heart that perhaps now felt the first itch of healing. But he didn't know that and cared less. The sigh seized his backbone, rippling up his vertebrae to his brain which felt delicately peeled, cold and clean. The feeling was so abruptly powerful that he decided not to examine it for fear that it would go away. He checked the temperature on the meat thermometer and went into the house to take the salad out of the refrigerator; he did not approve of cold salads. He put the small red new potatoes in water, ready to turn them on when he heard Sonia's car. He opened a magnum of Burgess zinfandel to check it out, then put his finger in a sauce dish to taste again the marinade he had swathed the leg of lamb in after he had boned it: a mixture of olive oil, rosemary, crushed garlic, Dijon mustard and a little soy. The pungency of the sauce crept up his sinuses and he turned at the scratching of a stray cat at the kitchen door. He prepared a bowl of lamb trimmings and set it out on the back porch for the cat, a frayed old tom with battered ears staring at him from beneath a flowering crab tree whose pink blossoms perfumed the backyard. A sharp gust of sea breeze loosened some petals and they fell on the unblinking cat. The cat approached slowly with three petals stuck to its fur and wolfed the lamb scraps with a low growl, then stretched and lay down thumping its tail and returning Nordstrom's stare. It seemed to him it was the first cat he had ever truly looked at in his life. They gazed at each other unblinking until tears formed to moisten his unblinking eyes. Then Sonia's car pulled into the driveway and the cat became a gray blur and slid through the porch railing, more reptilian than mammal.

The month fueled Nordstrom's departure from what he thought of as normal life. He awoke fairly early, took his coffee, then helped the maid who came with the house to tidy up from the night before. Sometimes the music from the night still drummed in his ears, tingled in his brain until he learned to recapture melodies as he began the day's shopping and cooking. Sonia was fluid enough to sense a change in her father's personality and did not question his behavior. Nordstrom had insisted that she and Phillip bring up all the houseguests they wanted from Cambridge because he felt like celebrating.

"What are we celebrating?" She laughed, then endured his stare, which seemed distant.

Nordstrom was thinking that with her tan Sonia looked more like her mother, that her hazel eyes were captious and a bit giddy. "I have no idea really. Why not? Maybe I know it's unlikely that there'll be another month like this. Also I want the excuse to cook for a lot of people, to be honest."

She walked up and kissed him on the forehead and laughed again. "I wish you wouldn't disappear every evening."

Nordstrom shrugged and watched the bright light in the room waver from a scudding cloud. She was the dearest creature on earth to him and still this didn't make him melancholy as it once did. "I like to sit and watch it get dark. Then when I go to bed I like to listen to the music through the floor."

Sonia looked away in embarrassment. "You ought to get a girl friend. I mean, you'd probably be happier."

"So strange in these modern times to have your daughter tell you that you need to get laid. I'm saving it for marriage."

"I didn't mean to be coarse. I didn't want you to think that Mother was the only woman in the world. You might even find something better, for Christ's sake."

Nordstrom rolled his eyes and Sonia stomped out of the room. There was a kind of half friendly bitchery between Sonia and her mother that he had found incomprehensible, as if they were trying to play a game with razors. He poured a dollop of bourbon and went to the window, abruptly turning away when he saw that two of Sonia's friends from college had taken off the tops of their bikinis. One of them, a rather plain girl all in all, had beautiful pear-shaped breasts that tilted up a bit and glistened with suntan lotion. Nordstrom felt a slight pulling low in his stomach that he was unable to blame on the whiskey. The girl had helped him with the dishes the night before and he had scarcely noticed her. In the past week or so, since the incident while basting the lamb, he had maintained with no particular effort the sensation of having just awakened from a lovely dream, but the difficulty was that certain things had become too utterly poignant to be borne up under. He would sit in the room in the dark listening to the music until it quit, sometimes not until near dawn. In between the records he heard the sea rising and falling against the breakwater. He found himself unable to read and without any interest in thinking. Thoughts, sensations and pictures passed through his mind but he let them float away. He wondered what a person blind from birth saw in his mind. He wondered about that sophomoric notion of what a man is, deprived of the input of the five senses. He wondered who was listening to the music from his bedroom, who was the listener and was startled. In sleeping the dreams of Laura had disappeared and he occasionally dreamt of women that didn't exist. How could that be? He would wonder in the morning. He rigged a setline down on the beach using a doorknob for a sinker and a chicken liver for bait, as he had done as a boy, but at dawn when he pulled in the line there was only a small dead shark tangled in a large clump of seaweed. He mourned his errant curiosity and buried the shark with the same reverence he had buried the soul of the crow thirty years before.

That night as he prepared dinner for a dozen absolutely stoned young people Sonia came into the kitchen and stared at him with her eyes flashing.

"You really pissed me off today. I wasn't trying to interfere in your life. You could at least talk to people. I keep telling them you're my father but they think you're the cook."

"There's nothing wrong with being a cook. But I'm going to take your advice and get a girl friend. A blond one with a huge ass that listens to country music."

Actually two of Phillip's friends had asked for turkey sandwiches one morning thinking Nordstrom was the cook. They had been embarrassed later and one, a short plumpish Sephardic Jew from New York, had helped Nordstrom with dinner. He was an habitué of the same restaurant in the Village where Nordstrom had eaten with Sonia and Phillip. The young man was a fine cook and while they were preparing the food (filet of sole Bercy aux champignons) Nordstrom asked him about the waitress that had caught his eye. It proved to be a fatal question.

"Oh my god just stay away. She's an absolute kike cunt, a dancer with those big dark Monet eyes. She'd put you in the blender. I mean my god every well-heeled fool in town comes around with flowers and she treats them like dogshit. She was married to this *schvartze* coke dealer, you know, a spade killer, and she had an affair with this writer who got his teeth beaten loose. But of course I'll introduce you if you love the masochism bit. You don't look like the type." The young man had given off a melancholy laugh. "I like these dipshit English girls myself."

The night of Sonia's anger Nordstrom capitulated and sat at the head of the table. He didn't mind that the people he cooked for smoked marijuana as it seemed to sharpen their appetites. He had roasted some quail he had stuffed with green grapes, halved and soaked overnight in Calvados. They were eaten greedily which pleased Nordstrom and he talked at length with two Harvard MBA's about the energy crisis and the consequences of Middle Eastern politics on oil imports. The two young men were surprised that the cook had been to Jidda, and had helped to negotiate an OPEC deal. They left rather hesitantly for a disco in Rockport with the rest of the crowd. Sonia kissed him and patted his back on the way out of the door.

Nordstrom watched their taillights recede into the warm darkness and then fed the tomcat that had emerged from under the backporch. If no one else were around the cat would now enter the kitchen which tonight was hot and muggy with a rank low tide smell hanging in the air, a seaboard reminder of what a swamp in summer smells like. The cat ate the last single quail that Nordstrom had been thinking about having for breakfast but had decided the cat would enjoy more than he did. The cat ripped at the brown-roasted skin and even crunched down the bones. Nordstrom petted the animal until it went rigid and dashed for the kitchen door. It was the plain girl with pear breasts in a pale-blue caftan. She shrugged at Nordstrom as he let the cat out the screen door. She poured a glass

of club soda and drank as if her life depended on it. Nordstrom didn't remember her at dinner.

"I got this perfectly goddamned sunburn today and felt
sick as shit." She talked out of the side of her mouth as was
the strange habit of her class. Nordstrom could think of
nothing to say so he put on his white cook's apron and
began the dishes. He had taken off his shirt while the cat
ate and felt a bit naked, now that the girl was there.

"Hope you're having a nice time," he said lamely.

"Sure. Faboo, if I hadn't fried the hell out of my skin
like a perfect nitwit." She paused and boldly appraised
Nordstrom. "You're a perfect dear to do all this cooking.
I mean Sonia's so lucky." She sat down at the kitchen table
and took a bag of papers from her purse and rolled a large
joint, lit it and inhaled deeply. "I'm going to Santa Barbara
tomorrow to visit my mother, if anyone gets up early
enough to run to Logan." She approached Nordstrom at
the sink and put the joint between his lips, ignoring his
shaking head. "This is pretty good shit, supposedly Hawaiian."

"I'll take you to the airport," he choked expelling the
smoke.

They looked at each other closely for a moment and
there was a glimmer of comprehension Nordstrom decided
not to admit to himself. He looked down at his hands
buried in the soapy water. She left the room and put on
a record, then returned and helped him with the dishes.
Above the music they could hear a thunderstorm approaching from the west. The air grew even more still and

warm. He felt the sweat flatten his hair and trickle down his back as he listened to her chatter about a career in fashion. She absentmindedly traced a finger down the sweat on his arm and he felt an involuntary shudder. Then she drew her caftan over her head and tossed it in the corner.

"I don't know about you but I'm perfectly suffocating and my burn itches."

She wore very slight, pale-beige panties and bra. She was burned, though not too badly, on the top of her breasts and just above and below her panty line. He reached out and touched a nipple beneath the fabric with a wet forefinger. She turned around and raised her arms. "My back isn't as bad." He wiped his hands on the apron and pressed them to the small of her back. Then she backed toward him, stumbling a bit in clogged sandals. He looked down at his hands and her buttocks craning outward. She reached behind her touching his hands, then slipped down her panties to just above her knees. "Go ahead. I've been thinking of this for an hour."

Nordstrom went ahead, as it were. On completion he collapsed backward to the floor with his pants around his ankles and the damp apron forming a small tent around his member. She laughed and he laughed. She lit him a cigarette and he smoked it without getting off the floor. She stepped out of her panties and took off her bra. She took a bottle of white wine out of the refrigerator and handed it to Nordstrom with a corkscrew. They abandoned the dishes and took a dip in the pool with the lights off, watching the approaching thunderstorm above the lights of Marblehead. They made love again with him sitting beneath her on a wicker lawn chair. The rain drove them indoors and they sat naked on the couch feeling the air cool gradually and watching the lightning and thunder explode above the ocean. They smoked another joint and danced. They fell asleep on the couch and did not hear the laughing voices that turned out the lights and record player.

Another week and the summer was over. Nordstrom made a melancholy bouillabaisse for twenty and the next day everyone disappeared. Another week in Boston and Sonia returned to Sarah Lawrence and Nordstrom returned to work. In the evening he was palpably lonely and began dancing alone to the records left behind and with the same bittersweet ache in his chest. In a little more than another month, in the middle of October, late one night he received a call from his mother that said "your father is dead."

Nordstrom took the first available plane out of Logan for O'Hare at dawn. He smiled remembering a previous dawn when he had taken the girl to the airport and had run into an old business associate from Los Angeles. He had been startled when the man had said "sorry about your divorce." and when Nordstrom had introduced the girl as one of his daughter's school chums it was plain that the man thought otherwise. But the meeting had made him feel buoyant driving against the traffic back to Marblehead; not only had he made love rather wonderfully, the word and idea of divorce no longer knotted his stomach or threw him into a fretful or melancholy state.

There was a five-hour wait at Milwaukee for a North

Central for Rhinelander so he chartered an idle Lear Jet, having enjoyed the plane when he was in the oil business as the closest domestic approximation to the thrill of a jet fighter. The fact of his father's death had not penetrated much beyond his intellect and in a difficult, blustery landing he thought he might join him. The copilot had radioed ahead and his mother and a cousin, a sallow barber with a truly dirty mind, were waiting there to meet him. There were tearful embraces, then the barber could not help himself and quipped "it must be nice" as he eyed the Lear. Nordstrom said nothing. In previous visits when he had tried to conceal his success all of his old acquaintances had been terribly disappointed. Those who had stayed home didn't want Nordstrom to be one of them—he was the stuff of their economic fantasies and any gesture to the contrary wasn't appreciated. Walking to the car with his mother in a cold, light rain he remembered when his parents had come to Los Angeles for a visit. They considered Nordstrom's home to be somewhat of a "mansion" as they called it, and on the next to the last day his mother had shyly asked him to see where Cary Grant lived. He drove her over a few blocks and pointed out an imposing home, having no knowledge or interest in the movie colony. He liked movies and novels, but had no curiosity about celebrities, actors, actresses or writers. His father had always wanted him to be a forest ranger and that still seemed to Nordstrom a noble pursuit. When his father was in Los Angeles he fished off the piers or took a headboat out of Santa Monica. Then his father would eat a great quantity of fried sand dabs just short of serious indigestion and talk about his first visit to Los Angeles in 1930. He had come from a poor family of Norwegian immigrants living in Chicago and when the Depression hit he spent four years as a young hobo drifting all over the troubled country.

After some brief civilities at the wake at his mother's house, jammed with friends and relatives, Nordstrom went to the funeral home and saw death itself. He stood at the open casket, the other visitors keeping distant to let the only son express his grief. He kissed his father's cool forehead and tears flushed out of him and his body shook. He was convulsed with loss and the unthinkable fact of death. He was a boy again and it was beyond his comprehension and he whispered "Daddy" over and over until there were no more tears left in his body and he walked out of the funeral home and down the street to the edge of town where he walked down past a lake rimmed with cottages to a log road that led into the forest. He walked up this log road for a mile or so until finally the sun came through the disappearing clouds and he took off his trench coat. Now it was suddenly Indian summer in the forest and the hardwoods were a brilliant deep yellow and red, shifting away in the haze to umbrous hills with splotches of white birch and green pine. He walked until his feet became sore and then he spread his trench coat on a stump and sat on it. He thought about his father, even felt envy for those Depression days when he had traversed the country to "look things over." Starting from nothing, everything was fine to his father beyond a subsistence level. He made money because he was competent, had wit and could not help making money. It was simply another world, Nordstrom thought. His own life suddenly seemed repellently formal. Whom did he know or what did he know and whom did he love? Sitting on the stump under the burden of his father's death and even the mortality inherent in the dying, wildly colored canopy of leaves, he somehow understood that life was only what one did every day. He seemed to see time shimmering and moving up above him and through the leaves and down around his feet and through his middle. Nothing was like anything else, including himself, and everything was changing all of the time. He knew he couldn't perceive the change because he was changing too, along with everything else. There was no still point. For an instant he floated above himself and smiled at the immaculately tailored man sitting on the stump and in a sunny glade back in the forest. He got up and pressed against a poplar sapling swinging back and forth to a harmony he didn't understand. He looked around the clearing in recognition that he was lost but didn't mind because he knew he had never been found.

He walked toward the lowering sun knowing that in October it was toward the southwest. He came to a pond he didn't recognize and flushed a raft of blue-winged teal. He walked around the pond through a blackberry thicket, snagging his suit a number of times. He walked up a small creek muddying himself to his knees in a seep until he reached higher ground where he dropped his trench coat and climbed slowly up a large white pine tree to get a vantage point. His hands were blackened and sticky from the resin that exuded from the tree but he could see for a dozen miles: he could see the white steeple of the Lutheran church where his father's funeral service would be held in two days, he could see a motorboat crossing a lake, a silo without a barn—the barn had burned when he was a senior in high school. He curled his arm around a limb for safety and lit a cigarette, hearing the shotgun blast of a partridge hunter far in the distance. A crow flew by and was startled by his presence, squawking away at a greater speed to warn others. There's a man up in a tree in a blue suit. Nordstrom looked down at his suit and was amused at how he had ruined it. He took out his gold pocket watch and aimed the 9 at the steeple knowing there was a section of road near the 12 if he needed to climb another tree for a sighting. His father liked to climb trees and was always creating deliberately lame excuses for doing so. Up in the tree for the first time in twenty-five years, Nordstrom thought it was part of his father's penchant for "looking things over." When Sonia was a little girl and they came to Wisconsin for a summer vacation she had brought along a diving mask. His father didn't care much for swimming and hadn't noticed diving masks before but he took to puttering around the lake with Sonia and diving overboard in his favorite fishing spots. At dinner he would say he saw a bluegill "as big as a goddamned frying pan" or a pike or largemouth bass "as long as your goddamned arm."

Nordstrom finally emerged from the woods just before dark near a small Indian reservation community outside of town. He walked down a gravel road toward a tavern thinking how his father would be amused at his ruined four-hundred-dollar suit not to speak of his Florsheim shoes now scarred and mud-caked. The last mile or so he had been concentrating on suits and the government and decided he no longer much believed in either. Suits obviously had helped to promote bad government and he was as guilty as anyone for wearing them so steadfastly for twenty years. Of late he had become frightened of the government for the first time in his life, the way the structure of democracy had begun debasing people rather than enlivening them in their mutual concern. The structure was no longer concerned with the purpose for which it was designed, and a small part of the cause, Nordstrom thought, was probably that all politicians and bureaucrats wore suits. He stopped in the parking lot of the tavern favored by Indians and regarded the dirty old jalopies and beaten pickups. Perhaps he should quit his job he thought, give all his money to his daughter and some to his mother whose small annuity was probably worthless in light of inflation. Then he cautioned himself for his wild thoughts, thinking that somehow they might be connected to death, to becoming lost and climbing a tree after a tiring flight and not having eaten all day.

The bar smelled of piss and sweat and Nordstrom blinked to focus on the drinkers. He heard his name called out. It was Henry who was appreciably into a binge. Nordstrom stood next to him wondering whether he should embrace the old man whose head seemed to nod with the jukebox and booze.

"You better call home. They're all looking for you."

"Henry, I want you to be a pallbearer," Nordstrom said, then ordered a drink for Henry, a bourbon and beer for himself. Henry downed his in a gulp and stared intently at Nordstrom.

"There isn't any fucking way I'm going into that church. I worked all day yesterday with your dad and he didn't look too good. So we had a few drinks. And he says, 'Henry I'm not feeling too good and I think my heart is going.' So I took him home and your mother called the doctor and then we went over to the hospital because he wouldn't ride in an ambulance. So they said it was bad and he could hardly breathe up in the room and they brought oxygen but he said he didn't want to die in an oxygen tent. He just lay there staring straight ahead with me and your mother on each side. Around about midnight the doctor said there is no hope. To call you. We went back in and he held our hands. He made your mother get up in bed beside him to be close as he went. He had ahold of my hand hard, so I stayed. He talked a little about fishing. I told him I would go along with him into death as far as I could but I would have to turn back. He said for me to tell you good luck and to say he loved you and to give you a kiss good-bye."

Henry stood then and gave Nordstrom a hug and kissed him on the cheek because he was short and could not reach Nordstrom's forehead. They had another drink in silence, then Henry led him out the door to his pickup.

A few days later Nordstrom flew back to New York with Sonia, who had come for the funeral, and then took the shuttle up to Boston. Laura had cabled her regrets from Mexico, saying she would have come but word only reached her on the day of the funeral. Nordstrom did not doubt it as Laura had loved his father and there had always been a playfulness and banter in their contacts that Nordstrom never quite comprehended. She had even stopped by for a visit in the past summer on her way through the Midwest. Laura had once said she found his father "sexy," a statement that had horrified him at the time. Laura had had the advantage of knowing that people died whereas even the most ordinary events, and death is the most ordinary of all, took Nordstrom by surprise.

CHAPTER
III

Now we have arrived where we began and are in continuous time, a wonderful illusion for those addicted to notions of yesterday, right now and tomorrow. Every evening after a long walk and light dinner Nordstrom dances alone, surely an absurd picture of a man of forty-three years, a father, formerly a husband, magna cum laude University of Wisconsin 1958, at thirty-five vice-president of finance for Standard Oil of California, and so on, as if such simpleminded clues were effective in tracking our mammal. But they are all discarded habits. Nordstrom means "north-storm" but it's not much more helpful than "crow." One learns little from a telephone book. It's winter in Boston, our St. Petersburg, and the man dances on, a bit clumsily to be sure, and with a witless tenacity. Sometimes he just jumps straight up and down. One night he went with the delicatessen owner to see a Celtics-Denver Nuggets' game to witness the greatest jumper of all, David Thompson. Thompson floated through the air in a three-sixty, and dunked the ball backward over his head and didn't even smile. The crowd rose to its feet, was hushed a moment, then exploded over this act that was not so much a defiance of gravity as a transcendence of what we have experienced of gravity. Sonia came up for the weekend and he took her and Phillip to the ballet to see Baryshnikov. Nordstrom wore a Cardin suit that Laura had selected for him years before but he had never worn out of embarrassment. In the lobby at intermission many lovely and not so lovely women smiled at him thinking Nordstrom must be someone they should know. They had a late celebratory dinner because Phillip had won a fellowship to spend the coming year in Florence studying at the Uffizi. Sonia would leave with him in June after her graduation. Phillip was prattling on about death at dinner. His own father had died when Phillip was fourteen and he had begun staying up very late, smoking cigarettes and wearing sloppy clothes. Lately he had read a certain French writer who talked about the "terrible freedom" that comes when the father dies. There is no one left on earth to judge. Sonia shushed him, thinking the conversation was insensitive to her father. Nordstrom said her concern was nonsense and though he found the whole notion appalling he guessed that it was probably true. He had been lucky with his own father who was all in favor of Nordstrom following his heart's affections, though it seemed odd that only recently had his son an inkling of how to go about it.

Late that night Nordstrom found himself sleepless because he hadn't had his two hours of dancing. He had enjoyed the ballet but he was losing what little of the spectator was left in him: he was becoming an amateur in the true sense—one who loved the doing, and had the beginner's openness about life that had been lost for transparent reasons since his childhood. Now in the middle of energetic insomnia he knew that he couldn't turn on the stereo at three A.M. because Sonia and Phillip were sleeping. He got up and tiptoed into the den in his pajama bottoms and danced an hour without music, hearing only a clock ticking and the shuffle of his bare feet on the carpet.

Feb. 17, 78: Have been planning this long trip for after I resign to include both S. America and Africa. Startling how close Rio is to Dakar. Desk covered with atlases, maps from *National Geographic*, guidebooks for a month now, but the energy is fast disappearing. Why should I want to know the strange when I am ignorant of the familiar. Really noticed my ankle the other morning for the first time in years. I like the crow on the cover of The Grateful Dead album but it is very difficult music to dance to. I bought a parka and snowmobile boots from a sporting goods store on Boylston and have been walking a great deal after work. The snow is wonderful this year despite the occasional near paralysis of the city. Between five and eight is the best time to walk. First the electric urge for people to get home from work, then the dinner silence and then the people going out for the evening. Have spent a great deal of time helping people get unstuck from their parking places. Wisconsin makes one an expert on snow and getting unstuck. Old man and wife buried in their Chrysler which I shoveled out as he was gasping, then rocked the car until it came free. He gave me a five-dollar bill refusing to take it back. He said it was for "a hot supper and a few drinks." Gave it to a bum a few blocks farther on. Bought a dozen Hawaiian shirts off the rack at Jordan Marsh for the trip I perhaps have lost interest in though I told the travel agent to go ahead. Always thought them in bad taste but now I like the silken feeling, strange colors though I haven't worn one out of the apartment not finding an occasion to do so. Have come to think in my cooking of the new *cuisine minceur* as narcissistic and partly silly though a few good ideas. People could eat what they chose if they did not ignore pushing their bodies a bit. Since dancing my belt has gone down two notches. Closely studied a flounder I filleted so as to get further sense of what I was eating. Fragile pearl-colored bones, spine in which through a filament of paste, the fish's body receives instruction from its tiny brain. Swim there and there and there. Wonder what he had seen in his watery life. Made a small *court bouillon* so as not to waste this carcass which had assumed outsize importance by the time I finished studying it. Then I cooked a handful of vermicelli in the stock and had it for a snack after dancing. Had a streak of tripe this week as I bought too much by the butcher's mistake: tripe Milanese, *menudo*—Mexican tripe stew—then the justly famed tripe *à la mode de Caen.* Old man in shipping department has cancer of liver so have put through an authorization for a bonus as he wants to die in his birthplace in Galway, Ireland, where his mother still lives. My own mother wrote to

say she is getting along fine and her cousin, also wid-
owed, is moving in. She said she had a fine letter from
Laura. Got a hard-on in a taxi thinking about Laura's
butt, more picturing it than thinking. She had small
breasts but was justly vain about her legs and butt.
How clearly I remember her Debussy dance so many
years ago in the hot gymnasium. It takes my breath
away now but there is no bitterness. I have been
having some intuitions about sex though ill formed as
a whole. For instance I saw the movie *Pretty Baby* and
though the girl is a superb beauty it was her mother
that owned sexual appeal. It is the life unlived that
makes men want so young a girl. To be twelve and
thirteen, be careless and silly, with floppy grace. The
world at face is so frightening no wonder. She
becomes her mother in a night. I longed so often for
that girl at the kitchen sink in Marblehead but it is
the nature of such things not to return. For instance
Ms. Dietrich as she chooses to be called is married to
a city planner, childless, in her mid-thirties and my
executive secretary though she could easily run the
company. Last Thursday we did a twelve-hour day to
prepare for audit, the last three hours at the apartment after I prepared a light dinner. It was hard and
tedious work and afterward we drank a bottle of Kor-
bel champagne to ease our sore necks and eyes. I have
known this woman closely for three years but was
startled by the effect of the wine on her. She wept and
said she was crying for me because Jews had taken
both my wife and daughter. So shocking it was funny
and I said now, now Ms. Dietrich that's utter nonsense. She embraced me and then I knew that she

wanted to tumble, and though she is a little chubby to be my type, I thought to myself why not. So we carried on at some length and once when we were up and down on each other I "awoke" with a start when I was looking plainly at her bottom and I said to myself "this is reality." The sensation lasted acutely for several days. And like the feeling when I was roasting the lamb last summer I decided not to doubt it as it seems to me that doubt is often an example of self-pity, a kind of whining about existence. Poor pitiful me, and that rot. Henry did not doubt that he could help my father into death, open the gate for him and shake his hand as he entered nothingness or whatever on earth eternity is. I don't read books on mystical matters as, like Lutherans, special powers are ascribed. My dealings in Tokyo with Orientals do not lead me to think they are any different from us. Henry is one Indian among a hundred sorry ones I have known. He gave me a turtle claw. It was wonderfully funny at the office when Ms. Dietrich pretended nothing had happened, all rather Germanic. Intimacies can be frightening in the light of day. As on the walk after I was lost and then found the gravel road, I'd been thinking solidly of giving up money and power. I would rather make an omelette. When I was young and had to hoe the garden or dig a garbage hole I would resent it and then get lost in doing these things for hours. Ms. Dietrich is so self-conscious because she is trying to be Ms. Dietrich every minute. Like Phillip trying to be unique and doing so by this stream of talk as if he would vanish if he stopped talking. How strange we all are. One minute we're

laboring over the accounts and the next moment
we're chewing on each other's bodies like dogs. Or
bears. Henry and Father once saw two bears make
love across a lake in Canada through binoculars. Read
the other day that whales commit homosexual acts.

Spring proved to be obnoxiously difficult for Nordstrom. It
was incredibly complicated for him to resign his job. The
owners of the company were a family of New Hampshire
aristocrats, crankish Yankees who plainly didn't want to be
abandoned by their managerial wunderkind. They offered
everything and when their largess was refused they grew
resentful. It was even more difficult and confusing to give
away the money. Sonia didn't want it and his mother was
hysterical. The E.F. Hutton man insisted he see a psychiatrist and Nordstrom readily agreed out of curiosity and his
understanding that, to others, he was committing an outrageous act. His mother's tearful attitude was that he had
worked so hard all his life for the money. The broker went
to New York to see Sonia, hoping that she could make her
father behave sensibly. Sonia came to Boston and they had
lunch with the broker whom Nordstrom actually had a
great deal of respect for. But Nordstrom was diffident and
ended up convincing them later that afternoon by giving
twenty-five grand to the National Audubon Society though
he had no special fascination for birds. He liked to watch
shorebirds by the hour on weekends near Ipswich but
wasn't curious about the names given them. When he saw
a particular species the second time he would remember

the first time he saw it. That saved him from having to carry around a birdbook.

And not that the concern for Nordstrom by others was unfounded. How were they, given their own natures, to know that Nordstrom wasn't another dipshit cracking utterly under all those pressures, known and unrecognized, that make up our lives? Sonia, with the cynicism of youth, thought it was too late for her father to change. Laura, who had been contacted, had refused to interfere, thinking the whole problem to be at the same time silly and charming, believing as did the broker all of the vulgar lingo attached to notions of mid-life change and so on, language as blasphemous to life as the central fact of the government in everyone's existence. His mother simply believed, within the framework of Protestant thrift, that people should hold on to their money for a rainy day. She wrote Nordstrom about how a prominent citizen of Rhinelander had come down with cancer and some seventy thousand dollars had been spent on the medical community in a hopeless effort to save his life. Ms. Dietrich's concerns were a bit more down to earth, centering on her hopes for another lovemaking session before Nordstrom cleared out. Her own husband was only nominally interested in sex and fell asleep after ejaculation whereas Nordstrom was a princely dallier who had obviously been well trained by his wife.

On the morning of his psychiatric appointment Nordstrom walked from Brookline to Cambridge. The fact of the matter was that in his arduous study of reality he had become a trifle goofy. He understood this and decided to go with it, as they say. It was a fine morning in early May and as he crossed Commonwealth he paused on the traffic island to study a jet liner passing above him on an approach to Logan. The silver plane looked lovely against the deep blue sky. He paused in Allston and ate an Italian sausage sandwich with green peppers and onions for breakfast. It was delicious with a cold beer and he exchanged pidgin Italian with the counterman who was trying to decide what number to pick for a dollar bet. As Nordstrom walked on he decided again that nothing was like anything else. One quantity could never technically equal another. No two apples on earth were alike, neither were the two cars at the stoplight, or any two of the three or so billion people on earth. He laughed aloud at the philosophical naiveté of these thoughts but that did not diminish their intensity. Neither were dogs, days, hours and moments ever the same. Finally, he was not the same as yesterday, and was at least infinitesimally different from a moment ago. When he reached the bridge near the business school he paused to stare down at the water dirtied by effluents and a heavy rain the day before. It was the Charles River and Nordstrom had always thought it lacked the charm of the·icy clear rivers of northern Wisconsin, though history buffs were quick to assure everyone that the Charles owned a great deal of history. Today Nordstrom had no opinions about the river. He just looked at it for a while. Of late he had become especially tired of pointless opinions and was trying to get rid of them. He would catch himself thinking as everyone does: too hot, too cold, too green, too fat, too spicy, ugly building, old slippers, loud music, homely woman, fat man. Not, he thought, that one couldn't discriminate but it had grown boring to get in a dither over rehearsing opinions about everything. To the degree that he had gotten rid of this propensity he felt a bit lighter and more fluid. The trouble was that life, the world around him, had begun to seem more fragile, almost evanescent. For instance, he looked at the river so long he forgot what it was. An old lady pushing a shopping cart paused next to him and looked over the rail to see what Nordstrom was looking at: he said "river," coming to what we think is our senses, and she continued on, a little alarmed.

Nordstrom walked downstream along the embankment and sat down on the grass on the far side of the Harvard boathouse. There was an old man with a gray beard sitting on a bench with his trousers rolled to his knees, basking his shins in the sun. The old man was staring at a young woman in a sleeveless blouse, sandals and a loose green skirt, who had her back turned to the old man and Nordstrom, and was rolling a softball back and forth with her infant son. When she bent over to pick up the ball the breeze from the west would billow under the skirt and the old man stared at the back of her smooth thighs. The old man did not mind that Nordstrom had caught him at his voyeurism, and Nordstrom himself only felt lucky at this noontime vision. After a little while the woman and her son scampered across Memorial Drive and were gone forever. Nordstrom felt more aroused generally than sexually, though there was that too, but added was the feeling of good food, good wine or another perhaps stranger feeling, that of letting a beautiful trout go after you had caught it. He was amused at the easy sentimentality the woman's thighs had brought over him.

The hour with the psychiatrist went rather easily, with none of the raw moments he expected. The man privately thought of Nordstrom as somewhat of a religious hysteric without a religion who did not seem in the least harmful to himself or others. The psychiatrist was a Jungian and not at all cynical about what he recognized as a pilgrimage away from an unsatisfactory life. He questioned Nordstrom on the possibility that he might be burdening his mother and daughter by giving them the money. Nordstrom wasn't particularly distressed by the question; he tended to be clinical about ironies, not forgetting their comedy and forgiving the often heartless questions they raised. The psychiatrist followed Nordstrom's gaze out the window to a fully leafed maple that was losing the final remnant of early May's pastel green. This hour's patient had a stolidity that reminded him of the commercial fishermen near his summer home up in Maine. He had put no stock in the broker's call—he treated the man's wife and considered him a cruel nitwit behind the patina of Hingham manners. For some unanswerable reason the Boston area seemed the capital of exotic neuroses and Nordstrom's problem had a refreshing tang of the ordinary.

"What are your immediate thoughts?" the doctor asked, taken by the intensity of Nordstrom's gaze out the window.

"Robin Hood. That maple reminded me of Robin Hood. When I was twelve a friend and I built a tree hut in a maple and played Robin Hood. Then my friend quit the game in favor of throwing a baseball against a barn in

[157]

hopes of becoming Hal Newhouser. I was hurt because we had made cuts in our arms and become blood brothers. So I moved the hut so no one would know where it was but my father caught me hauling lumber and told me to build in a beech, not a maple, because lightning never strikes a beech for some reason. But I said that a beech doesn't have enough foliage to hide anything. My dad said then you'll have to take your chances and that when he was young he always wanted to build a hut at the bottom of a lake so he could look out the window and see fish."

"Do you still enjoy fantasies about being Robin Hood?" Nordstrom had made a long pause and the psychiatrist wanted to continue this interesting train of thought.

"Oh god no. I don't think about being anyone. I don't have that much imagination. Young boys admire outlaws because they don't have to do anything except what they want to. Outlaws pull a job and then just sit around at a hideout cleaning weapons, you know? Every day they simply do what they choose and make a good living at it, at least that's the childhood notion. Outlaws think the law is full of shit which is not an unpopular suspicion. But to be honest I thought today of Robin Hood's girl friend, Marian or Miriam? Up in the hut I had two photos, one of a woman's front and one of her back. That's what we used to call it, front and back. I paid three dollars for these pictures as a nude was hard to find and three dollars was a lot of money. This woman I saw bending over down by the river reminded me of Marian or Miriam because she wore a green skirt. I used to be a little amazed in my hut knowing that Marian or Miriam had a front and back by natural law and very probably Robin Hood had taken advantage of the fact."

"Did you have a fantasy about the woman by the river?"

"No, not really. Again I'm not too imaginative and then I like to avoid fantasies so that it's more of a surprise when it happens. Sometimes it's a little difficult when you see a lady as lovely as today. Maybe it's a simpleminded oddity of mine. I noticed the other day that if I forget to wind my watch I am always interested in the exact time the watch stops. I remember the year when I stopped finding pennies in my pocket that were older than myself. I was thirty-three. I feel a little silly taking up your time, though I'm paying for it. To be frank, I became tired of this money thing when my wife left me. I started to look at it coldly. I loved her terribly and then it all disappeared, especially for her and not so much for me. I thought my ambition ruined us though hers helped in the ruin. It's such an ordinary story. I didn't so much lose faith in it all as I totally lost interest."

"What are you interested in now?" The psychiatrist interrupted another of Nordstrom's long pauses. "Oh Jesus I don't know. My dad who died in October always said he liked to look things over. Maybe that's what I want to do. I might take a long trip. I sort of came to life again last July and it's been pleasant. Most days I'm quite excited about living for no particular reason. I've taken to cooking rather elaborately."

Nordstrom stared at the psychiatrist for a full minute and smiled. "In the evening I dance alone, most often for two hours. Sometimes I just jump around, you know?"

May floated along easily. Nordstrom's replacement arrived from Chicago. There was a modest dinner honoring his departure with many in management finding reasons not to attend. There was a fine set of luggage for Nordstrom. A tearful Ms. Dietrich got drunk and had to be sent home in a cab, her plans for the evening awry and the concealed lingerie bought for nought. Nordstrom ended up in Dorchester after a tour of honky-tonks and played poker until dawn with a group of men from the shipping department. He made the long walk home at daylight, a dim and misty morning with the Atlantic palpable in the air, the breeze causing only the slightest tremor in the leaves. He felt a nagging compassion in quasi-dangerous Roxbury for an old black man lying in a pool of bloody vomit watched by sparrows. A block later it was a diseased tree that upset him, trying to remember in puzzlement why Jesus killed the fig tree. When you got past the surface civilities of even a state religion you weren't far from the tom-toms. The long gray empty street was a different sort of river. He could whistle and make his own music, despite the flavor of gin in his sinuses. An old dog followed him for a block and he paused to allow it to sniff his pant leg.

He reached his apartment in two hours, took a shower and made a cheese omelette which he washed down with a slug of white wine. He went to bed but couldn't sleep. He made a pot of coffee and leafed through his diary with disinterest. "Saw pretty girl at Crane's Neck Beach. She had extraordinarily large feet. She will no doubt spend the summer burying them in sand out of view. The cruelty of genes. That classmate with the huge dick who was the secret envy of all in the locker room after gym class was teased to a shamefaced idiot. Now a bachelor driving county snowplow and gravel truck nicknamed Dork." Nordstrom paced the apartment and saw the girl across the courtyard stretching in her shorty pajamas. He got a hard-on that more closely resembled a toothache than something pleasant. He regretted that he found self-abuse so unsatisfactory. He leaned out the window and breathed deeply, his cock nudging the sill unpleasantly. She smiled and waved. He waved back, his heart thumping. She stretched and retreated into the darkness of her apartment. He sighed and went back to the kitchen and turned on the radio. An unnamed man sang "Don't Say *Mañana* Unless You Mean It," and Nordstrom longed for the Caribbean though he'd never been there. Joe Carioca or something. He'd rent a small apartment, drink rum and cook seafood. The sun would be hot, the water blue. Despairing of sleep he pulled a bottle of Montgomery Calvados from the cupboard and began to write.

May 78: Holy Christ I can't sleep and it's nine in the morning. Drank more than I usually do in a week or so but not sedated. It's because I'm usually awake now and I don't like these old man's unchangeable habits. I used the same shaving lotion for twenty years. Walked from Dorchester in a trance. Old drunk Negro grieved me, made throat well with tears. Wrote Henry a note asking him to please accept Dad's fishing tackle and deer rifle. Got a picture post-

[161]

card back that said "thanks Henry" and that was all.
Asked Mother to have him looked after if he takes ill.
Hard drinkers go fast sometimes. Dad said that once
to Henry out on the lake and Henry said nobody is
born and nobody ever dies. Dad said, "Henry, you are
full of shit to the sideburns," and we all laughed. I
have not forgotten the idea that he might have been
serious. Read in *The New Yorker* how this man
walked thirty-five days into the Himalayas facing nu-
merous perils to see a snow leopard and never saw one.
He saw many tracks and spoor, though. Saw a bobcat
once from the tree hut. Also a badger snorting along.
The bobcat floated. I made a noise and he did a
three-sixty like Thompson and vanished. Bobcats are
always ready. Called my summer friend the Sephard
to arrange graduation dinner party for Sonia. He suggested the Village restaurant where I saw that girl.
But he said she was back to dancing and no longer
worked there but should he invite her as a lark to
thicken the stew of the evening? I said of course and
sent a check leaving the menu to his good taste.
Thinking of her now puts heat into my stomach. Felt
like I'd levitated when the money was gone but now
the feeling is gone and there's no sensation but a
slight lightness. Are we truly allowed to start over?
We'll see, as Dad used to say. I'm so hopelessly slow
to change. All those years with Laura and the gradual
deadness and then three years of true deadness. Then
the lucky break which I am not interested in compre-
hending for fear still that it might disappear. I have
just lit some dope Sonia left me, like an antique hippie, in hopes it will rest my brain. She thinks it's good

for me though I don't do it more than once a month. Can't ever remember wanting a woman so much. Deranged by fatigue. They are the best thing there is for better or worse. My heart aches. It would be good even now to have that older black woman in the Green Bay whorehouse on that obligatory trip in high school. I hugged her and wanted to smooch which she thought was funny. Girl in green dress on river bank was heartless. Now I am what they call stoned. The apartment is almost packed. The storage people are coming. On Tuesday after Decoration Day now called Memorial Day for reasons I forgot. Decorating graves on a warm day. Now an image of Laura again. Almost can smell her. That summer in pine board cabin by a creek in Montana with Sonia playing in the yard. The creek was loud but soothing. She was making coffee, wearing only her underpants. She tied up her hair and washed the sleep away at the sink. She stretched. Sunlight from the window on the back of her legs.

CHAPTER
IV

The world does not suffer fools gladly, thought Nordstrom at four in the morning in a corner suite seven stories up in the Carlyle Hotel in New York City. He sipped bourbon with not too much relish. He was half waiting for the phone though unwilling to take the initiative himself. There was no getting a jump on reality. He had imagined the day otherwise, which is okay if you're by yourself and in control. You only approach total control in the toilet, Nordstrom thought and laughed. Outside the toilet there were bound to be surprises and not all of them pleasant. Some of them left a vacuum in the stomach as if one were falling off earth backward. Something that will inevitably happen anyway. Now he wanted Laura to call but knew she wouldn't. And he wouldn't call her. Sonia and Phillip and Laura had just dropped him off in a cab. There was an abyss he had almost forgotten between what his heart wished would happen and what would probably occur in the hours that came toward him before sleep.

The first surprise was seeing Laura at all. No one had told him but then he hadn't bothered to inquire. There she was sitting beside him, having flown in from Paris. He hadn't seen her for nearly four years. During the studied banality of the ceremony and the reception afterward, Nordstrom thought that a whole world was occurring behind your back and it was best to be on your toes. She looked very good though he felt it only as a surface impression rather than in his stomach. When graduation was over they took a cab down from Yonkers to the Pierre where Phillip and Sonia were staying with Laura before they would all leave the next day. They talked and then Nordstrom made a bad move caused by his inherent sentimentality. Safely pinned in the pocket of a linen sport coat was fifteen thousand dollars in one-hundred-dollar bills. It was for the BMW he had promised Sonia seven years ago in their Los Angeles den. He had made inquiries and it was recommended she fly up from Florence (Phillip already pronounced it Fee-renz-ee) and buy the car in Munich. The gesture brought the room to a halt and he felt very clumsy and old-fashioned, say like Sid, the owner of the delicatessen to whom he had bequeathed his whole wardrobe in a touching moment. He wanted to travel light. They all went at him at once and he felt insufferably gauche: Phillip said an expensive car might provoke violence given the troubled state of Italian politics. Laura said no one cares about cars. Sonia said he had already given everything away and they wouldn't need a car in Florence. Nordstrom retreated to the bathroom and felt no control. He didn't feel as hurt as he felt misplaced with what remained of his sense of family. Sonia and Laura embraced him when he came out of the toilet and there was a sudden shockingly sexual urge toward both of them. They would disappear tomorrow and it was the lust brought on by death. Phillip broke the strange mood by snapping a photo of the "charming" family.

A further surprise came at the restaurant. The waitress-dancer he had so looked forward to meeting had a sort of feral coldness about her when they met, and now, seated at the far end of the table between the Sephard and Laura, she regarded the table with an unmistakable hauteur though she couldn't have been much older than the graduates and their dates. She was plainly a woman of the world with Levantine features tending toward thinness, and whatever warmth she might have was well concealed. Nordstrom was pleased with the meal (a galantine of duck, mussels steamed in white wine, striped bass baked with fennel, leg of lamb that had been boned and butterflied then stuffed) but the crowd was giddy and drinking too much to concentrate on food. They all had plans. They were excited to a degree almost equal to Nordstrom's excitement about having no plans. The raw point of the evening was that everyone, through the graces of Phillip's mouth, knew that Nordstrom had given away all of his money and was going on a long trip. In fact, he thought, they had a certain advantage over his future as he wasn't at all sure about the trip—departure day three days hence —though the sheaf of tickets was back in a leather folder at the hotel. But it was the fact of his giving the money away that made him, in their eyes, a monkish wild man off on a pilgrimage. He was appalled. He knew most of them from last summer in Marblehead but he noted that he had become radically changed in their eyes. The girl next to him assumed he was going to India and expressed disappointment at his itinerary. He had thought of them previously as *au courant* and rather far to the fashionable Left but now they seemed to stand decidedly more than himself as smack-dab in the middle. He remembered how so few of the sixties' radicals did anything so rash—say not pay their taxes—as to actually end up in jail for their beliefs. It was a hoax in that most of them seemed to own boutiques now. There was something amusing here that couldn't quite be traced. Everyone is just fucking around as usual, he thought. If I were home, which no longer exists, I'd be dancing now. He began to get an inkling that the point was to be dancing in your brain all of the time when his daughter who was seated next to him sensed his bleakness, squeezed his hand and kissed him on the ear, saying please come visit. He felt the intensity of her concern and nodded yes.

The evening wore itself garishly thin. He noted that Laura and the waitress-dancer—Sarah by name—were making frequent trips to the toilet, he guessed for snorting cocaine. A number of couples left for a disco and the party closed in together but still lacked the ease and camaraderie of wine. They were in an anteroom and the Sephard had the waiter close a partition. Phillip lit a joint and passed it. Another couple left and now there was only Laura, Sarah, the Sephard, Phillip, Sonia, the close friend of Sonia who wanted desperately for Nordstrom to go to Katmandu, and

Nordstrom. The party warmed as the Sephard told witty stories, so deft that Nordstrom laughed deeply and forgot himself. He saw Laura's eyes motion to him and then over her shoulder to the rest rooms.

Nordstrom made his way to the rest room and stood mugging in the mirror for no reason. There was naturally a toilet in there which meant he was in control again. If one sat on the stool, he thought, that made one the king of a dubious country about six-by-eight feet, but only if you could lock the door and in this case you couldn't. Even the lock on the stall was broken. It might be better to give up the idea of kingship before it went awry. The mirror revealed a man much stronger than the man felt. He knew it didn't matter if the image was himself or not. Jo-Jo the Dogface Boy, Marvin, Farley Cudd—any name would do. The dog was there at suppertime without being called. Anyone knew that when you had to be called it was usually for something unpleasant. Before they cut a tree down the timber cruiser made a mark on the tree for the lackeys with chain saws to follow, and the mark had to be construed as the tree's name. Nordstrom was grinning at the idea of names when Laura and Sarah entered. O these days. Women in men's rooms. What next? he thought. Sarah poured a line of cocaine along her forearm and offered it up to him.

"Frankly, I'd rather fuck."

Sarah widened her eyes mockingly and looked at Laura whose eyes glittered. Then she laughed.

"I heard you've become a lunatic," Sarah said.

"I thought you didn't like rich businessmen."

[168]

"They have definite advantages over poor business-men."

She lifted her arm closer to Nordstrom's nose. He snorted it off as he imagined a crazed pig or dope fiend would. Laura laughed leaning against the urinal.

"Nobody addressed my first suggestion," Nordstrom said.

The two women looked at each other and he was intrigued that they were taking him seriously. He had simply been trying to keep control of his country by mounting an offensive.

"Let's flip." Sarah drew a quarter out of her purse.

"Okay." Laura drew closer and kissed him on the cheek. "Of course it's adultery for me but there are extenuating circumstances. I'll take heads."

Nordstrom slid his hand down Laura's buttocks feeling the cheeks clench a bit as they used to do. When the quarter was in the air Phillip blundered in.

"What's happening in here?" he said with a drunken leer.

The ladies bustled out and Nordstrom wondered what the final penalty might be for strangling his future son-in-law. The quarter jangled against the wall but he did not look down as he walked out. The coke made him feel like he had been locked in some sort of hyperthyroid refrigerator.

Back at the table the ladies looked at him and laughed. He slowly concocted his most murderous stare that had been used to good effect against business opponents in the old days. They became nervously silent but Nordstrom persisted until everyone at the table was alarmed. He had won the round, as paltry as that might be, but it was somehow important. Phillip returned to the table mumbling about having found a quarter. The Sephard's face stiffened as the partition abruptly opened. A tall black man looked in, elegantly dressed in a gray pin-striped suit. Behind him and staring over his shoulder was an Italian, a cutout from the movies of a gangster psychopath. The tall black man eased around the table and grabbed Sarah's wrist squeezing it painfully. Then he walked away dragging her, a half ambulatory doll, the pain of her twisted arm bright in her face.

"See here . . ." Nordstrom said, moving away from his chair.

"Fuck off, dude," the black man said.

Nordstrom hit the man rather too hard, low on the cheek, and the man spun around losing his grip on the girl. Then his knees buckled and he sat down hard before bouncing up still dazed. Laura and Sonia began screaming and Nordstrom turned to see the Italian very close with the muzzle of a pistol aimed at his stomach. The black man rubbed his jaw and stared at Nordstrom.

"You'll die," he said smiling.

Two waiters and the manager rushed in belatedly at the screaming. There was no point in taking a chance.

"It's just a family quarrel," Nordstrom said. The black man accompanied by the girl pushed past the waiters. The Italian followed and the manager shrugged.

* * *

Back at the hotel Nordstrom had thought of the event as the last nasty surprise of the day. But then a death threat was rather striking in its own unique way. He would have to deal with it. Things were bound to happen if you lived in the open, if you walked very far off your porch. He jotted down some contingency plans as they used to call it in the oil business. After he had deservedly punched the man it had taken a full hour, a magnum of Dom Ruinart and two of Phillip's joints to calm down what was left of the dinner party. The Sephard had insisted on a frantic consultation in the toilet where he kept insisting, "Oh my god I told you." But Nordstrom's ho-hum self-assurance even calmed the Sephard. He simply resented the intrusion on the evening, very probably his last family gathering.

In the hotel suite there were a number of options though they lost a little of their clarity in the mixture of wine and cocaine, also the feel of Laura's bottom in his left hand as some sort of electrical stigma. Perhaps after more than twenty years the hormonal confusion of love was gone, the lump in the throat and the void beneath the breastbone, but one could hardly negate the happy sexuality that had become hapless but still there for reasons no one understands. The first option was to call the security chief of his former company, at one time an FBI chief in Los Angeles. His advice would be clinically expert and friendly. The two men would be in jail by first light. Nordstrom rejected this because he hadn't really liked the man. There was something unctuous and utterly crooked about him and he

didn't want to owe the man a favor. The second choice was
a bit more sensible and he might have made a call had not
Laura and Sonia been leaving at noon the next day. It was
the former bodyguard and factotum of a Texas oilman. He
now occasionally exchanged recipes with the man who
lived near Corpus Christi and raised quarter horses. They
had had a fine time quail hunting and Nordstrom had
entertained the man and his wife when they came to Los
Angeles. The man was sort of Texas A&M linebacker type
from Del Rio. He now maintained his family by what he
euphemistically referred to as his "specialties." He was an
intelligent character and collected editions of Dickens and
Thackeray. Nordstrom had never minded that the man
was a major league arbiter of the kind of extortion case that
never hits the press and an occasional killer. But then the
threat, direct as it was, didn't seem important enough.
Then the phone rang.

"Darling, did I wake you?"

"No, I was reading. My nose is still awake."

"Well it's just that I was worried about you. That girl
Sarah called. She wanted to warn you to be careful. The
man is very dangerous . . ."

"I already had him checked out. He's a nickel ante dope
pusher," Nordstrom lied.

"You're so smart, darling. Anyway I told her where to
get in touch with you . . ."

"That wasn't smart," he interrupted. "She's married to
the man. But it doesn't matter. Get some sleep."

"I'm sorry. Oh my god." There was a longish pause. "Do
you want me to come over?"

"Of course I do, but I'd have too much sense to open the door. You looked wonderful today."

"So did you. It was a little crazy but I would have gone ahead with it at the restaurant."

"So would I but we didn't. Good-bye darling."

"Good-bye. Be careful."

Nordstrom felt a little bleak over his strength in not letting Laura come over. His family was disappearing in a jet plane. It suddenly occurred to him that he could get Laura back if he so chose. During dinner Sonia had dropped an obviously planted hint that her mother was unhappy. After they had left the restaurant there were frantic inquiries by Laura over his plans. The cab stopped at one point so Phillip could retch in the gutter. He wasn't a drinker and had gulped far too much wine. Nordstrom had said he'd probably cash in the tickets for his trip and go to a cooking school for a few months. Then he would get a job in a restaurant by the ocean. He got carried away by the wine and the coke and the speeding taxi: he would cook near the ocean, buy a small boat to fish from in the off hours. He hadn't decided whether the Atlantic, Pacific or Caribbean. Probably the Caribbean since he had already bought the shirts. Laura and Sonia had eagerly interrupted, saying since he had given away his money they would buy him a restaurant but he said no, I don't want to own a restaurant, just want to cook in one. They seemed a bit sad after that and he couldn't help them.

Sarah called then and said though it was five A.M. she wanted to come over and explain certain things. He said he'd meet her for lunch at Melon's at one the next day. She seemed startled but agreed. He was reasonably sure they thought they had a turkey and were setting him up. He knew he had a certain advantage contrary to appearances: he lacked the usual misapprehensions about people that are caused by preconceptions. Sarah, her husband and the Italian thug waltzed around New York like violent peacocks. People that tripped most often and fatally did so out of greed, not understanding that it was a limited though convoluted game. Nordstrom had learned this in the oil business if not before. Still sleepless he drank a cold beer and made a few notes in his diary.

June 15, 78: A new and interesting problem. I have been threatened by death. I saw this basically as an insult and will have to deal with it on those terms. Otherwise I would simply go away as there is certainly nothing to hold me here. But that is not the point. People diminish themselves so horribly by letting themselves get pushed around by nitwits, whether by the government or the thousand varieties of criminals. Surprised I refused Laura, the first time ever, but then life is a matter of fine, hard lines. I remember tonight fishing for bluegills and perch with Mother, how I had to bait the hook as she couldn't bear wigglers and earthworms, and also take off the fish. She didn't mind cleaning fish, birds or rabbits. Also when we went blackberry picking and saw that bear she said get behind me and I said Mother I'm sixteen and bigger than you. Must call her tomorrow, maybe go see her, also Henry then go south in the fall. Dear

Mother I'm in a pickle. Henry would probably wait until dark and shoot them. None of the young men ever dared tease him even when he was drunk as a hoot owl. Doubt if I really need cooking school though am weak on certain sauces and desserts. This random violence saddens the heart. Here I had arranged a wonderful dinner for my daughter. I could take the plane to Rio the day after tomorrow but the threat would follow me everywhere like a toothache. Of course it's not limited to the City. Heard at Dad's funeral that huge drunken pulp cutter that lived in shack near the sawmill got tired of his neighbor's barking dog so one night tore the dog's head off with his hands and beat the master senseless with the carcass. Served thirty days and moved to Duluth. Laura could be here now talking about random violence. What an astounding lover she was, probably still is. Once we read a modern sex book but found nothing we hadn't already done. Long for my dancing. How biologically flimsy we are. We go along for forty-three years then someone pokes a knife in us or a .38 slug and it's good-night. That deer-hunting accident when I was sixteen. Two Milwaukee factory workers out by Wells Lake. One shot the other thinking it was a deer. I was nearby and carried the doctor's bag for him. I told the ambulance guys they didn't need the oxygen but they carted it into the woods anyway. It was a 30.06 and the bullet entered below his belt, struck the hipbone and deflected upward scrambling along the way and coming out below a shoulder blade in an apple-sized hole. The air was cold, the wound smelled and his eyes were open. I can imagine Sonia

strolling around the Uffizi with a notebook, so intense
and lovely. What is that river in Florence? Must get
some sleep. It's first light and I need to be on my toes.

In the morning Nordstrom shaved with his straight razor,
using his soft leather belt as a strop, as his father taught
him to do insisting it was the only way to get a good shave.
He stuck his head out the window while drinking his three-
dollar pot of coffee to taste the late morning warmth. Far
below a man in a dirty white apron was smoking a cigarette
in an alley. A cook should smoke his cigarettes looking at
the ocean he thought. He dressed in a grandiose Hawaiian
shirt (surfer against a setting sun) and baggy chinos. Into
an ankle-high pair of desert boots he slipped the razor,
which would discomfort his walking but might prove
handy in a pinch.

He reached the restaurant purposefully a half-hour early.
He spotted the Italian down the street in a parked car and
paid a waiter ten bucks to take out a note that read "Hi!
Be careful." Sarah was beautiful when she entered and
many heads turned. They sat near the corner window and
he noted the thug was gone. They talked about dancing
while Nordstrom ate a double steak tartare for strength and
she trifled with a salad. She had begun dancing at ten,
studying with Andre Eglevsky who had only recently died.
She hoped to go to Jacob's Pillow for July and August. She
was the daughter of a New York University law professor.
She had been married to Slats for three years. He was an
exciting man though a bit volatile. Nordstrom thought that
she had given no indication thus far of actually being a

human being. There was the quality of a photograph or mirror image about her. She said she needed to talk to him in the strictest privacy and perhaps his hotel room would be better than a restaurant.

They walked the six or seven blocks to the hotel with Nordstrom hobbling a bit from the razor in his shoe. He decided he liked New York very much and if things cooled off a bit and after a visit to Wisconsin, New York would be the place to go to cooking school. Even the nasty air was good, somehow addictive in its mix of ozone and oxygen, the smells coming out of restaurant and subway vents, looking at Rodin's bust of Balzac with the indigestion of a big lunch, and up here on the East Side, the most striking ladies in the world. If you couldn't live in the woods for reasons of unrest this had to be a good place. Suburbs everywhere were murderous with torpor. Nothing vivid and all the trees looked planted. He paused in a shop to buy Normandy goat cheese; wrapped in straw, its odor seeping out of the package. He was amused at her impatience and accurately predicted what would happen: she would seduce him and then afterward in a parody of concern she would make an extortionary offer. She wasn't a very good actress. He was lighthearted and bouncy despite the razor, doubting that anything bad could happen before dark.

And that was how things did happen. In the room she snorted some coke and Nordstrom refused. She was girlish, turned on the radio and demonstrated some dance moves. She shed all but her underthings and pranced around. She talked about how much she liked Laura and Sonia and it

[177]

was too bad that terrible thing had happened. They made love and for a half hour or so she broke through her bad acting into simply making love in silence. While she was in the bathroom Nordstrom removed the .32 from her purse with his handkerchief and slid it under the mattress while whistling the old tavern song "Heart of My Heart." When she had done her toilet she came out affecting a troubled mien and had two more lines of cocaine.

"I don't know if I can help you . . ."

"Help me what? I doubt I can get it up again. You are one crazed little windmill. My god." He yawned deeply.

"I mean protect you from Slats. He's really pissed. In fact no one ever hit him and lived."

"Not even his mama? Didn't he ever get spanked? I bet you spanked him before."

"You better get serious. He could have offed you last night but I said, no Slats. He didn't mean it. But I can only do so much." She was getting angry.

"But I did mean it. He fucked up my daughter's graduation dinner. I'd sort of like an apology. Tell him that. He has bad manners . . ."

"That's not the way it works, you hick fuck. If it wasn't for me you'd be dead. I pleaded with him and he finally said this morning he'd accept ten grand not to kill you. That's a final offer. You got until tomorrow at midnight. And don't run. He'll find you. He's got connections everywhere."

"Tell him that's my offer, too."

"What the fuck you talking about?" she spit out.

"I won't kill him by tomorrow night. That makes us

even. No one kills anyone. No one has to go to the bank. Everyone saves his money."

She left in a snit after writing out a number and saying she hoped he'd come to his senses. Nordstrom turned off the radio and fixed on the idea of coming to his senses. He had never felt more within his senses, as a matter of fact. He had fixed his point on earth as dead center in New York while at the same time his family diminished high above the Atlantic. His mother and his dad's best friend Henry were in northern Wisconsin. He had already had lunch and made love. Next came a much-needed nap, a long stroll and a late dinner. Perhaps a movie. But there was the slight aftertaste of asking the Sephard about Sarah the summer before, the increased curiosity after the warning. He toyed with the idea of the airport, or simply renting a car. Or calling Corpus Christi, imagining alternatives without interest. Then he made up his mind for good and called the desk to arrange to have the room next to his bedroom added to the suite. Then the Sephard called in a state of concern adding that he had a psychopathic second cousin over in Brooklyn that might be of help. Nordstrom assured him that everything was "lovey-dovey," and that he'd call if there were problems. The bellhop appeared with the new key, and Nordstrom prepared for his nap. He discarded the idea that this whole thing wasn't fair and that the extortion attempt was too clumsy to take very seriously, even with the threat. Later in the evening would be the test; if there was no move to freshen things up he would let it go.

Seven hours later he was sitting in a chair in the new room reading *Audubon* magazine. He had read hastily through the entirety of E.M. Cioran's *A Short History of Decay*, a book Phillip had left behind for him. Cioran immediately became Nordstrom's favorite author and he meant to scour the city for additional books. He had spread his weapons around the room; the razor on a windowsill beneath a wide-open window, Sarah's gun still wrapped in a handkerchief—the prints might prove useful—and before him on the desk a bottle of wine wrapped in a wet hand-towel to use as a sap. He was mindful of the total absurdity of what he was doing. It was impossible not to smile despite the apparent danger but then he figured he might own some modest sort of amateur's advantage: his concentration was complete because he had either lost or given up everything on earth. He went through the un-locked double door and made a pass beside the street window and turned off the light. Now if anyone were watching the window they might assume he was going to bed. He had placed a number of empty beer cans around on the floor with spoons stuck in them as a childish early warning system. He picked up his diary, went through the bedroom and into the new room, leaving the inner door ajar. He doubted if any interloper could resist the bait of the new room. He refused the urge to have a drink.

June 18, 78: The girls with Phillip took off for Europe at noon today. I am sitting here waiting for Slats' man, probably the Italian, to show up and threaten me further—probably a mild beating for the insolence of my reply to the extortion. What a sur-prise he'll have assuming I'm successful. Will check out cooking schools tomorrow, also Cioran books. Like those sections titled "The Arrogance of Prayer," "Crimes of Courage and Fear," "The Mockery of a 'New Life,' " "Non-Resistance to Night" and "Turning a Cold Shoulder to Time." Despite the fact that Phillip is an utter asshole I must send him a thank you note. Wish I had some fried bluegills. A drink. A pretty woman. Wonder what Cioran does everyday writing out of that abysm of despair. Presumptuous to write and ask though I suspect he's reasonably happy having gotten it out of his system as they say. I am not a violent person and I'm not interested in violence. The media romanticizes this nonsense constantly. Never read anything about anyone I knew that was accurate. The world is haphazard. You can see the strain of resisting this principle if you study faces at all. My first warning should be the elevator cable unless he comes up the stairs. But that door is locked on the inside. Locks are useless except against the most slovenly criminals. Wish I had that huge Bouvier that got hit by a car down at the beach. Terrible to keep a dog like that in the city. Sephard talked about a Spanish restaurant that makes first-rate stewed squid. Maybe tomorrow night. Forgot I had all that dough until I paid the bill at Melon's and felt lump. Sarah owns one of those truly beautifully formed pussys. A marvel of wise design amen. Remembered I could call my old friend high up in D.E.A. and have Slats rousted. But I oddly hate to see anyone locked up. And it's best to learn how to do things on your own in this new life I have so studiously chosen. Midnight now.

[181]

Nordstrom got up from the desk and stared in a slow half-circle at the locations of his weaponry. Dressed in his pajama bottoms he did a little jig and shuffle in front of the mirror before turning out the light. If things went well he would get a room or a small sublet apartment and a radio so he could begin dancing again. He had prepaid for the suite for a full week: over two hundred dollars a day—thinking he might need to entertain—but now he knew he must economize. He began to force everything from his mind so that sitting there he could dwell entirely within his ears. He had purposefully left his watch in the bedroom —such things moved on a different time and a watch was a pointless distraction.

It was interesting for him to note that in the darkness, barring thought, pictures still floated lazily across his mind. He discovered that if he didn't fix on these mental images, no matter how fascinating they were, they would disappear. They came from left to right: Sonia on the bassinet, thunderstorm on the lake with a crane flying across the metal plate of water, Mother picking wild strawberries, a wreck on the San Diego Freeway, dancing in Brookline, asparagus in Marblehead, a distracting woman he had never seen in life. Now his eyes fixed on a cuticle of light peeping above the next building. It became the moon, nearly full and its flowering nimbus showed him the room and his feet on the floor. A beer can tipped with its spoon. He rose and flattened his bare back next to the doorjamb. The future came at five breaths a minute and his heart seemed too high in his ribs. There was a small itching now inside just below his pajama drawstring. Then the door opened and the man made three slow steps in, paused half turning, and made three more. Using the wall for a fulcrum Nordstrom bolted through the room catching the man low in the back; two long heavy steps and he bore him quickly to and out the window before the man even began to struggle, and catching only the window jamb with an effort to save himself. In the first few stories of his plummet the man was silent, then a scream began that diminished in distance until his body struck the trash cans. Nordstrom had the odd thought that it was like casting out a huge anchor in a very deep place where for some strange reason there was no water. He dropped Sarah's pistol out the window, then wiped his sweating face with the handkerchief. The moon shone clear and sweet on his face and chest. Visitors often forgot the moon shone down on New York City.

In the morning he had just gotten out of the shower and was having his coffee and talking to his mother when the detectives came. He let them in and quickly finished the conversation; she was planning on a trip to Hawaii with her cousin Ida in November. They hoped to see Jack Lord work on *Hawaii Five-O*. One detective accepted a cup of coffee while the other looked out the window. They were both very bored. No, Nordstrom hadn't heard anything. Sound asleep. Too much celebrating. His daughter had graduated eighth in her class at Sarah Lawrence. Why the extra room? He thought his ex-wife and daughter might stay an extra day. He went to the window and looked down with them. O what a shame. Some poor soul. A suicide.

Perhaps but not a hotel guest or model citizen. A thug in fact and they were trying to figure out what he was doing in the neighborhood. It was a hot morning and Nordstrom offered them a beer but they refused politely. They had a lot of floors to cover. Thank you.

The detectives were barely out of the room when Sarah answered the call he had made to Slats before he went to bed the night before. Nordstrom was very grave. The prisoner had made a full confession before, out of grief, he flung himself out the window. Maybe he hadn't counted the floors on the elevator. Who knows. He insisted she and Slats join him for lunch at the Japanese restaurant at the Waldorf. Then they could settle up. Then Nordstrom arranged to have dinner with the Sephard, thinking he might have some good tips on a cooking school.

To tell the truth he had mixed feelings about what he had done but there seemed no alternative. These criminals might have finally threatened his family. And he had been prepared in his soul if the night had gone otherwise. But it was no small thing to hurl another creature into eternity. Only rarely did a man occur on earth bad enough to die. He dressed and combed the bookstores in the area looking with some success for books by E.M. Cioran, finding them finally at the newly opened Books and Company near the Whitney.

When he arrived at the Waldorf Sarah and Slats were already seated, having no doubt arrived early to case the joint. Nordstrom had barely been seated by a brightly painted geisha when an old, florid colleague from the oil industry stopped at the table. Nordstrom introduced his table mates but the conversation faded dismally when he admitted readily that he was doing nothing but thinking about going to cooking school. Slats was elegant in a blue cord Haspel summer suit. The oil man left and drinks arrived.

"Now you're a murderer," Slats tisked knowingly and Sarah nodded in agreement.

"Righto," Nordstrom said with a weird musical lilt. He meant to make them uncomfortable. "Right now under this table cloth I got a .44 aimed at your balls and I'm thinking of blowing your ass off in self-defense." Slats' eyes widened in alarm and disbelief. Nordstrom winked crazily at Sarah and yelled "bang." Heads turned in alarm and Slats tipped over his drink. A geisha rushed over. "I was just telling a joke that ended with 'bang,'" Nordstrom explained to the room at large. "I want three sashimis and one large squid tempura. And get the man another drink." The geisha bowed.

"You are a fucking lunatic," Slats insisted.

"Righto. I wanted your complete attention."

"Oh, man, you are in real trouble," Slats nodded.

"Yes, you are . . ." Sarah began to chime in but noted Nordstrom's crazed stare and paused. He stared at both of them with his head strangely atilt.

"You both have to cut this jive shit or I'm going to tear out somebody's heart. There's only so much shit I can take, you know? You sent that numb-nuts wop to my room and I proved he couldn't fly, not even a little bit. Now I got this confession . . ."

"This man would never talk," Slats interrupted, for the first time fully getting into what was happening at the table.

"That's how much you know, fuckface." Nordstrom was enjoying the purity of his acting performance, unexampled until now in his life. "I interrogated for Special Forces in Da Nang in sixty-seven. Sometimes we pitched them out of Hueys, and sometimes I strangled them. They had thin necks." Nordstrom made a strangling motion with his hands. "Your friend was a hard case. I sapped him and when he woke he wouldn't be nice so I knotted a wet towel and got it in his mouth so he wouldn't bite. Then I put four fingers in and jerked up and got the front teeth. The confession with a gold tooth is in a safety deposit box at Chase Manhattan." Nordstrom remembered the gold tooth from the restaurant. "Then I pitched the cocksucker out the window. And then I called you and went to bed."

The sashimi arrived and Nordstrom advised that they use the horseradish mustard sparingly. Slats gazed at him feeling a bit trapped. It had been a little stupid all along and the angles were disappearing. "This is raw fish isn't it?" Nordstrom nodded. Slats was tentative, and then, liking the fish, he began to eat quickly.

"Maybe it's a draw. Shit, Berto had a grand of mine on him. Some detective is at the track today with my money. You need any toot?"

Slats signaled to the waitress and pointed at his place. "More," he said.

"No thanks. I don't think so. Or maybe I could buy

some for a friend." The tempura arrived and Nordstrom
served.

"Here I am gobbling this shit and my dad died on Iwo
Jima," Slats laughed. "For you it's five hundred bucks for
a quarter. I can see this detective feeding his old lady
lobster on my money."

"I'm actually sorry I hit you. I don't usually think that
fast but I had some coke in the toilet and I forgot you were
married."

Sarah explained it was only a way of making money, a
gig, and that they weren't married. Rich men sympathized
with her mistreatment and advanced her money to get out
of Slats' clutches. With Nordstrom they decided to esca-
late because they were convinced he was simpleminded.
Slats was curious about the itinerary of the trip he had
forgotten. The idea of foreign travel suddenly reminded
Nordstrom of the pictures of vigorous men shearing sheep
in the *National Geographic* in faraway places. They talked
on for another half hour and Sarah suggested a cooking
school on Waverly Place for when he returned. Slats insisted on paying for the meal. Nordstrom counted out
fifteen hundred bucks from Sonia's BMW money on his
lap. Sarah slid him a small sack of coke under the table.

"I added the grand for what you lost on Berto. I wanted
us to be even up. Now everyone is even except Berto."

They walked out of the restaurant into a hall off the
Waldorf lobby. Slats patted Nordstrom on the shoulder.
"Don't sweat it. He was an asshole."

* * *

At midnight Nordstrom was sitting in the dark in his hotel bedroom looking at the moon and thinking about lily pads. Sonia had insisted he go to the Museum of Modern Art to see these huge paintings of lily pads by Monet and he had gone after lunch, staring at them utterly blankminded for an hour. Now in the moonlight all of the lily pads on the lakes of northern Wisconsin revolved before him. Sometimes they had small buttery-yellow flowers and sometimes they had large white flowers, strong with an eerie perfume he could smell twenty-five years later in a hotel room. He didn't know if in the morning he would leave on his trip or go to Wisconsin for a few weeks. Bass hid under the lily pads and he used to swim under them and look upward so that the pads looked like small green islands in the air refracting the light. He had given the cocaine to the Sephard over dinner. The Sephard had been relieved but puzzled when Nordstrom insisted that Slats and Sarah were "nice people." There was a neurotic English girl with a perfect fanny with the Sephard. She wanted to call a friend for Nordstrom but he said no. He was really quite tired. Just breathing on the bed in the moonlight seemed quite enough for the moment. First you breathed in, then out, and so on. It was easy if you tried to keep calm.

EPILOGUE

He drove south in late October, one year after his father's death, in a sixty-seven Plymouth he had paid seven hundred dollars for. In no particular hurry and nothing to guide him but a Rand McNally, he stopped in Savannah, bought two new tires, and thought the town rather too pretty for his taste. He wanted to avoid a self-conscious location. In the trunk there was one suitcase, one box of books, and one box of assorted cooking equipment he could not bear to part with in his urge to travel light; he was neither happy nor unhappy as he rejected one place after another, just looking things over. Finally, in late November, he got a job in a small seafood restaurant in Islamorada, Florida, of good reputation at an abysmal wage. His fingers were soon sore from cleaning shrimp and picking crab. He got nailed rather painfully in the palm by a stone crab and learned to be careful. Within a month he was allowed to cook a daily specialty. His home was a one-room tourist cabin at the end of a lane of crushed shells lined by dank mangroves bordered by an unnavigable lagoon. There was a small gas stove, a double bed, Formica table, linoleum floor, black leopard lamp, rickety air conditioner, three rattan chairs. There were a lot of mosquitoes which he didn't mind, having been trained for them in Wisconsin. He kept his money in an upturned frozen orange juice can in the refrigerator freezer, not wanting to bother with the bank. He didn't kill the palmetto bugs that crawled around, having figured that they didn't eat much or sting. One day he was pleased to see a large rattler back in the bedraggled palm scrub. He bought a rowboat and nearly died when an oarlock broke and he was swept out to sea in a strong tide and a heavy sea and spent an entire day bailing with his hat and paddling with one oar. He was rescued by fishermen and spent two days in a hospital being treated for severe sunburn, feeling like a stupid shit. It paid to keep on your toes, he thought, in this new life where he was utterly unprotected. He unfolded a lot of ice-cold money and bought a Boston Whaler and a sixty-horse Evinrude, after determining it was the most stable boat available. With the help of a push pole he kept strapped to the boat's gunwhale he could skid it across the lagoon in a medium tide and keep it beside the cabin. He bought a spinning rod and some jigs, mask and flippers and a book on marine biology. He waded tidal flats looking at the bottom, fished channels, identified his catch in the book and released it. He worked six days a week but had mornings and Monday off for his explorations. When he felt more comfortable in these strange waters he bought charts and a boat trailer and went off to Big Pine on

Mondays, an area richer in mangrove islets and tidal cuts. One warm still day in a deep tidal creek he hooked a tarpon and was shocked as it hurtled out of the water near the boat, twisting its big silver body and its gill plates rattling before it broke off. That day he thought he counted a thousand shades of turquoise in the water. He had become a water, wind and cloud watcher in addition to being a cook. Late at night he danced to a transistor radio. He was the source of respectful local amusement. He had a wonderful affair with a Cuban waitress his own age. She had a small portable stereo and taught him Latin dances. He got more local respect when he threw two burly drunks out of the restaurant one night, punching one senseless, but it reminded him unpleasantly of Berto and he wept a few minutes when he got home. He wrote and received chatty letters from his daughter in Florence, exchanging apercus with Phillip on the great author E.M. Cioran. After the Cuban waitress abandoned Islamorada for Miami he had a brief three-day fling with a college girl who was a bit sullen and really didn't like to fuck. His mother wrote that she had actually seen Jack Lord in Honolulu. She and Henry planned a two-week trip down in April when the tourist season slackened and Nordstrom would have more time. They would have to take the bus as Henry considered planes an insult to his life and the life of the sky. One day while driving Nordstrom saw a moray eel and a black-tipped shark and was thrilled to the core.

One evening while he was taking a cigarette break behind the restaurant, Nordstrom watched two waitresses approach, then pause while they whispered. It was his habit during the evening break to sit on a huge piece of dredged coral, hundreds of pounds of tiny antique, crushed marine invertebrates. He would drink a tall, cold piña colada, smoke a cigarette and watch the ocean. In his position of chef none of the other help usurped his sitting place. Now the waitresses came up to him, both a little plump and giggling but one with fine olive features. They offered a joint and he took a long, noncommittal puff. Their problem was that there was a dance tonight in a bar just down Route 1 and they had no one to go with and they didn't want to walk in the bar alone. Nordstrom was disturbed. He had never danced in public. Oh Jesus why not, he said to himself. At the bar he danced with the two girls and anyone else willing until four in the morning when the band stopped. Then he danced alone to the jukebox until four thirty in the morning when everyone had to leave.

LEGENDS
OF THE FALL

CHAPTER
I

Late in October in 1914 three brothers rode from Choteau, Montana, to Calgary in Alberta to enlist in the Great War (the U.S. did not enter until 1917). An old Cheyenne named One Stab rode with them to return with the horses in tow because the horses were blooded and their father did not think it fitting for his sons to ride off to war on nags. One Stab knew all the shortcuts in the northern Rockies so their ride traversed wild country, much of it far from roads and settlements. They left before dawn with their father holding an oil lamp in the stable dressed in his buffalo robe, all of them silent, and the farewell breath he embraced them with rose in a small white cloud to the rafters.

By first light the wind blew hard against the yellowed aspens, the leaves skittering across the high pasture and burying themselves in a draw. When they forded their first river the leaves of the cottonwoods stripped by the wind caught in the eddies, pasting themselves against the rocks.

JIM HARRISON

They paused to watch a bald eagle, forced down by the first snow in the mountains, fruitlessly chase a flock of mallards in the brakes. Even in this valley they could hear the high clean roar of wind against cold rock above the timberline.

By noon they crossed a divide, a cordillera, and turned to take a last view of the ranch. That is, the brothers took in the view not the less breathtaking in the raw wind which blew the air so clean the ranch looked impossibly close and beautiful though already twenty miles distant. Not One Stab, though, who feared sentiment and who stared straight up in disdain when they crossed the railroad tracks of the Northern Pacific. And a little further on when they all heard the doleful cry of a wolf at midday, they pretended that they had not heard it for the cry at midday was the worst of omens. They took lunch as they rode as if to escape the mournful sound and not wanting to sit at the edge of a glade where the sound might descend on them again. Alfred, the oldest brother, said a prayer while Tristan, the middle brother, cursed and spurred his mount past Alfred and One Stab. Samuel, the youngest, dallied along with his eyes sharp on the flora and fauna. He was the apple of the family's eye, and at eighteen already had one year in at Harvard studying in the tradition of Agassiz at the Peabody Museum. When One Stab paused at the far edge of a great meadow to wait for Samuel to catch up, his heart froze on seeing the roan horse emerge from the woods with its rider carrying half a bleached buffalo skull against his face and his laughter carrying across the meadow to the old Indian.

On the third day of their trip the wind let up and the

air warmed, the sun dulled by an autumnal haze. Tristan shot a deer to the disgust of Samuel who only ate the deer out of instinctive politeness. Alfred, as usual, was ruminative and noncommittal, wondering how One Stab and Tristan could eat so much meat. He preferred beef. When Tristan and One Stab ate the liver first Samuel laughed and said he himself was an omnivore who would end up as a herbivore, but Tristan was a true carnivore who could store up and either ride or sleep or drink and whore for days. Tristan gave the rest of the carcass to a honyocker, a homesteader, whose pitiful barn they slept in that night preferring the barn to the dense ammoniac smell of the cabin full of children. Typically the honyocker did not know there was a war going on in Europe, much less owning any firm notion where Europe was. Untypically Samuel took a liking at dinner to the oldest daughter and quoted a verse of Heinrich Heine to her in German, her native language. The father laughed, the mother and daughter left the table in embarrassment. At dawn when they left the daughter gave Samuel a scarf she had spent the night knitting. Samuel kissed her hand, said he would write, and gave her a gold pocket watch for safekeeping. One Stab watched this from the corral when he saddled the horses. He picked up Samuel's saddle as if he were picking up doom herself, doom always owning the furthest, darkest reaches of the feminine gender. Pandora, Medusa, the Bacchantes, the Furies, are female though small goddesses beyond sexual notions. Who reasons death anymore than they can weigh the earth or the heart of beauty?

They rode the rest of the way into Calgary in the full

flower of a brief Indian summer. There was a bad incident at a roadside tavern where they tethered their horses to have a beer to cut their dusty mouths. The owner refused to let One Stab inside. Samuel and Alfred reasoned with the owner, then Tristan entered after watering the horses, sized up the situation and pummeled the beefy tavern owner senseless. He flipped a gold piece to the porter who nervously held a pistol, took a bottle of whiskey and a pail of beer and they had a picnic under a tree outside. Alfred and Samuel shrugged, long accustomed to their brother's behavior. One Stab liked the taste of beer and whiskey but would only rinse his mouth with it before spitting it on the ground. He was a Cheyenne, but had spent his last thirty years in Cree and Blackfoot territory and had decided he would only get drunk if he ever returned to Lame Deer before he died. His spitting brought laughter from Samuel and Alfred but not Tristan who understood and had been close to One Stab since the age of three while Samuel and Alfred tended to ignore the Cheyenne.

In Calgary they were given an uncommon welcome for enlistees. The major forming the local cavalry came from the same area of Cornwall as their father, in fact, he shipped out of Falmouth on a schooner the same year, but for Halifax rather than Baltimore. The major was baffled by the refusal of the United States to enter the war, which he accurately saw as more monstrous and enduring than reflected in the easy optimism of those Canadians who envisioned the Kaiser and his Huns in flight the moment the locals landed on the Continent. But then such simpleminded braggadocio is appreciated in soldiers, who are largely cannon fodder for international economic and political machinations. In the month of training before shipping by train to the troopships in Quebec, Alfred quickly became an officer, Samuel an aide-de-camp due to his scholarly German and ability to read topographical maps. Tristan, however, brawled and drank and was demoted to wrangling the horses, where he in fact felt quite comfortable. Uniforms embarrassed him and the drills bored him to tears. Were it not for his fealty to his father and his notion that Samuel needed looking after he would have escaped the barracks and headed back south on a stolen horse on the track of One Stab.

Back near Choteau, William Ludlow (Colonel, Engineers U, Army. Ret.) spent sleepless nights. He had taken a chill the morning the boys left and spent a week in bed staring out the north window waiting for One Stab to return with some news however feeble and scanty the news would be. He wrote long letters to his wife who wintered in Prides Crossing north of Boston, also keeping a house on Louisberg Square for her evenings at the opera or symphony. She loved Montana from May through September, but equally loved to board the train back to the civilities of Boston, not an uncommon thing for rich landholders in those days. Against the popular misconception, cowboys never did own ranches. They were not much more than the expert, wandering hippies of their day, cossacks of the range who knew animals much better than each other. Some of the grandest ranches in north central Montana were actually owned by largely absentee Scottish and English noblemen.

(A loutish Irishman, Sir George Gore, of suspicious noble birth had enraged the Indians by killing a thousand elk and an equal number of buffalo on a "sporting" trip.)

But Ludlow wrote his wife in a state of grief. She had insisted that Samuel be kept from the war. The year before she had cherished their Saturday lunches in Boston, talking of his always exciting past week at Harvard. She had babied her last born while Alfred had been stodgy and methodical from youth and Tristan uncontrollable. In September, a month after Sarajevo, she had quarreled with her husband then left after the three days it took to pack. Now Ludlow knew he should have kept Samuel and sent him back to Harvard if only to please his mother. The young second cousin, Susannah, she had brought from the East in hopes that Alfred would make a good marriage, had instead become engaged to Tristan. This amused Ludlow who secretly favored Tristan's misbehavior even though after the engagement dinner Tristan inexcusably disappeared with One Stab for a week on the track of a grizzly that had taken two cattle.

Ludlow lay under the comforter looking at the scrapbooks of his life, his mind enlivened by a mild fever. He had reached the age where his habitually romantic frame of mind had turned to the ironies; the past had become a dense puddle out of which he could draw no conclusions. Though he was sixty-four his health and vigor had not diminished and his parents, both in their mid-eighties, were alive in Cornwall, which meant barring an accident, he was likely to live longer than he cared to. In his scrapbooks he read a sappy poem he had written in his

Vera Cruz days and noted with amusement it was pasted next to a newspaper clipping about "The Fecundity of Codfish." As a mining engineer he had ranged from Maine, to Vera Cruz, to Tombstone in Arizona and Mariposa, California, to the copper country in Michigan's Upper Peninsula. He had not married until thirty-five and then the choice had been mutually unlikely—the daughter of a vastly wealthy investment banker from Massachusetts. And not that wealth was a part in this absurd nesting influence—he still drew some five hundred pounds a month from a Vera Cruz silver mine, nearly four thousand dollars in the exchange of the time. But it gathered in a bank in Helena where he traveled several times a year to look after his investments and carry on at the Cattleman's Club. His marriage had burned out, had gradually transmogrified from its previously Keatsian fire into a remote and cranky elegance. Their extended honeymoon voyage to Europe had civilized them to the point that he did not greatly care if she took a winter lover in Boston, usually far younger than herself. Her most recent discreetly scandalous affair would be a Harvard student, John Reed, who would become a famed Bolshevik and die in Moscow of typhus. Like many wealthy feminists of the time her interests were ardent and captious. After the first son had been properly named after the grandfather, the second caught the brunt of her few impulses, being named "Tristan," gleaned from medieval lore in her years at Wellesley. Somewhat typically she was the first woman to play polo with anything equal to the capabilities of those male horse sybarites who take the world as their stable. But she was a grand one, even in her fifties, a preposterous beauty with her once thin body verging on lushness. She had tried to make poor Samuel an artist but he owned his father's scientific bent and wandered around the ranch with his nature guidebooks studiously correcting their Victorian inaccuracies.

For the first time since the boys left Ludlow came down for dinner and noted with despair the single place set at the head of the dining room table, the coolness of which the roaring fireplace did not allay. Roscoe Decker, his foreman, sat drinking coffee with his wife, nicknamed Pet, a Cree noted for her beauty whom Ludlow's wife had taught to cook well over the past few years from an antique French cookbook known as the Ali Bab. Decker (for no one called him Roscoe, a name he disliked) was about forty with the slender legs of a horseman but with a bullish chest and arms, got from a youth full of digging fence-post holes.

Ludlow said he was lonely and wondered aloud if they all might eat together in the dining room. Pet poured him a cup of coffee and shook her head no. Decker looked away. Ludlow felt his face redden thinking he might have to order them to eat with him no matter the ten years they had spent in each other's distant good graces. So Ludlow and Decker drank their afternoon coffee under strain, disarming the odor of a Normandy venison stew Pet was cooking in cider in the wood range. Decker attempted to talk about the cattle but Ludlow stared into the distance unhearing in his anger. He watched Isabel, Decker's nine-year-old daughter, named after Ludlow's wife, make her way across the barnyard carrying something. She came through the pump shed and in the kitchen door and the something turned out to be a little badger a few weeks old that Tristan had given her. Pet told her to take the beast outside but Ludlow interrupted out of curiosity. The badger seemed ill and Ludlow said the milk must be warm and it might take meat ground into paste. Pet shrugged and began rolling biscuit dough while Ludlow warmed some milk and Decker examined the creature. They found a cache of old nursing bottles and nipples in the pantry and Isabel fed and rocked the badger which ate hungrily. Now Ludlow was happy and took out a bottle of Armagnac and poured himself and Decker glasses to add to their coffee. Isabel refused to go to school because of a certain half-breed onus, so Ludlow said he would finally undertake to tutor her starring the next morning at eight sharp.

The mood lightened so markedly that Ludlow went into the cellar for a good bottle of claret to go with the meal. For years he had been indifferent to his wife's taste for good wine, then having become a gradual convert, he read a vinology book and went on a binge to the point his cellar was chocked, partly from a derailed Northern Pacific bound for San Francisco that he cagily bought from a railroad official. And in the cellar he solved the problem; they would all eat in the kitchen including One Stab when he returned. That way he hoped that his sons' absence would not be so raw and glaring. He construed it back in the kitchen as a natural winter fuel measure. The dining room would be closed off. Decker's family would move to the guest room and the three ranch hands could have Decker's cabin. They all knew One Stab would not move from his hut which only he entered short of Isabel when she was sick at three and One Stab asked to perform some private ceremony. Ludlow knew, though, that One Stab owned a coup bag full of scalps, not a few Caucasian, but he privately approved.

After dinner they played pinochle all evening with Pet and Isabel winning owing to the wine and brandy Ludlow and Decker had consumed. Ludlow announced that Decker must take tomorrow off and they would take the setters and go grouse hunting. Decker said he expected that One Stab would be back in a few days. Pet served a pudding made from ripe plums from the orchard and Isabel fell asleep in her chair with the badger staring from his blanket on her lap. At midnight Ludlow went to bed with a warm steady feeling that the world indeed was a good place, that the war would be quickly over, and that he and Decker would have a good hunt the next day. He said his nightly prayers, adding for a change One Stab, who as a pagan was no doubt impervious to their influence.

At a little after three A.M. he awoke in a night sweat after a dream so crisply actual that he was still shuddering a half hour later. In his dream he had seen his sons die in a battle while he stood helplessly on the outcrop of a butte; then he had looked down and noted that he wore elkskin leggings, and was, in fact, One Stab. He wondered as he lit his pipe watching the shadows of the kerosene lamp flicker against the wall where he himself had been in the dream all the more poignant because in 1874 he had been encamped at Short-Pine Hills and One Stab had arrived and rather casually said that Sitting Bull with five thousand braves was coming south toward them from the Tongue River. So they rode hard day and night for three days to escape the trap with some men tying themselves to their saddles in exhaustion.

Ludlow drew his robe close and left his room, walking down the hall and peeking first into Alfred's room with all its sentimental bric-a-brac, dumbbells, self-help books, and then Samuel's, littered with microscopes, stuffed animals including a snarling wolverine, botanical specimens, a piece of driftwood drawn from the river in his youth that owned a startling resemblance to a hawk. Tristan's room which Ludlow had not entered in recent memory was stark and bare; a mule deer skin on the floor, a badger skin covering the pillow on the bed, and a small trunk in the corner. Ludlow grimaced, knowing the skin on the pillow was from Tristan's pet when he was ten years old that Ludlow had shot after it had killed his wife's lapdog and she had gone into hysterics. Normally a most truculent animal, Tristan's pet would ride horseback with him, perched rotundly across the pommel of the saddle and hissing gutturally at anyone who came near except One Stab. Ludlow stooped holding the lantern over the trunk. He felt a bit like an old snoop but could not resist his curiosity. Inside the trunk the lamplight caught the glitter from the sterling rowels of a pair of Spanish spurs Ludlow had given Tristan on his twelfth birthday. There were some cartridges for a Sharps buffalo rifle, a rusty handgun of unknown origin, a jar of flint arrowheads, and a bear claw necklace, no doubt a gift from One Stab whom Ludlow often felt was more the boy's father than he himself.

On the bottom of the trunk wrapped in antelope hide Ludlow found with surprise his own book printed in 1875 by the Government Printing Office with "my father wrote this book" in a childish scrawl inside the cover.

He stood abruptly with the lantern teetering dangerously in his hand. He had not opened the book in three decades mostly out of grief that his recommendations on the Sioux had been not taken, even scorned, after which he resigned his commission and left for Vera Cruz. He noted that Tristan had underlined and notated the pages and was curious about what so unlearned and obdurate a lad would make of what he considered a technical work. He took the book back to his room and poured a glass from a demijohn of Canadian whiskey kept under the bed for insomnia.

The title itself was bland if one neglected certain historical ironies: *"Report of a Reconnaissance of the Black Hills of Dakota,* made in the Summer of 1874 by William Ludlow, Captain of Engineers, Bvt. Lieut. Colonel U.S. Army, Chief Engineer Department of Dakota." As a scientist, or what passed for one at the time, he had been attached to the Seventh Cavalry under the command of an officer of his own rank, Lieut. Colonel George Armstrong Custer. Ludlow with his Cornish reticence loathed Custer and kept the company of his scientific group which included George Bird Grinnell of Yale College, a boon companion. When Custer became especially worried or angry he would mimic Ludlow's English accent, an inexcusable frivolity in a fellow officer. Ludlow privately celebrated when he heard of Custer's demise at Little Bighorn three years later in

'77. His own recommendations in the conclusion of his report had been terse and direct. After enumerating the obvious advantages of the region, including the protection it afforded against the torrid heat and arctic storms of the neighboring prairies, Ludlow advised:

> To this, however, the final solution of the Indian
> question is an indispensable preliminary. The region
> is cherished by the owners as hunting grounds and
> asylum. The more farsighted, anticipating the time
> when hunting the buffalo, which is now the main
> subsistence of the wild tribes, will no longer suffice to
> that end, have looked forward to settling in and about
> the Black Hills, as their future permanent home, and
> there awaiting the gradual extinction which is their
> fate . . . The Indians have no country farther west to
> which they can migrate.

He sipped deeply from his whiskey, more interested in Tristan's squiggles than the horrors and chicanery of the government which had made him a near recluse. He remembered well the plague of grasshoppers Tristan had found interesting:

> I counted twenty-five one morning on what I judged
> to be an average square foot of ground. A brief calcu-
> lation at that rate over a million to the acre . . .
> exceedingly rapacious, their capacity for destruction
> to living vegetation may be imagined. Their powers
> of sustained flight, too, are wonderful . . . they appear
> able to keep on the wing of a whole day, always

moving with the wind, and filling the air to a vast
height . . . the wings reflecting the light make them
appear like tufts of cotton floating lazily in the wind
. . . in descending through the slanting rays of the sun,
they resemble a fall of huge snowflakes.

Ludlow remembered Custer making an erratic speech to
the troops with his long blond locks punctuated with cling-
ing grasshoppers. He read on, fixing only on the portions
Tristan had underlined, including a passage on a blood-red
moon that fired the beige landscape, to which Tristan had
added "I seen this phenom. once with Stab who would not
talk at campfire." The most haunting paragraph, though,
was a description of buffalo skulls which Ludlow recognized foresaw One Stab's Ghost Dance superstitions and
Tristan's boyish passion, "A man who shoots a buffalo and
not eat the entire body and make a tent or bed of the skin
should himself be shot, including the bone marrow which
Stab says restores all health to the human body." Ludlow
recalled the skulls and the light on the feathers of a pere-
grine falcon that had flown under his horse in pursuit of
a doomed passenger pigeon: "It is but a few years since the
country through which we passed was the favorite feeding
ground of the buffalo, and their white skulls dot the prairie
in all directions. Sometimes these are collected by the
Indians, and arranged on the ground in fantastic patterns.
In one of these collections which I noticed, the skulls had
been painted red and blue in stripes and circles, and were
arranged in five parallel rows of twelve each, all the skulls
facing the East."

He finished his drink and dozed, not extinguishing the lamp because he was afraid the dream would return with its fatal questions, the wildly colored and operatic doom. Ludlow was not fool enough to try to order a life already lived, but he was rawly conscious that his secondary life lived through his sons had been mismanaged, not so much with Alfred and Samuel who merely were what they were, but with Tristan. Ludlow would entertain, at least temporarily, any scientific notion touched by the bizarre and there was an idea current that character often skipped a generation. Ludlow's own father had been a schooner captain, in fact at eighty-four still was, of unremitting fierceness and charm whom they tended to see in off years while growing up. His own tamer wanderings had been engendered by his father's tales of seeing giant squid fighting in the moonlight in the Humboldt swells off Peru, and how a man is never the same after rounding the Horn in a seventy-knot gale. One year Ludlow's Christmas present would be a shrunken head from Java and the next a small gold Buddha from Siam and a constant flow of mineral specimens came from throughout the world. So perhaps Tristan in a genetic lapse had become his own father and would like Cain never take an order from anyone but would build his own fate with gestures so personal that no one in the family ever knew what was on his seemingly thankless mind. At fourteen Tristan had quit school and trapped enough lynx to buy anything but had the pelts made into a coat and sent off to Boston to his astounded mother. Then he borrowed Ludlow's Purdey shotgun and disappeared, arriving back at the ranch three months later with

JIM HARRISON

a sack of money he won at competitive trap and skeet shoots at sporting clubs. That money had gone to buy One Stab a new saddle and rifle, Samuel a microscope, and Alfred a trip to San Francisco. The whole family was sheltered with perhaps too much money, but Tristan had his own golden touch. The sheriff in Helena had written that Tristan had been seen in the company of prostitutes at age fifteen and his mother had had a nervous fit and Ludlow had given an obligatory lecture that degenerated into his curiosity over whether the whores had been attractive. Ludlow's own bimonthly trips to Helena always included a few nights spent with a schoolteacher he furtively had courted for a decade. To his old cronies at the Cattleman's Club he liked to quote Teddy Roosevelt's "I like to drink the wine of life with brandy in it" and felt foolish afterward, considering as he did all politicians to be knaves. But now Tristan was beyond his sphere of influence and he knew that there was small chance of hearing from him, just as they had never heard from his own father. A few years back his father had gone aground in the Orkneys and Ludlow had arranged the purchase of another ship to which he got small thanks, only a note: "Dear Son. I trust your family is well. Send the boys over for seasoning. God-damn your money. You'll get back every cent." And the small amounts arrived periodically at his bank in Helena from places as varied as Cyprus and Dakar. As his eyes dimmed with sleep he knew he would have to write Susannah, Tristan's betrothed, to get any news. She was a frail, lovely girl of surpassing intelligence.

Ludlow slept late and was embarrassed knowing that

Decker had been ready to hunt for hours. He looked out the window and saw how his lemon-ticked setters sleeping on the lawn gave the effect of sunlight coming down through the leaves of birch trees. They were fine dogs, shipped straight from Devonshire by a friend who came every other year to shoot.

By noon they had shot seven brace of ruffed grouse and both dogs and men were fatigued from the rare late October heat though the northern horizon was dark and they knew that snow was possible by nightfall in the vagaries of Montana weather. While roasting two grouse Decker suggested they buy a thousand calves the next spring because the war would up the price of beef. Also he needed two new hands just to replace Tristan and Pet had cousins over near Fort Benton, one being half-black, if Ludlow didn't mind and they were fine cowboys. Ludlow fed his dogs the hearts and livers of the two grouse and agreed with everything Decker suggested, wondering idly what a half-black Cree would look like. Probably wonderfully ugly. He dozed in the sun smelling the grouse skin roasting on the coals. Decker noticed One Stab far up the hillside of the box canyon and knew he would not come down until after lunch out of etiquette because there were only two cooking grouse. It was One Stab who brought Decker back from Zortman and Ludlow took him on even though he knew he must be on the lam from some unnamed crime. Ludlow was prodded awake and ate with relish. He loved this box canyon and intended to be buried here near where a small spring seeped from the canyon wall. He had been able to buy the twenty thousand acres—not really very large for a

ranch in the area—for a song because of his mining connections when it was determined that there was nothing
of mineral value on the land. There was plenty of water,
though, and the ranch could support cattle to a degree that
equaled ranches three times its size though Ludlow limited
the number sharply out of a lack of greed and not wanting
the problems of too many hands. Also if cattle foraged on
the ridges the game birds would leave. The dogs scented
One Stab as he descended the hill and wagged their tails
frantically. The old Indian took a drink from Decker's flask
and spit it on the fire where it flamed upward. Decker was
always amused that One Stab spoke with a strong trace of
Ludlow's English accent.

Late that night winter came. And the next day brought
an angry, imploring letter from his wife begging him to use
his influence to free Samuel from the army. Her sleep was
troubled though Alfred had written from Calgary that all
was going well. But what in God's name did the boys have
to do with defending an England they had never seen and
Ludlow's own misbegotten sense of adventure had pushed
them off with no thought of her feelings. These letters
continued through the late fall into January with a
menopausal hysteria becoming so extreme that Ludlow,
who anyway was full of dull foreboding, no longer opened
the letters. He had skipped a pre-Christmas trip to Helena
and short of any impulse of romance he read and brooded
except for the few hours each morning he had taken it
upon himself to teach little Isabel to read and write. He
sent Decker off to Helena to buy supplies and presents and
the day after he left, a United States marshal had stopped

by inquiring if he might know the whereabouts of a Jon Thronburg wanted for bank robbery some years ago in St. Cloud, Minnesota, and rumored to be in this area. Ludlow showed no surprise at the early photo of Decker and replied that the man in fact had passed through three years before on his way to San Francisco to catch a boat for Australia. The marshal nodded wearily, ate a big meal and rode off in the gathering dark for Choteau.

Ludlow waited an hour in case the marshal might be waiting then sent One Stab off to Helena to warn Decker to avoid all towns and main roads in his immediate return. Things seemed to be going badly. By an absentminded mistake he had caught Pet standing drying herself after her bath which conspired to leave him feeling weak, heavy and congested. He would have gladly given his ranch to have even one son back.

In Boston Isabel had taken up with an Italian basso profundo. He had no English so their affair was conducted with her minimal tourist Italian. They would lie back in a pretentious oriental chaise before the fire, his head on her breast, and talk about opera, Florence and the wild redskins he hoped to see on his concert trip to San Francisco and Los Angeles. She, in fact, had become bored with him: his brief, strenuous lovemaking did not suit her for she was far less spiritual than her lovers supposed. She had dreamed unpleasantly of her son Tristan and the singer's head against her breast reminded her how as a boy when he had pneumonia she cuddled and read to him in the same position, a closeness that was fatally rended in the fall of his

JIM HARRISON

twelfth year when she opted to return to Boston for the winter. And how the passionate boy had tortured her for her decision, writing in the winter that he had prayed daily for her return by Christmas and when she hadn't returned by Christmas he had cursed God and had become a steadfast nonbeliever. In the spring when she returned he was cool and so distant that she complained to Ludlow who couldn't get a word out of Tristan on the subject of his mother. Then she feigned illness and when the boys filed into her room to kiss her goodnight she detained Tristan and brought him to temporary heel by an onslaught of sentiment and weeping, using the total arsenal of her wiles. He told her that he would love her forever, but he could not believe in God because he had already cursed Him.

The first tentative blow reached the parents individually in late January when they received word that Alfred, never a very good rider, had shattered his knee and broken his back in a fall from his horse near Ypres. The prognosis from the field hospital however was good and they could expect him home by May. The major from Calgary sent a special note of condolence to Ludlow. Alfred had been a brilliant young officer and would be sorely missed. It was unfortunate that Tristan's recklessness diminished the effects of his bravery but the major assumed he would further mature in battle. Samuel had proven spectacularly useful and the major feared losing him to a general as he was such a golden boy all officers had taken note. Ludlow read through the lines to the extent that he understood the degree Tristan was chaffing under army discipline. He felt momentarily guilty when he found himself wishing that it was either Samuel or Tristan returning in the spring, rather than Alfred. In France the Canadians were camped between Neuve-Chapelle and St. Omer. Still in the early and optimistic stages of the war they were considered a bit haphazard and clumsy by their English counterparts, especially the curt and dashing officers from Sandhurst who rather typically saw the war as part of their own brilliant military careers. Such Teutonic nonsense had never been limited to the Huns. But no one faulted the Canadians on the matter of aggressiveness in battle—if anything, their courage was excessive.

Tristan was tented with the worst of the ruffians in his company. Alfred was embarrassed when Tristan visited him in the field hospital, swaggering and sloppily dressed with manure on his boots. Tristan had smuggled in a bottle of wine which Alfred had refused. One of Alfred's fellow officers came for a visit and Tristan had failed to salute, sitting there drinking the bottle of wine and leaving without saying good-bye except to have Alfred tell One Stab to take his favorite horse if he didn't return. Outside the hospital tent Tristan's companion, a huge French-Canadian named Noel, a trapper from British Columbia, waited with downcast eyes in the rain. The news that Samuel and the Major were dead had just reached camp. They had been on a reconnaissance up toward Calais with a group of scouts when they had been hit with mustard gas, then cut to ribbons by machine gun fire as they wandered numbed in a glade of a chestnut forest. A lone surviving scout had come back with the story and was now being debriefed. Tristan stood there dazed in the rain and mud with his friend embracing him in sorrow. The scout who was from their tent approached with an officer in tail. They raced to the paddock and quickly saddled three horses. The officer commanded them to stop and they knocked him aside in full gallop northward toward Calais reaching the forest by midnight. They sat still and fireless through the night and then at dawn in the fine sifting snow they crept forward in the snow and wiped it from the faces of the dozen or so dead until Tristan found Samuel, kissed him and bathed his icy face with his own tears: Samuel's face gray and unmarked but his belly rended from its cage of ribs. Tristan detached the heart with a skinning knife and they rode back to camp where Noel melted down candles and they encased Samuel's heart in paraffin in a small ammunition canister for burial back in Montana. An officer interrupted, but left wordlessly when it occurred to him he would be strangled if he interfered. When they finished, Tristan and Noel drank a liter of brandy from their booty from a farmhouse and Tristan then left the tent and howled Goddamn God until Noel subdued him and he slept.

In the morning Tristan awoke and heartlessly refused to commiserate with Alfred when a messenger came to bring him to the hospital tent. He wrote a note and taped it to the canister saying, "Dear Father, this is all I can send home of our beloved Samuel. My heart is broken in two as yours will be. Alfred will bring it back. You know that place he should be buried up near the spring in the canyon where we found the horns of the full curl ram. Your son Tristan."

Then Tristan went mad and there are still a very few old veterans up in Canada that remember his vengeance, because he was captured and restrained before it reached full flower. Tristan and Noel first feigned new seriousness as soldiers and volunteered for the scouts on nightly reconnaissance missions. At the end of three nights seven blond scalps hung in various stages of drying from their tent pole. On the fourth night Noel was fatally wounded and Tristan reached camp at mid-morning with Noel over the pommel of his saddle. He rode past crowds of soldiers to his tent where he laid Noel on his cot and poured brandy down his lifeless throat. He sang a Cheyenne medicine song One Stab had taught him and a group of soldiers gathered around the tent. Alfred was brought on a stretcher by the commanding officer to reason with Tristan. When they opened the tent flap Tristan had made a necklace of the scalps and had laid his skinning knife and rifle across Noel's chest. They put him in a straitjacket and sent him off to a hospital in Paris where he escaped within a week.

The doctor who attempted to treat Tristan in Paris was a young Canadian from Hamilton who was given the psychiatric ward somewhat by default. In his postgraduate studies at the Sorbonne he had dabbled a bit in this new science of behavior but was ill-prepared for the shell-shocked and hapless victims of fear that arrived daily. His youth and adopted Parisian cynicism at first led him to believe that the men were merely cowards, but their odd behavior soon disabused him of that notion. They were traumatized puppies who either cried out for their mothers at night or retreated into a permanent and inconsolable silence. The doctor so doubted his ability to knit up their souls that he became almost bored with his patients and did all he could to have them shipped home. Thus he was fascinated with the arrival of Tristan when the ambulance driver advised him that a true "crazy" was waiting to be unloaded. The doctor sent attendants and read the report from Tristan's commander. He felt himself oddly unmoved by the scalpings and was surprised at the commander's horror. How could mustard gas be considered normal warfare and not scalping, in reaction to the death of a brother? All the doctors had been prepped on the medical complications of mustard gas which in fact constituted the beginning of truly modern warfare. The doctor had studied the classics at Oxford and felt himself learned on the subject of vengeance. He had Tristan brought to his office, excused the attendants and released the man from his straitjacket for which he got a polite "Thank you" and "May I have a drink?" The doctor loaned Tristan a uniform and they walked through the Bois de Boulogne to a small café where they ate and drank in silence. Finally the doctor said that he was aware of what had happened and there was no need to talk about it. Unfortunately it would take a number of months to process Tristan out of the army and send him home but he would do the best he could to make Tristan's stay as pleasant as possible.

* * *

It took several weeks for the news to reach Montana. One afternoon late in February on a day that was cold but sunny and clear after a storm had abated, Pet was driven by one of the new hands to Choteau for groceries and to pick up the mail. Ludlow wiped the frost from a kitchen window and stared at the mere ounce of sun he figured to be hovering above the bluish snowbound shadows of the barn. Decker and One Stab sat at the table drinking coffee and arguing about altitude with maps spread before them. One Stab was correcting the maps because he had covered the area from Browning to Missoula with a Cree friend known reverently as One Who Sees As A Bird, a man with an uncanny topographical perception of territory. One Stab disliked the altitude numbers attached to mountains. How high above which of the seven seas Tristan had told him about? What did the numbers mean if there were no sea near them? Some large mountains have no character while certain smaller ones are noble and holy places with good springs.

Then One Stab released them from the argument by asking Decker to read to him from *In the Grip of the Nyika* by J. H. Patterson who had also authored *The Man-Eaters of the Tsavo*, both books about adventures hunting and exploring in East Africa by the British colonel. Decker was bored by the books but Tristan had started years before and One Stab would close his eyes and listen with deep satisfaction to his favorite parts, including the lions that would jump on a moving flatcar to grab railroad workers to eat, the rogue elephant with one tusk that gored the horse named Aladdin, and best of all, the rhinos that died in great numbers from charging the new train that passed through their territory. The latter gave One Stab visions of thousands of buffalo charging the Northern Pacific railroad and tipping over the train. Many years before when he was involved in the tattered remnants of the Ghost Dance movement, One Who Sees As A Bird told him that he had created a new buffalo by throwing a buffalo skull in a sulphurous fumarole at Yellowstone when Ludlow measured the great waterfalls for the government. The trip had been humorous to One Stab who looked at the great mass of falling water and yelled numbers until the disquieted Ludlow asked him to be quiet. Tristan had promised to take him one day to the place where the animal fights the train.

Pet came in the door stomping the snow from her boots. She handed Ludlow the letter from Tristan and looked away. So did Decker. Only One Stab watched Ludlow open the letter, not fearing the worst possible or probable because he owned the Cheyenne sense of fatality that what had happened had already happened. You couldn't change it and trying to was like throwing stones at the moon.

Still very much in his late prime Ludlow grew old overnight. His stunned grief lapsed in and out of anger, and he took to drink which exacerbated his remorse. In a certain state of drunkenness his anger would turn into rage and this broke the threads of his vigor as if his tendons had been sprung, and he became stooped and careless of his appearance. He read Tristan's fatal letter so many times it became frayed and soiled. When the official letter of condolence came he did not open it nor did he respond to his wife's daily stricken letters. He was not beside himself so much as he was submerged in his own powerlessness. And how could they lock Tristan up before he scalped every Goddamn Hun on the continent. And what was this mustard gas that killed so that men ran around helplessly with blinded eyes and burning lungs and the horses screamed under them. The world was no longer fit for a war and he privately seceded from it. Pet mourned and little Isabel stayed out of the way, reading children's stories to One Stab who one evening joined his friend and mentor in drinking, not spitting it out for a change. But within an hour Decker had to restrain him, then give him more drink so that he would sleep and carry him to his hut after One Stab sang a song in Cheyenne about Samuel's life and his forest hikes and microscopes that revealed invisible worlds, then moved into the Cheyenne death song at which Ludlow broke down not having heard the song since forty years before in the Mauvaises Terres when a scout had died.

In Paris Tristan began to plan his escape after the first night in the ward, the noise of which was a symphony of the deranged. Unlike Ludlow who was wealthy and of a generally sentimental nature, the wealth in recent years protecting him from the actual machinery of civilization, Tristan's guilt was specific and limited to the dead body of his brother, the heart sunk in a canister of paraffin. Only

Alfred as a child of consensual reality escaped this guilt. So Tristan told the doctor by the third day that he could not bear the asylum and would travel somehow to his grandfather's in Cornwall. The doctor said you can't do that but without conviction. He spoke of the matter to his superior officer who knew of Ludlow's reputation—the military world being somewhat clubbish in those days. The colonel said merely to let Tristan escape saying that the man was totally disabled and should be given swift passage home.

On Tristan's daily walks through the Bois and over to the nearly deserted stable of Longchamps he had watched horses being ridden and exercised. One day he bought a fine mare, knowing that the trains demanded official passes. He told the doctor his intentions and the doctor wrote a note. At dawn Tristan packed his meager duffel and slipped by a sleeping attendant. It took him five days to ride to the coast through rain which changed to sleet and periodic snow. He rode swiftly through checkpoints saluting wildly at a full gallop, the horse throwing a shoe at Lisieux which was quickly repaired at an exorbitant rate by a blacksmith. At Cherbourg he caught a freighter with relative ease to Bournemouth outside of which he bought another horse riding west to Falmouth on the coast of Cornwall. One cold midnight with the Atlantic roaring outside the breakwater he presented himself at his grandfather's door. This late night knocking brought his grandfather in his nightshirt armed with a Beasley purchased in New Orleans. Tristan said, "I am William's son, Tristan." And the grandfather held the lantern high and recognized him from photos and said, "So you are." The captain woke his wife who made a meal and the captain drew out his best bottle of Barbados rum to welcome this madman he had heard of for twenty years.

Tristan spent a taciturn month in Cornwall with the word reaching Ludlow he was safe after his escape. The first morning the captain had him working on the schooner at the most menial jobs, Tristan not knowing anything about ships but quick to learn of hawsers, knots and sails. The captain had a load of rebuilt generators bound for Nova Scotia, in March, to return with a load of salted beef to be picked up in Norfolk on the way back. He would drop Tristan in Boston to be with his grieving mother and he could make his way home from there. They set sail in March on their antique ship crewed by four old sailors and tight watches—able men were needed for England's war effort. Tristan hacked ice from the rails for a week before the weather turned only a shade warmer, but fair. He was dropped without ceremony in Boston after three weeks at sea. Tristan made his way to South Station and nursed a bottle of rum on the mile run to Dedham where Susannah fainted when he arrived at her father's door. She did not know that he had promised to meet the old captain three months later in Havana.

Tristan, Alfred, Isabel and Susannah sat in a darkened parlor in Louisberg Square; two sons, a mother, a betrothed lover who felt she had improperly invaded their grief. Tristan was stiff and abrupt and Alfred gray and somehow coarsened, and Isabel could not control herself. They readied themselves to attend a memorial service arranged by

Samuel's Harvard College friends. Then Tristan announced he would marry Susannah in a few days and his mother denied him permission saying that it was improper to marry even before the funeral. Tristan was curt and manic telling her she might attend if she wished.

Tristan and Susannah married at her family's country place near Dedham and the occasion was hopelessly solemn. Only Susannah's two sisters understood how she could marry a man her parents disliked though they had long been friends of Isabel's.

One late April morning Ludlow went to meet the train in muddy clothes which betrayed his increasing eccentricity. He had been repairing the frost damage to the Cornish stone fence surrounding the ranch house. It was not that he had any sentimental dislike for barbed wire, only that he did not like to look at it. Isabel had requested the Presbyterian minister for the funeral the next day but Ludlow hadn't contacted the man, failing to understand what he had to do with Samuel.

Tristan and Susannah scarcely had left their compartment on the train trip which Isabel thought was indecent and which enlivened Alfred's secret jealousy. Tristan had in mind the making of a son to replace his brother and that was the sole purpose of his marriage, in essence a cruel impulse he knew, but could not help himself. When he embraced his father at the railroad heading he trembled but did not weep until he embraced One Stab.

Early the next morning, a brilliant spring morning with the fresh green pastels of budding aspens and new grass, they buried Samuel's heart up in the canyon near the spring. Isabel saw all their lives becoming history in units of days and nights so fatally private there was no one left for her to love. One Stab watched Decker fill the hole from up on the hillside. When everyone left he walked down the hill and looked at the stone but could not read the words.

SAMUEL DANT LUDLOW 1897–1915
WE WILL NOT SEE HIM
BUT WE SHALL JOIN HIM

CHAPTER

II

Tristan's midsummer dreams were full of water; the rolling cold Atlantic swept through his sleep in green unfurlings. If he awoke in the night he would slide his hand hopefully across Susannah's belly. In the two months of their marriage he had been a truly crazed lover though not for any biological reason, but the wound in his brain over Samuel. He idly considered prayer then laughed to himself thinking that God would likely give him a muskrat for a son. He was a week from his unannounced departure to Havana to meet his grandfather, a matter he knew to be unshakably perverse but he could not help himself. A hundred years before he would have been content to travel the land, the mountains and rivers seemingly without end, but now at twenty-one in 1915 there was little or none of that left, and his compulsion was to see beyond the seven millionth wave and further. And not that he didn't love where he was: in fact short of Canada north Montana was his sole option. And perhaps he loved his wife as much as a young man of his unique nature could. He doted on her, kept her to himself, and they talked for hours of mostly imaginary (on his part) plans for the future: to ranch and raise a family and blooded horses and, of course, cattle to support the venture. Susannah would sit near the corral under a parasol to protect her fair skin and watch Tristan and Decker break and train horses aided by the strange half-black Cree who stuck to most difficult mounts like a burr in a setter's hair.

Ludlow had been kept busy entertaining Susannah's father, Arthur, who had come west on a sporting expedition with a large trunk full of H. L. Leonard fly rods. It seemed odd to Ludlow that the man seemed openly to care more for Alfred than Tristan. Alfred's back had repaired itself, but he still needed a cane for his leg. After a few weeks fishing, though, the financier having enjoyed himself so thoroughly looked for something to buy in that curious tradition of the rich who in a state of general good feeling cast about for something to buy. He settled on a large adjoining ranch calling it a wedding present for his daughter and son-in-law though he retained a half share to insure what he referred to as "prudent business practices."

Ludlow became courtly again with his wife: their grief finally too large to be held privately. The rawest time had occurred one hot Sunday afternoon when they were having a picnic on the lawn and a girl in a cheap summer dress rode bareback up to the gate. Tristan immediately strode out and lifted her from the mount, recognizing her while the others watched puzzled but mildly bored: it was the honyocker's daughter from up near Cut Bank to whom

Samuel had given his gold watch for safekeeping. She approached the table hugging her satchel to her breast. Tristan introduced her, brought her a plate of food and a glass of lemonade. He sat down beside her and balefully watched as she drew Samuel's watch from her satchel. She had heard of his death in the Helena newspaper and had made the three-day ride to return the watch, and if anyone cared to, they might read Samuel's letters to her. There were a hundred or so, one for each day of his service, and each in his meticulous script. Isabel began to read, then was overcome. Ludlow paced the lawn cursing while Alfred stared at the ground. Susannah took the girl off to give her a bath and a rest. In the middle of the afternoon she said she had to leave and asked that they send the letters to her when they were finished. She would accept nothing, not clothing, money or the gold watch though she asked for a photo of Samuel because he had neglected or was too shy to send one. Tristan rode silently with her a few miles wishing that she were pregnant and that would somehow bring back Samuel, but no, he died pure and virginal. And now she rode off with only a photo to console her. He wanted to strangle the world.

Tristan returned from the short ride in a mood so foul that he tried to break a young stallion that they had had no luck with. It was a tough beefy-looking animal that years later would be referred to as a quarter horse. He intended to breed it to three of his father's thoroughbred mares which Ludlow thought to be an interesting idea, but which Susannah's father, an aficionado of racehorses, thought outrageous. Tristan worked through the late afternoon until it occurred to the watchers at twilight that one of the beasts in the corral, whether the horse or Tristan, would likely end up dying in the match. Susannah's father quipped that the horse would serve a better purpose as dog meat, and Tristan stared at him and said he would name the horse in his honor Arthur Dog Meat at which he stomped off refusing to join them all later for supper and demanding an apology which he didn't get.

Late that night the ocean again entered Tristan's dreams: he tossed his bruised body and saw the black sky and immense rolling swells of the night watch, the rattling of an ice-stiffened foresail, and later the sky shot with stars too large to be stars. He awoke with Susannah covering him and the curtains blowing as if they were sails. He went to the window and stared down at the stallion in the corral; in the moonlight he could see the outline of its thick swollen neck. He told Susannah that he would be going away for a few months, or perhaps even a year, to meet his grandfather's ship in Havana. She said that she could tell that he needed to go and she would wait for him forever. At breakfast he kissed his father and mother good-bye and rode off with One Stab to Great Falls to meet the train. One Stab gave him his skinning knife and Tristan remembered that his own was buried with Noel at Ypres. He embraced the old Indian and said that he would return, to which One Stab only said, "I know it," as he rigged a lead line for Tristan's horse.

The voyage never really ended, except as it does for everyone: in this man's life, on a snowy hillside in Alberta late in December in 1977 at the age of eighty-four (a grandson found him beside the carcass of a deer he had been gutting, his hand frozen around the skinning knife One Stab had given him that day in Great Falls—the grandson hung the deer in the tamarack and carried the old man home, his snowshoes sinking only a little deeper in the snow).

Tristan took the train east to Chicago, spent a few days out of curiosity studying the Great Lakes ships at the docks, then went south to New Orleans and over to Mobile where he spent a few days on a schooner owned by a Welshman out of Newfoundland and on down through Florida to Key West where he took a night ferry to Havana after watching a load of green turtles being unloaded at a kraal from a Cayman's schooner, a graceful but filthy ship.

It was his first time in the tropics and on the night passage to Havana he was sleepless, spending the hours pacing the deck and wondering at the moist dense heat which the slight breezes of the Gulf Stream did not dispel; and beneath the bow where he walked to escape the smell of coal smoke from the stacks, the waves were phosphorescent. In the first light with Havana in distant view he sipped rum from his flask watching his first porpoises cut across the bow, lie back, then hurtle across the wake: turning he saw the strange vast purple penumbra of the Gulf Stream casts in the sky. He was red-eyed and strained from his travel but for the first time in half a year he felt something akin to ease in his soul, as if the dawn shore breeze laved the surface no matter the currents and turmoil below. He smiled at the water and the thought of his grandfather's schooner which though relatively new held so small a place in the world of the great steamers anchored off Havana. But it was a matter of less money and going where you wanted, the ports undesirable to the large shipping companies, or bays too shallow for big drafts and heavy tonnage. Besides the old man said he disliked the smell of smoke or the sound of engines at sea and it was too late for him to develop an interest in the grotesque.

People finally don't have much affection for questions, especially one so leprous as the apparent lack of a fair system of rewards and punishments on earth. The question is not less gnawing and unpleasant for being so otiose, so naive. And we are not concerned with the grander issues: say the Nez Perce children receiving the hail of cavalry fire in their sleeping tents. Nothing is quite so grotesque as the meeting of a child and a bullet. And what distances in comprehension: the press at the time insisted we had won. We would like to think that the whole starry universe would curdle at such a monstrosity: the conjunctions of Orion twisted askew, the arms of the Southern Cross drooping. Of course not: immutable is immutable and everyone in his own private manner dashes his brains against the long-suffering question that is so luminously obvious. Even gods aren't exempt: note Jesus's howl of despair as he stepped rather tentatively into eternity. And we can't seem to go from large to small because everything is the same size. Everyone's skin is so particular and we are so largely unimaginable to one another.

Thus Tristan had not more than a shred of comprehension of the agony he caused Susannah. On the morning of his departure she took a long walk and became lost. One Stab found her at nightfall and after that Ludlow asked One Stab to keep an eye on her if she left the yard. Her walking continued for weeks and her father truncated his vacation out of disgust when she refused his plan to have the marriage annulled. But Susannah's character owed more to the early nineteenth than the early twentieth century and as an abandoned lover she was unwilling to commiserate with anyone; this resolve was impenetrable and she spent her time either walking with Samuel's botanical and zoological handbooks or sitting in her room reading Wordsworth, Keats and Shelley, favorites from the two years at Radcliffe before her marriage to Tristan. She enjoyed talking to her mother-in-law whose intelligence was as extraordinary as her own as long as the conversation didn't lead to Tristan. But most of all she enjoyed her long summer walks and such were her preoccupations that she never noticed One Stab following her. Sometimes she invited little Isabel along and she marveled at the child's quick wit and her knowledge of the natural world gathered from her mother and observation rather than from books. One especially hot afternoon while they were bathing in a pool formed by the spring near Samuel's grave Isabel noticed One Stab back in the forest and waved. Susannah cried out and covered herself then was embarrassed by the child's puzzlement. Then Isabel laughed and said she was going to marry One Stab when she grew up if he didn't get too old because Susannah had already married Tristan and there were no other choices on earth. Susannah slipped back to her neck in the water remembering how one day in this pool Tristan had imitated an otter chasing the fingerling trout and eating watercress. Isabel was saying that One Stab only followed to prevent her from getting lost or straying inadvertently between a sow grizzly and her cubs.

In Havana that morning Tristan took breakfast then walked the streets until noon came, the appointed time when his grandfather would make his daily visit to the shipping office. The meeting was casual at first but when they stepped away from the clerks out into the crude heat of the day his grandfather became grave and walked quickly tilted forward as a man in a rainstorm. The crew had been sent home and he had been ill with dysentery, the only complaint Tristan had ever heard from his mouth, but it was a veil over the inevitable: the schooner would be seized on its return to Falmouth for the war effort. To keep control of the ship they must cooperate. When they passed the guards at the British Consulate the old man paused and looked at Tristan with his cold blue eyes and told him not to say anything: the bargain had been struck. Then the old man pulled long from a flask of rum and offered it to Tristan saying that his senses had to be dulled a bit to bear these nitwits.

Later that afternoon they loaded supplies on the schooner with a new first mate, a Dane down from San Francisco named Asgaard, and three Cuban deckhands of evident experience. The captain of record was now Tristan and his grandfather was listed as a passenger bound for Falmouth. They slipped from their mooring after dark,

raising an American flag before the mainsail and recording
their heading in a brand new logbook. In a strong
northeaster they rounded Cape Antonio the next morning
and headed southwest down the Yucatan Channel toward
Barranquilla to pick up a neutral cargo of mahogany and
rosewood, and not incidentally, an important British subject. Then they headed east, passed south of the Caymans,
up the Windward Channel and out the Caicos Passage
turning north to catch the Gulf Stream whose current
would aid them toward England.

In his cabin the old man barked an occasional order up
to Asgaard and continued to school Tristan relentlessly.
They took double watches keeping awake with Jamaican
coffee. For a month all else was wiped from Tristan's mind
except ingesting sixty years of his grandfather's experience:
his sleep was troubled by imagined line squalls, frayed
mooring lines, split masts, the strange giant waves found
off Madagascar on occasion in the winter. They saw no sign
of a German blockade as they neared the southern coast
of England. They slipped into Falmouth at night where
they were met by British intelligence. It was the old man's
last arrival and he took permanently to bed that night
aided by Tristan and his wife who had tallied his returns
for over a half century. He was nearly merry when he took
her hand and said that he was home for good.

Tristan was briefed the next day by an officer who had
formerly been a factory manager in the Midlands. The
officer was deferential and poured Tristan a drink as he
nervously fingered a file. Then he asked if Tristan minded
showing him how one went about scalping another human

being; in his youth he had read a great deal of the literature of the American West but none of the authors had described the precise technique and he was curious. Tristan silently moved his hand in a slicing motion beneath his widow's peak and then made a swift ripping motion. It attracted his rarely used sense of humor and he said that one waited until the man was dead or nearly so depending on the degree of one's dislike and that you couldn't scalp a beheaded man because you needed an anchor to gain a good fulcrum. The Englishman nodded appreciatively and they went on about their business. The next morning the schooner was to be loaded with wooden cases marked tinned beef but which in fact held weaponry of a certain advanced nature. The cargo was bound for Malindi on the Kenyan coast to aid the British in their anticipated problems with the Germans at Fort Ikomo in Tanganyika. In this relatively early stage of the war they should have no trouble with the Germans in that they were flying an American flag but the situation could change momentarily and if Tristan were under fire he must scuttle the schooner. If the skirmish were of a minor nature as they neared Kenya a case of hunting rifles and shotguns consigned for Nairobi might be used in defense and that he should school his crew for that eventuality.

Tristan spent the afternoon sitting beside his grandfather's bed waiting for his midnight departure. While the old man slept he wrote Susannah and his father that he was on a mission for the government not realizing his letters would be censored and that he had been followed everywhere that day by an intelligence officer disguised as a

Cornish fisherman. And writing the notes brought a strange sweep of sentiment over him as if for a moment his destiny was no longer so inalienably private and buried within himself. He imagined his father and Decker arguing about breeding lines and his mother in the parlor with the gramophone playing *Cavalleria Rusticana*. He saw Susannah sitting up in bed and stretching her arms in the first light, how her slight figure walked to the window to look at the weather surrounding the mountains and how she would come back to bed and look at him a long time without saying anything.

Some of our strangest actions are also our most deeply characteristic: secret desires remain weak fantasies unless they pervade a will strong enough to carry them out. Of course no one ever saw the "will" and perhaps it is a cheapish abstraction, one blunt word needing a thousand modifiers. When Tristan set sail for Africa that morning after a silent lamplit breakfast with his grandmother—she gave him a Bible wrapped in an untreated lambswool sweater she had knitted—he was fulfilling a number of inevitabilities. Since his sixth grade geography class in a country schoolhouse he had dreamed of going to Africa, not for the hunting because One Stab had taught him a much more honorable and functional sense of hunting than to shoot an animal to gratify his ego, but merely to see it, to smell and feel and know it, to see how it jibed with the dreams of that child crazed with maps he once was. Another obsession was caused by the tales his father told of his few short youthful trips with his own father: a trip to Göteborg in Sweden one summer and another to Bordeaux and of the whale seen breaching in the North Sea. Always the expert horseman, once in his dreams Tristan envisioned a schooner as a giant seafaring horse jumping wave froth and pitching full tilt against swells. And there was the unspoken, unthought, unrehearsed sense that time and distance would reveal to him why Samuel died.

A week of brisk chill winds brought them around Cape St. Vincent where they headed southeast toward Gibraltar. Asgaard figured they had been averaging a hundred and fifty nautical miles a day, a grand pace that would slacken somewhat when they entered the Mediterranean. Twice they had dropped the sails for rifle practice. Tristan had been delighted on opening the case to find seven Holland & Holland rifles of varying caliber including an elephant gun plus four shotguns. But the seas were too rough and it was nearly impossible to time the aim on a rising or falling swell to hit the bottle off the stern. Only Tristan and one of the Cubans who was later revealed to be an exiled Mexican could do it. Asgaard, the peaceful Dane, closed his eyes as he pulled the trigger; one of the Cubans couldn't stop giggling and the other was stiff and serious but inexperienced.

A day and a half into the Mediterranean passing Alboran, a German destroyer in the early evening signaled them to reef and heave to but a squall and the gathering dark gave them a clean escape. For safety Asgaard thought it wise to skirt the Algerian and Tunisian coast beyond which point they would supposedly be safe, at least until they reached the Indian Ocean. It proved true though Tristan was enervated and sleepless when they were becalmed for three days off Libya. Against orders they stopped in Crete at Ierapetra long enough to take on fresh water to replace their brackish supplies. At the wharf an obviously German shopkeeper studied them furtively and the Mexican offered Tristan to cut the man's throat. The crew had not been apprised of the mission but none of them believed the cases in the hold held beef. And to Asgaard's dismay Tristan dispensed totally with the shipboard formalities that separate captain from crew, formalities that he had loathed and chaffed against in the army. He ate with the crew, occasionally trying his hand at the cooking, played cards with them and had begun taking guitar lessons from the especially shy and taciturn Cuban who called him *caballero* instead of captain. Neither was the liquor rationed to the time-honored two ounces a day: the liquor stores were left unlocked though no one abused it. Asgaard was pleased two days out of Falmouth, though, when Tristan announced at dinner that anyone who didn't work out would simply be pitched overboard. But the crew was swift and efficient with a high morale partly because they were headed south into the warmer climes they loved.

The schooner arrived one dawn at Port Said and passed into the Suez Canal uneventfully. Only Tristan and Asgaard were disturbed by the extreme heat of the Red Sea. The heat was mitigated a great deal when they made the Strait of Bab el Mandeb and entered the stiff southerly breezes of the Indian Ocean in the Gulf of Aden. Two weeks later they reached Malindi only to find that the rendezvous had been changed to Mombasa two days' sail further south. Tristan had relapsed into grief to the point that he secretly wished to encounter a German gunboat, but the exchange in Mombasa was hitchless. The British officer said they were under no immediate further obligation for a partial reward for the danger of their voyage. The officer said he was recommending a decoration at which point Tristan became heartsick and walked from the room. After more than a month at sea the sight of this officious popinjay sickened him. Asgaard had been to Mombasa before and was spending his shore leave with a French widow so Tristan with the two Cubans and a Mexican in tow took the new train to Nairobi where they spent three days drinking and whoring themselves to exhaustion. Tristan made a deal to take a load of ivory, elephant tusks and the false ivory of rhinoceros' horns thought to be to the Chinese an aphrodisiac, to Singapore. In Nairobi he smoked some opium and rather liked its dreamy mind-banishing propensities. On their way back to the port Tristan had his photo taken at a fuel stop with a dead rhino's head across his lap. He paid a frayed, alcoholic English photographer twenty dollars to send the photo to One Stab, c/o William Ludlow, Choteau, Montana, USA. The message was to read, "Here is a dead one who stopped the train if only for a moment."

Back in Montana it was autumn again, only a fated year since the boys left for the war. Isabel and Susannah had left for Boston after Susannah was cured from a bout of pneumonia caught on a long cold walk in the rain. That year there were only three days of true Indian summer and one afternoon on the porch Ludlow was fiddling with a crystal set while One Stab and little Isabel gravely watched. When the first strains of music came over the airwaves from Great Falls they were simultaneously appalled. The sleeping bird dogs on the porch stood and barked, the male with his shoulder pelt ruffed in threat. Ludlow nearly dropped the set which he had spent two days assembling. Then Isabel laughed and clapped, jumping in a circle. One Stab lapsed into a deep brooding state as Ludlow explained the notion that everything owned its own sound. Within an hour of thought One Stab considered the crystal set to be as essentially worthless as the gramophone.

Susannah spent the winter in Boston at Isabel's Louisburg Square address. Still alienated from her parents over the matter of her marriage, she found Isabel to be a good companion and their relationship progressed from the artificiality of daughter-in-law and mother-in-law to close friends. Isabel had decided to take no lovers that year and had instead devoted her energies, other than to the usual symphony and opera, to the learning of French and Italian and to the questions of feminism and suffrage. She held a dinner for a distant cousin, the poetess Amy Lowell who was somewhat a scandal, given as she was to smoking cigars in public. Susannah, whose health had been weak, was delighted with the grand orotund lady who asked for a goblet of brandy after dinner, lighted a cigar and read her slight, fragile poetry so absurdly different from the bearer.

Susannah never received the letter from Tristan from Falmouth, only a note from the British government that the letter would be held until such time as its sensitive nature would not endanger the war effort. This puzzled and grieved her and she nearly contacted her father who had received news of Tristan of a somewhat congratulatory nature. The British Consul in Boston had advised him that Tristan would receive the Victoria Cross for successfully undertaking a mission of an extremely perilous character, the exact nature of which could not be revealed. Susannah's father could not help but mutter "damned adventurer" when he heard the news though it came out at a Harvard Club luncheon and he was roundly congratulated for having so noble a son-in-law. He was cut somewhat from the same cloth as J. P. Morgan and Jay Gould though from a decidedly smaller pattern. The war in Europe would clearly provide him with his financial heyday, and he plunged heavily into cattle and grain from a base of mining and manufacturing. He had set Alfred up with an office in Helena, encouraged him to enter politics and to send him weekly reports on any economic intelligence he might garner. Alfred had already made him a nearly extortionary profit on a wheat deal and Susannah's father could not help but think what a fine son-in-law he would have made. Arthur was heavily into Standard Oil which had bought the Montana copper interests from Anaconda, forming Amalgamated Copper. Alfred clearly understood the prerogative of those who owned the capital while Ludlow who tended to dotter was sentimental about miners' wages and living conditions. When scab vigilantes hanged a Wobbly from a bridge in Butte, Arthur saluted them.

In the spring Alfred came east for Arthur's counsel in mapping out his future, to see his mother and not incidentally Susannah whom he loved in secret. Alfred was a bit cloddish compared to Tristan and Samuel but he was steadfast in his admiration of his brothers, and of a loving and faithful nature. He wept one evening at bedtime when he found himself wishing that Tristan wouldn't return and Susannah would somehow fall in love with him. In fact Alfred was a bit too guileless, a characteristic his political career would speedily change. It hurt him deeply in Boston when Susannah seemed almost not to notice him across the dinner table at a celebration over the reunion of the family. In the days that followed she was friendly but distant on a number of April walks across Boston Common when it seemed his heart would burst. She gave him on parting a book of Amy Lowell's poetry which his essentially stodgy nature could make nothing of, but the inscription, "Dearest Alfred, you are such a good, noble man, love, Susannah," kindled his spirits to a point that in the privacy of his compartment on the long train ride home he opened the book jacket, smelled her inscription and trembled thinking he caught the scent of her.

The schooner was not fairly beyond sight of Dar es Salaam where they had loaded the ivory when Tristan was struck with acute dysentery so virulent that he fainted at the wheel. The first stage of the disease flattened him and he ran a temperature of over a hundred and five during a week when the seas ran so high Asgaard feared both for the life of the captain and the boat. And had not Tristan and the schooner both owned nearly supernatural constitutions they both would have rested unshrouded on the bottom of the Indian Ocean. At the end of the first week the fever did not break but diminished to the point that Tristan was at least ambulatory in his tropic nightmare. In his waking dreams he had seen the gates of hell and wanted to walk through them and God alone knows what held him back one midnight when he perched naked on the bowsprit like a gargoyle with the warm spray of the ocean cooling him only a little until the Mexican sapped him with a belaying pin and put him back to bed.

For Tristan the dead were on deck and in his cabin he drank, despite his fever, and heard their footfalls. Samuel laughed and talked about botany but there was snow in his hair and his white hair blew in the shore winds as they neared Colombo in Ceylon. Susannah appeared with blue wings and One Stab howled off the bow wake. He heard them, even saw them, through teak and white-oak slabs. He did not know what was delirious sleep or delirious waking so that both his waking and sleeping dreams were soul chasers. One dawn Asgaard found him down in the hold nude, clasping a huge elephant tusk to his chest and examining the bloody root which had darkened and smelled horrible. Tristan grappled upward to the deck and tried to heave the tusk overboard when Asgaard restrained him and he was confined to his cabin with the Mexican on guard.

Tristan had in his fever achieved that state which mystics crave but he was ill-prepared for: all things on earth both living and dead were with him and owned the same proportion, he did not recognize in any meaningful sense his naked foot at the end of the bed, or the ocean under whose lid it was always night even at high noon, the blood at the end of the great tusk did not belong on the schooner and throwing it overboard would somehow return it to the elephant's head. Susannah arrived as a pale pink sexual ghost and her womb covered him, saline like the spray off the bowsprit until he was a ghost, too, and he was the ocean, Susannah herself, the bucking horse beneath him, the wood of the sea horse beneath him, both wind ripping the sails and the moon above the sails and the light of the dark between.

He had largely recovered by the time they hit the entry of the Strait of Malacca and sailed in fair soft winds toward Singapore. The ivory was dumped without ceremony at a shipboard conference not the less profitable because of the Chinese businessmen's fear of the cutthroats that watched the bargaining. Tristan was stretched thin by his disease as cable about to be sprung but fully in command. He agreed to take at an exorbitant price a trunk of pure opium to San Francisco to be accompanied by one of the businessmen. Asgaard hedged but over dinner Tristan made an even split of the ivory profits with the crew, saving out an extra share for his grandfather as the owner of the schooner. He said the same would happen with the opium profits and Asgaard lapsed into a dream of a small farm on the coast of Denmark that could easily be his own. The Cubans celebrated thinking how overwhelmed their families would be with this new wealth. Only Tristan and the Mexican were rootless, cared next to nothing for the pile of money before them because they wanted nothing that could be bought with it: one could suppose that the Mexican thought of his far-off and beloved country he could not return to without dying. And God knows what Tristan wanted other than to revive the dead: his brain was the remnant of carnage, a burned city or forest, cold scar tissue.

The schooner headed north through the South China Sea stopping at Manila for fresh supplies and water. The opium courier was panicked at that infamous port, so Tristan set Asgaard and the two Cubans armed with hunting rifles on deck. He then went down to his cabin and wrote a short but fatal note to Susannah (Your husband is forever dead, please marry another) which he posted with the captain of a fast steamer he met when he and the Mexican began their binge in Manila. Just before dawn on the way back to the ship they were set upon by four thugs near the dock and might have died were it not for the Mexican disarming one of the assailants while Tristan attacked the largest man. The Mexican cleanly beheaded one with the man's machete and the others, save the one Tristan was strangling, fled, but not before Tristan received a severe leg wound, a deep slice across the side of his knee which cut the tendon. The Mexican applied a tourniquet and they made their way singing back to the dinghy which they rowed drunkenly to the mooring. Asgaard cleaned and sewed up the wound with catgut improvising knots around the tendon. The wound had healed by the time they reached Hawaii though ever after Tristan walked with the trace of a limp.

No one but his far-flung crew knows much of Tristan's next six years except for a few details, all the more teasing because of their incompleteness: we know he reached San Francisco then headed south to Panama hoping to pass through the new canal but the landslide at the Gaitland Cut had temporarily closed the new passage so he rounded the Horn and had a small steam auxiliary put in at Rio. Then the schooner had a relatively stable three years in the Caribbean working as an island trader ranging from Bermuda to Martinique over to Cartagena. Tristan bought a small ranch on the Isla de Pinos then set off for Dakar on another escapade for the British government in the last year of the war. He rounded Good Hope returning to Mombasa where he took aboard a Galla woman for a week but she feared the rocking of the schooner and was put ashore with a small sack of gold in Zanzibar. He was repeating his ivory and opium run as he made his way again east to Singapore, Manila, Hawaii and San Francisco, down through the open canal late in 1921 and thence back to Havana where Asgaard and the rest of the crew left him except for the Mexican. He spent a few months on his ranch and when he returned to Havana he learned of the death of his grandfather five years before and that his father had suffered a stroke and that he wished him to come home so that they might see each other before Ludlow died. Tristan and the Mexican hired another crew and made their way to Vera Cruz where the Mexican now had enough money to bounty his life with power. Tristan put the schooner in the Mexican's care and journeyed north by horse and train arriving in April of 1922, still sunblasted, limping, unconsoled and looking at the world with the world's coldest eye.

It is not for us to comprehend Ludlow's speechless delight when he and One Stab sat on the porch listening to the symphony on the radio one warm April afternoon and saw Tristan's horse picking its way around the melting snowdrifts in the road and up through the gate. Tristan jumped from the horse and caught his father falling into his arms from the porch and he repeated father over and over but the old man was truly speechless now because of his stroke. One Stab stared straight upward and felt the first tears of a life so rough as to be incomprehensible as Ludlow's delight. One Stab began singing. Decker ran from the corral and Tristan and Decker tried to lift each other at once. Pet came from the kitchen hearing the noise and tried to bow as Tristan embraced her. A girl of sixteen with a long pigtail wearing men's clothing came around the corner carrying a bridle: windburned but not quite Indian in her darkness. She stared at Tristan who caught her glance but then she walked away. Decker said it was his daughter Isabel but she was shy.

Pet killed and dressed a spring lamb, built a fire behind the kitchen and began roasting it. They sat on the porch drinking but mostly silent. Ludlow wrote questions on a slate board with chalk. His hair was white but his carriage erect. Decker looked off in the distance and explained that Tristan's mother was in Rome, then paused adding as a false afterthought, that Alfred and Susannah had been married the year before and were on an extended though belated honeymoon tour through Europe and would be at Cap d'Antibes for the summer. Decker was relieved and drank deeply when Tristan seemed unconcerned. Tristan walked a circle on the lawn and said he wanted to take a quick ride and hoped they wouldn't be too drunk by dinner.

He rode quickly up the creek that led to the spring in the box canyon. The remnant of a snowdrift covered Samuel's grave and a magpie flew off the stone as he arrived and unhorsed. He watched the invisible tracery in the air the bird made climbing to the canyon top above his head. He decided he wasn't good at graves because the grave under his feet was merely snow and earth and a stone dulled by the weather. On the way back to the house he watched Isabel grooming three spring foals in the sunlight. Decker called her Two to avoid confusion with Tristan's mother. He asked her where the badger was and she said the animal disappeared but his children still lived up behind the orchard. She took him into the barn and showed him an Airedale puppy Ludlow had bought for her birthday. Though only ten weeks old the pup advanced growling on Tristan and he swept it up gradually calming it until it chewed on his ear. Then he stared at her closely until she flushed and looked down at her feet.

At dinner Ludlow carved the lamb ceremoniously, then wrote "tell us tales" on his slate board and passed it to Tristan. Oddly, and like many men compelled to adventure with no interest in the notion of adventure but only a restlessness of the body and spirit, Tristan did not see anything particularly extraordinary about his past seven years. But he had an extravagantly accurate idea of what the table wanted to hear so he talked on for his father: the beheading of the Filipino thug, a typhoon off the Marshall Islands, an anaconda he bought while drunk in Recife that wound itself so tightly around the mast that it could not be detached until they offered it a piglet, the beauty of some of the horses he left in care of his crew hands in Cuba, and how some of the citizens in Singapore eat dogs, which shocked everyone at the table except One Stab who asked Tristan about Africa. After dinner he distributed some presents from his saddlebags including a necklace of lion's teeth which he placed around One Stab who set off a few days later on a three-day ride to Fort Benton to show the necklace to One Who Sees As A Bird. Tristan impulsively gave a ruby ring meant for his mother to Two, placing it on her ring finger and kissing her on the forehead. The table was silent and Pet started to interfere but Decker calmed her.

Later that night after everyone had gone to bed Tristan walked far out in the pasture in the moonlight: the snow patches were a ghostly white and far to the west he could see the even whiter peaks of the Rockies. He listened to the coyotes yelping and chattering in pursuit and occasionally a short howl. Back near the corral he heard the puppy crying and went into the barn and picked it up. He took it in the house and up to his room where he put it on the mule deer skin and built a nest around it with a comforter against the chill of the night. Tristan slept then until the middle of the night when the puppy growled and in the moonlight from the window he saw Two standing at the foot of the bed. He reached for her hand and after a while she joined his deep and dreamless sleep, wound about each other with all loneliness faded at last from the earth.

Tristan's life seemed to be moving through time in increments of seven: and now he was to have seven years of grace, a period so relatively peerless and golden in his life that far into the future he would turn back to that time; the minutiae of the book of days, a hieratica relived slowly so that each page was turned with some eagerness. No grace is isolate, and it was to a greater part the people he loved, but could scarcely comprehend as people when he left, who led him into light and warmth; but on that first morning he could see them clearly from the window after Two slipped back into her nightgown, kissed him and left the room: first there was a loud unidentifiable noise far out in the pasture which proved to be a Ford flivver jouncing over the rocks and through mud in great circles with One Stab at the wheel and Ludlow sitting erect beside him in his buffalo robe. Decker leaned against the barn in an Irish wool cap having a morning smoke in a patch of sunlight and scratching the nose of a Hereford bull as it poked through the slats of the fence: Pet scattering grain to the chickens and a few geese and shooing away the pup who chased the chickens. And when he came down for breakfast the wood cookstove was warm and sunlight flowed through the south window with a view of the valley. Two poured him coffee and he looked into the crockery bowl of herring Roscoe Decker was addicted to and fetched a piece with some pickled onions. Two served him fried trout that One Stab had caught at dawn. He stared at her back and the black shiny hair in a single plait as she washed the breakfast dishes. He closed his eyes and the floor rolled beneath him for the moment as the sea and he could smell brisk sea air at northern low tide in the herring. He opened his eyes and asked Two with a smile if she would marry him soon and thus avoid scandalizing the house with nightly visits. She dried her hands and took her ruby ring from the window sill as if she were holding a chalice and said yes if he were sure of himself, and yes if he weren't sure of himself.

There was a grand early October wedding, delayed until then so Isabel could get back from Europe and at Pet's insistence because she feared that Tristan would leave at any whim, an idea remote from his thoughts. Tristan spent the summer building a lodge house up in the box canyon overlooking the spring. A group of Norwegian carpenters came from Spokane along with three Italian stonemasons from Butte. The lodge was simple in design with one huge main room with a kitchen and fireplace at one end, and on the other end a wall-sized fieldstone fireplace. There were two wings of three bedrooms apiece. Two was embarrassed at the size of the place and One Stab and Ludlow visited daily in the flivver carrying lunch for the workers. Ludlow had taken to writing longish, eloquent letters to which Tristan would answer around the fire after dinner.

In Montana the Depression came ten years early. On the eastern plains the grain market goaded to affluence by the war collapsed totally aided by two years of severe drought. Banks failed and the cattle market inflated as the hunger of soldiers dwindled. Decker pared the stock back to registered Herefords, but the sole income of the ranch was the get of the foundation stallion, still referred to by all as Arthur Dog Meat, that Decker bred to the thoroughbred mares. The offspring didn't own the strength or the sturdiness of the quarter horse but they were exquisite cutting horses and class pleasure mounts, pretty faced and spirited. And they were powerfully fast at the quarter mile and Tristan and Decker raced them at fairs in Montana, Idaho, Washington and Oregon. With gambling winnings, Tristan bought Ludlow a Packard touring car that One Stab drove with dignity and care, still in his lion's tooth necklace. Men came from as far as San Antonio and Kingsville, Texas, to buy horses for amounts that Decker and Ludlow found boggling, but which Tristan insisted upon with shrewdness.

The fall wedding had passed into memory without the presence of Alfred and Susannah. In fact it was four years before Tristan saw Susannah over a polite but festive Christmas dinner. Alfred arrived from time to time when he was in the area campaigning for the United States Senate, a contest which he won handily helped not a little by the coffers and influence of his father-in-law. No one but Two and Pet saw Susannah's grief that Christmas. She was still childless and when Tristan's children, Samuel Decker and Isabel Three, caressed her yellow hair in the parlor, she wept.

The economics of the time grew more questionable and on Arthur's advice Ludlow slowly withdrew his capital from the Helena Bank and for want of a better idea buried gold beneath a huge stone on Tristan's hearth. Tristan with his habitual though charming arrogance insisted the ranch be self-supporting. He still sent formal notices and amounts of money to Susannah and her father for the use of the land they mutually held.

CHAPTER
III

What doomed him again (for there is little to tell of happiness—happiness is only itself, placid, emotionally dormant, a state adopted with a light heart but nagging brain) was a trip to Great Falls with Two and the ranch hands to drive a group of fall steers to the railhead. It was a pleasurable trip, not the less happy because of its almost antique nature. It was October and the stock market, whatever that was, had just collapsed. But Tristan had got a small amount of cash for the cattle and they all—Two, Tristan, Decker, the half-black Cree, a Norwegian who remained on from the carpentry crew years before—stayed to celebrate after an arduous hot summer. They had the best meal in town with plenty of drinks, but were put off by the finery and wealth of a neighboring ranch crew that had gotten rich by smuggling liquor in from Canada in defiance of the Volstead Act.

One Stab was coming next day in the Packard to take Two home with her fall shopping, so Tristan told the smugglers' leader he would take ten cases of whiskey for his own use and to sell to his neighbors. He told his crew he would split the profits and they were drunk with pleasure thinking of the quick money, ordering even more whiskey to carry in the panniers of the packhorses.

They made a strange procession filing down a narrow canyon into a valley near Choteau, the horses not far behind the Packard bogged and slowed in the October rain. Then at the mouth of the canyon near where the road turned north toward Choteau, the law with two armed men and a Ford coupe blocked the road. They fired vaguely into the air as they had been instructed as Federal officers. And the procession still in good humor stopped. The Federal officer said they had learned of the shipment and Tristan would have to give up the whiskey. They recognized Tristan and were apologetic saying he would face charges in November in Helena but they would have to destroy the liquor. Tristan turned from the officers hearing One Stab wail. He walked to the Packard, looked at One Stab's face, then at Two where she sat in the back with the supplies and gifts. She sat there as if built of stone with a ricocheted bullet from the canyon wall neatly piercing her forehead like a red dime.

Tristan went berserk then, reached for a nonexisting gun, then slugged each startled officer, putting one of them near death for months. He drew Two's body from the Packard and ran with it down the canyon. The procession followed him as he carried her body for miles through the cold rain. He carried her body howling occasionally in a language not known on earth.

* * *

Three days later the marshal came to Ludlow's house saying that Tristan would have to serve thirty days in the Helena jail because of the severity of the crushed skull of one of the Federal officers. The lightness of the sentence was due to Alfred's enormous influence in Montana politics. Pet interrupted to say that Isabel Three was gone. Tristan rode out covering a dozen miles until he found her close by up in the woods near the spring. One Stab was singing his Cheyenne death song and she was joining in with a voice so high and plaintive that the remnants of Tristan's heart broke in half. He lifted her slight body to the saddle and carried her home.

It is still argued by old men in the area whether it was alcohol, jail or grief, or simply greed that made Tristan an outlaw: but this is only gossip to nurse the drinks of pensioners and interesting in that forty years later Tristan was still an object of fascination, somehow the last of the outlaws, rather than a gangster.

In fact after he found six-year-old Three up at the spring singing with One Stab, he was mute for a number of months, except with his children. He was mute in jail refusing all visitors, including Alfred who came to offer his condolences and those of Susannah in a letter. The Helena press covered the meeting under the heading "Senator Visits Bereaved Brother in Jail."

In fact, Alfred was hoping for some solace and intervention from Tristan. He had arrived at the ranch the day after the funeral and only a few hours after the Marshal accompanied Tristan to jail. Ludlow stayed in his room and would

[255]

not see his eldest son. He sent Pet down into the parlor
carrying his slate saying he could not talk to Alfred as long as
he represented the U. S. Government and its base practices.

Ludlow in fact had thought of Two as a daughter and
had loved her as a daughter. Years before he had been
delighted to teach her to read and write and was constantly
to Pet's and Decker's dismay trying to spoil her with gifts.
It was Ludlow who wrote Isabel and told her to bring from
Boston the grandest and costliest wedding gown possible.
Now when he rode out to the grave with One Stab in the
flivver he felt far more than his seventy-five years thinking
of another October when he sent the boys off to war, and
then the beautiful October afternoon seven years before
when Tristan and Two had been married in a grove of
cottonwoods, the sun glistening off the white gown against
the sere colors of autumn, faded grass and yellow aspens.
Two deaths in fourteen years of loved ones are not all that
uncommon except to the mourner who has lost all sense
of common and uncommon and is buried in the thoughts
of things left out and how it might have been.

Alfred returned to Washington spending a long train trip
in a sleepless turmoil. As a political issue, Prohibition had
been a senseless obscenity to him and had only served to
promote the interests of the criminal element, all the more
evident in the waning years of the Volstead Act. His father
had always been a hero to him. And he liked to quote the
elegant old frontiersman in speeches to the Senate though
Ludlow, to be sure, had no such notions of himself. Popular
ideas as basically silly as "cowboys" or "frontiersman" or

the law of Prohibition itself came after the fact in self-congratulatory phases of history, when the energies turned toward labeling and social order.

But Alfred's problems were more profound in nature than politics and an alienated father. Susannah in fact was quite ill, had always been ill in a quiet nonobvious manner. And Washington, the social demands of being a senator's wife exacerbated her problems. Alfred had bought a country house and stables out in Maryland where they boarded many of his father-in-law's racehorses. She stayed there most of the time with twice-weekly visits from a professor of forensic psychiatry from Johns Hopkins, an old French Jew sworn to secrecy, as a mad wife has always been a political liability. In the blindness of his affection, Alfred had refused to admit the severity of the problem. One afternoon years before when they were being driven from Vallauris to Nice to take the boat home, Susannah insisted the driver stop and they walked off into a wooded hillside and made love. She had seemed terribly happy for weeks though there were intermittent fits of weeping. Despite this Alfred thought himself never so gloriously happy, but then Susannah had descended into her particular torment, refusing to leave the stateroom for the entire two-week trip back to New York. The country place and release from the immediate pressures of Washington seemed to help.

But in each of the nine years of their marriage there had been periods of what must be called insanity of varying degrees of severity. The psychiatrist hadn't been encouraging though in the past few years Susannah had been his most endearing patient. He had pushed her activity with the racing stable, understanding as he did that a preoccupation with animals tended to calm a patient, that the horses benignly seemed to draw the poison away at least temporarily.

The weeks that followed Alfred's return from Montana had been totally hellish. Susannah had reached the pinnacle of her manic phase where all things on earth had become too vivid to be borne up under: she could see a horse's heart through the skin, muscle and bone, and the moon was only a foot beyond the window; cut flowers in vases were dead and terrifying and certain paintings from France had to be turned to the wall; she claimed she lacked an imaginary child no matter how hard she tried to invent one and she used Tristan's refusal to answer her note of condolence as a lever to descend into depression.

In April Alfred came back west ostensibly to visit his constituency. He bought a large house in Helena, thinking that if Susannah began spending her summers in Montana it might help. Isabel would be there and Tristan and Pet might allow Susannah to help with Three and Samuel. As he drove into the muddy yard near Choteau his heart, always optimistic, lifted at his plan and at the beauty of the ranch.

Tristan and Decker were outside the shed building frames for packsaddles while Ludlow and One Stab watched smoking their pipes. When Alfred got out of his car Ludlow slipped through the fence and walked far out in the pasture with One Stab following. Tristan, Decker and Alfred watched Ludlow make his way around the melting drifts as if he intended to walk to the end of the

world. Tears streaked down Alfred's cheeks and Tristan
took his arm. Alfred asked for his forgiveness but Tristan
was matter-of-fact and only said, "Forgive you for what,
you didn't shoot my wife." Decker sat on a sawhorse and
watched Tristan and Alfred walk into the pasture after the
receding figures of Ludlow and One Stab. Decker's own
sorrow owned a harder Nordic remorselessness. (He waited
three years until he was at a cattle auction in Bozeman
before he had the opportunity to shoot one of the Federal
officers on the Bozeman to Livingston road the officer
traveled every day. He sat on a rock up in the loblolly pines
with a .270 on his lap, first shooting out a tire, and when
the man got out of the car he shot him ten times with great
satisfaction. The other Federal officer had been transferred
east and Decker had to be satisfied with the one.)

Halfway into the pasture Alfred stopped and in a rush
of words explained that Tristan must write Susannah and
relieve her of her twisted guilt. Tristan nodded in sympa-
thy for his brother. When they reached Ludlow, who was
leaning exhausted against a boulder, One Stab walked away
out of earshot. Tristan took his father's arm and asked him
to forgive Alfred who was his son and not the government.
Ludlow shivered in a chill and stared at Alfred with hard
but watery eyes, nodding at Tristan and looking away. He
was without his slate so he merely embraced Alfred and
began his walk back home.

When Alfred left the next morning he felt airy and
positive though it was raining. He had been forgiven and
they had a fine evening with Tristan's children sitting on
Alfred's lap as he told them stories of life in the great cities

of the East. He paused on the way to the main road to let a large band of packhorses and mules pass driven by two hands he recognized, the negroid Cree and the huge Norwegian carpenter. He wondered idly why Tristan wanted so many pack animals.

By early May when it was sure that spring had solidly broke and that any mountain storms would be short and fitful, One Who Sees As A Bird came down from Fort Benton and led Tristan, Decker, the Norwegian and Cree from Choteau up past Valier and Cut Bank to Cardston in Alberta where they loaded fifty packhorses with four cases of whiskey each, cut back down past Shelby and Conrad to Great Falls where Tristan got rid of the whiskey for six thousand dollars. The large profit was due to the fact that the whiskey was first-rate Canadian blended, not cut into working-class rotgut, a practice of the more venal smugglers. The other factor in the large profit was the scarcity of roads in northern Montana making it a relatively easy area for police. One Who Sees As A Bird made it an assured run though his friend One Stab was sad that Tristan had insisted he stay home to take care of Ludlow and the ranch.

Unfortunately, Tristan wasn't satisfied. Without realizing it he had half hoped to meet some resistance. Then Decker counseled him to think of his children and the fact that the small population of Montana would lead to their eventual capture. Tristan agreed though Decker's quiet anger was such that he only voiced these reservations at the insistence of Pet who feared for her grandchildren. Tristan made one more run in high summer and when they got home One Stab said Pet had disappeared with the children. One Stab said he would have followed but Ludlow had been ill. So Decker and Tristan rode up to Fort Benton in the Packard with the hole in the back seat and brought Pet and the children home.

Tristan laid off then after wiring the Mexican in Vera Cruz to bring the schooner to San Francisco by the following spring. There was money to be made. Isabel had come west for the summer helping Susannah settle in an appropriate house for a senator in Helena. Isabel had her grandchildren and Pet down for a month and Susannah's tentative health thrived caring for them and Three and Samuel adored her in return. No one knew that Susannah's apparent health was based on the most fragile of misconceptions. When Tristan had answered her letter at Alfred's insistence he had dwelt overmuch on the fact that fate had separated them and despite what had happened they must live with it with grace. The letter was unwittingly cruel because it somehow gave her hope; she had entered a period again when her world was somehow too errantly vivid, peeled back so that her days were a sequence of the essence of things. Alfred was planning a big dinner and party for all his political and social friends in Montana and she went rather manically about the preparations with the help of Isabel who was an expert at such matters.

Tristan went down to Helena to see a representative of a Canadian distiller he had met up in Cardston. The man had discussed with Tristan the trouble caused by a group known as the Irish Gang based in Seattle and the apparent stranglehold they had on the liquor distribution in the Northwest and California. Certain demanding clients in San Francisco were unable to get the first-class whiskey their clients preferred. The two men had tentatively agreed that Tristan would make a schooner run from Vancouver Island to San Francisco and Tristan intended on this sunny day in Helena to strike an exorbitant deal. He had brought along five cases of Haig & Haig as a gift for Alfred though he had declined to attend the party. He had always been repelled by the ostensibly important friends that Alfred had brought up to the ranch for hunting season: they played cards and drank all night, got up late and with few exceptions, the Cree filled their elk and deer licenses, though Tristan refused to cooperate any longer after a rich haberdasher shot a grizzly sleeping on a hillside.

Tristan had his meeting then drove around Alfred's ornate Victorian mansion until he found the back entrance. He intended to greet his mother, deliver the whiskey, avoid Susannah somehow and get back to the ranch. Helena unnaturally enervated him, all those men dubiously referred to as civil servants wandering around, not to speak of the cold limbo of his month in jail there when his throat and chest were continuously on the verge of choking him with his memories of Two. Even after bearing the children she would spring to her mount on a horse without using the stirrups and when she rode the roan gelding hard her hair would fly out in the back as the mane of a wild animal. But he was well past simple notions of vengeance and perhaps grief had coarsened and poisoned him to the point that he knew there was no evening the score with the

[262]

world, because even if he could that would not recreate the woman whom the rain had beat against until her long black hair had swung against his legs.

So for this man it was no more than rather belligerently fateful that he should walk into his brother's kitchen and find Susannah laughing and talking with Samuel and Three. He greeted and hugged his children, then they ran off to help their grandmother direct the hanging of the decorations for the party. Susannah and Tristan sat there in a condition of discomfort so extreme that it seemed the kitchen would explode. Susannah half lied and said she dreamt that she had become the mother of Samuel and Three, but Tristan shook his head no and she stood clasping her hands as if to pull her shoulders together. She left the table and walked into the pantry. Tristan sat at the table sweating in the close August heat and then she called his name in her soft clear voice. He pressed his hands hard against his face and went to the pantry where she stood naked with glistening eyes, her hair released around her shoulders, her clothes about her feet. He closed the pantry door and tried to calm her, then gave up without hesitation when she said if he did not make love to her she would begin screaming and scream until she died. They sank in each other's arms, their skin sticking to the cool tile floor.

Later when Tristan left, Susannah cut off her hair with sewing scissors and was confined to her room for the duration of the party under a doctor's and nurses' care. Early the next morning Susannah was driven north to Choteau with the doctor, Isabel, Pet and the children. They drove in two cars and Alfred was distraught, but kind, utterly uncomprehending. When they arrived Tristan took the children up to a hunting cabin he had built some dozen miles into the mountains for a few days.

But when he returned Susannah was excited and graceful again, and everyone was relieved and Alfred left in a few days to return to Helena to take care of his political business. Tristan was only a week away from leaving for San Francisco to meet the Mexican and the schooner. He would keep the crew thin, taking the Cree and the Norwegian because he trusted them.

It was now early in September, and a brief cold spell had arrived and left within two days dusting the foothills with snow that had melted off the aspens by mid-morning. Tristan sat alone in the lodge after One Stab and Ludlow had picked up the children to take them down to have lunch with Isabel. He brooded over the smoldering log in the fireplace thinking bleakly of his betrayal of his brother, no matter the circumstances. He placed not a shred of blame on Susannah recognizing that she was periodically less responsible for what she did than the youngest of children. His heart ached over the confusion and pain he had caused on earth. He poured a glass of whiskey, and began packing for San Francisco early, knowing that it would be best to be far from Susannah if she collapsed again.

Tristan quickly packed, noting to tell Decker where he hid his money should he not return. But when he got back to the main room Susannah was sitting on the couch before the fire. He called her name but she didn't answer. He walked to the couch and looked at the fire and down at her short rain-dampened hair and clothing. She spoke low and clearly, asking his forgiveness for what she had done. She couldn't help herself because she loved him so terribly and knew at one time he had loved her and it wasn't fair so she broke down just to be with him once more on earth. She was unwell and a senseless torment to everyone so when things had settled down and she and Alfred returned east she would take her life. She assured Tristan that there was no self-pity involved, only that she could no longer bear the phases of insanity and his absence.

When she stopped Tristan tried to gather time for a few moments with his brain whirling in panic. He rushed his words and thoughts, feeling his heart dull and sinking further from reality. He said that she mustn't take her life because life was so awkward and complex that one day they might be together again. He would at least return in a year and they would see each other again when their spirits and minds had cleared and they could talk calmly.

So he left, and she had hope again, and held his lie that saved her life close. She had more hope than when he had left so many years before because she thought she knew how desperately he wanted to be with her again. Her health took an abrupt upturn and when they got back to Washington Alfred and the psychiatrist were delighted by her behavior over the next ten months and had hopes as ebullient and false as her own.

In San Francisco Tristan, the Cree and Norwegian quickly made contact with the Mexican, boarded the schooner and left under cover of darkness. On the advice of the distiller's representative, the Mexican had given the impression on the dock that the schooner was headed for Hawaii for delivery in Maui. They made their way in cold stormy weather north up the coast and reached the inlet near Church Point on Vancouver Island in a week of brisk sailing. They loaded in the dark and headed back toward the rendezvous point in Bolinas Bay just north of San Francisco.

Their luck held at Bolinas and the unloading and full payment were uneventful. Tristan and the Mexican were driven down to San Francisco by a man who was helping to arrange the next shipment to be paid for by a group of restaurant owners. After a meeting in an apartment above a speakeasy on North Beach the man drove them back toward Golden Gate, stopping against orders at a wharf restaurant for a quick meal. The Mexican was nervous thinking he recognized a dusty Model A from earlier in the afternoon. When they got out of the parking lot four men quickly surrounded them and beat Tristan and the Mexican senseless with blackjacks and dumped them back in their car, cutting the throat of the other man. Before the beating the most elegant of the attackers said they best keep away from the liquor business on the coast. Tristan remembered his gray suit and smiling eyes, his Irish brogue, when he awoke in the car after midnight. Tristan revived the Mexican and they dragged the man with the cut throat out of the car, drove back to the speakeasy and asked if the deal was still on. It was.

* * *

When they returned to California from Canada, this time to Tomales Bay near Point Reyes, they were ready when at dawn a launch approached their anchorage. Those in the launch did not know that Tristan had already unloaded a few miles further up the coast. As the launch drew near the schooner Tristan and the Mexican lay under wet canvas watching, with the Norwegian and Cree down below ready for a second wave of assault if necessary. The launch raked the main house with a short burst of machine gun fire before Tristan and the Mexican opened up unerringly with the elephant gun and a .375. He recognized two of the men that had beat him and they went first with the five-hundred-grain shells designed for the largest walking mammal on earth blowing them in shattered pieces out of the boat. The Mexican worked on the waterline of the launch, then potted the heads of the remaining two men as they dog-paddled in the incoming tide.

They sailed south for Ensenada then, with Tristan recognizing that though he had won the battle he could not win the war. He spent a winter of utter dissolution and the Mexican returned to Vera Cruz, his wallet full but knowing the game was over. After a month Tristan had sent the Cree and Norwegian home to the ranch with a long letter to his children and the message to Ludlow and Decker that he would return home after visiting Alfred and Susannah during the racing season at Saratoga. He hired an old Mexican fisherman and his wife to take care of the boat and cook for him. He drank and thought of Susannah and what he might possibly tell her in June when there was nothing to tell her. He began to miss his children and allowed the fisherman and his wife to move their three grandchildren on board when their mother abandoned them. He spent his days drinking and fishing with hand lines with the old man in a small scow powered by sail. Early in May he came not so much to his senses but to the realization of how much he missed his children so he left the schooner in the care of the old couple and traveled north. He had not an inkling of how he might urge Susannah to longer life, but he would go home before traveling east to Saratoga.

Tristan had not more than a few hours of ease in the Montana June when he reached the ranch. Everyone seemed fine after a hard winter though it was obvious that Ludlow was failing somewhat and Isabel had come by mid-May with that thought in mind. Then at dinner Decker mentioned that two old friends of Tristan's, Irishmen from California, had stopped by the day before but unfortunately he had told the friends that Tristan was already headed for Saratoga. Tristan felt a deathly cold flow up his spine, also anger knowing that all those he loved had been in grave danger.

By dawn the next morning Decker and One Stab had driven him to the train station in Great Falls. Decker was fearful and wanted to come along but Tristan said no that he must watch the ranch. Before they left late in the evening the Cree and Norwegian had been stationed on the porch and told to shoot strangers on sight. Tristan got on the train in an old suit of Samuel's (he owned none) and a satchel full of money and underwear, a Beasley pistol owned by his grandfather and One Stab's skinning knife.

When Tristan reached New York he hastily bought clothes and a car and drove north at top speed to Saratoga Springs. The racing season was in full tilt despite the Depression and he couldn't find accommodations, so he settled on a tourist cabin near Glens Falls. He shaved his mustache and the next morning he bought some clothes from a groom and changed them under the stands with the roar of the crowd above him. Between the races he carried a pail of water and a currycomb and watched the stately parade of horses on the mowed grass behind the grandstand on show for the next race. He studied the crowd closely and picked out Alfred and his father-in-law, Susannah under parasol, standing with a group of fashionable horse owners, including a sprinkling of Whitneys, Vanderbilts, Guests and Wideners: then he spotted what had to be one of the Irishmen standing near an ornate flower bed, nattily dressed but still somehow obvious. Tristan walked to the paddock near the barn, passing a large florid man talking to a jockey. When he passed he recognized the voice of the third man who had beat him on North Beach. Tristan did not turn but walked into the stables where he was told to keep busy cleaning stalls. Then the man came into the barn and looked around diffidently. He walked into an empty stall to piss. Tristan followed and slammed his head to the wall catching his head with two tines of a heavy manure fork. Tristan buried him under straw and manure in the corner of the stable and went back to the grandstand toilets and changed his clothes. He located the second Irishman and followed him to a tourist home after the man had looked around for his companion until the racing grounds were nearly deserted. Tristan followed the man until late in the evening for want of an opportunity until the man walked home from dinner and drinks on a shady sidestreet near the tourist home. Tristan broke his neck, emptied a garbage barrel and stuffed the man into it, gently replacing the lid.

The next morning after a sound sleep helped along with whiskey, he drove back to Saratoga wearing an expensive suit bought in New York. He hoped to separate Susannah for a little while and somehow assure her of his love enough to keep her alive. His chance came after lunch when she stood alone staring at a bay stallion favored in the first race. He stood beside her until she noticed him but she showed no surprise, saying only that she knew he would come.

They quickly walked away from the racing grounds to a house a few blocks away her father kept for the racing season. Tristan was hesitant but she said that it would be at least an hour or more before she was missed. Unfortunately, Alfred had assigned one of his Senate aides to keep a continuous eye on Susannah because of her mental problems. After the aide watched Susannah enter the house with a strange man he rushed back to the track to notify Alfred.

Susannah led Tristan to the master bedroom to avoid any intrusion by the maids. At first she was cool and demanding, asking that Tristan meet her in Paris by the middle of October. He refused, saying that the time was not yet appropriate. She became hysterical and he offered the following spring as a compromise beyond which she could not go. Then there was a long unbearably painful silence at the end of which he recognized again the signs of her impending madness. He forestalled it by drawing her to him and assuring her that by the following May he would be ready. She shuddered in his arms and as he gazed over her shoulder Alfred walked into the room. Susannah felt Tristan's hands tighten on her back and heard the door close. She guessed what had happened and her heart lightened thinking that at last it was all over and she could go with Tristan.

They were still as marble figures in a garden hearing their own breathing and the distant noises of the race grounds. Alfred said only to Tristan, "I want to kill you," and Tristan released himself from Susannah and handed Alfred his pistol. Alfred stared at the pistol then pressed the muzzle to Tristan's temple. They looked at each other and Susannah came to them as if sleepwalking. Alfred turned the pistol to his own head and Tristan knocked it from his hand. Alfred slumped to the floor weeping and Susannah stooped beside him and with cool and detached words said that it was a terrible misunderstanding, that she would stay with him always. Alfred stood then and he and Tristan exchanged a strange look that went beyond any comprehension they might have been able to voice, but Alfred's look held not a little hate. Susannah followed Tristan into the hall, kissed him and laughed saying perhaps they would meet one day in hell, or perhaps heaven, wherever people go if they go anywhere.

On the trip home Tristan stayed dulled by his thought and liquor, laughing once in Chicago when he changed trains and saw on the newsstand that the Volstead Act had been repealed, Prohibition ended. Back home he worked hard with the horses, amused his children and hunted with One Stab who owned the false and waning agility of the aged who refuse to accept age.

Near the end of September Tristan received a telegram from Asheville, North Carolina, from Alfred saying, "You have won her. I am sending her home . . ." He rode to Choteau and checked the return address by phone, and found out disturbingly that it was the address of a private asylum. He borrowed a Ford truck and drove over to Great Falls to meet the train, a little puzzled but somehow imagining that he would spend the rest of his troubled life caring for Susannah though he envisioned that she might finally get well at the ranch. He met the train feeling cold in his stomach but disregarding it. A politician friend of Alfred's approached Tristan, led him to the baggage car, handed him a list of burial instructions as the porter unloaded the highly polished rosewood coffin.

There's little more to tell. Susannah was buried next to Samuel and Two and the reader, if he or she were a naive believer, might threaten God saying leave him alone or some such frivolity. No one has figured out how accidental is the marriage of the blasphemy and fate. Only a rather old-fashioned theologian might speculate on Tristan damning God so many years before in France when he and Noel encased Samuel's heart in the paraffin. The contemporary mind views such events properly as utterly wayward,

owning all the design of water in the deepest and furthest
reaches of the Pacific.

One warm Sunday morning in mid-October a few weeks
after the burial Samuel and Three were playing on the
porch swing with their ponies saddled and tethered to the
railing. Isabel had brought breakfast upstairs to Ludlow
who wasn't feeling well. She was reading to him from
Melville's *Pierre, or the Ambiguities*. Ludlow loved Melville while Isabel found the author tiresome.

In the kitchen Pet packed lunches for Tristan and the
children's outing. She listened carefully to the talk of
Decker and Tristan. They were trying to speculate themselves out of an impossible quandary: the fact that the Irish
could very well return out of simple vengeance. Tristan
stretched and walked over to Pet and asked her opinion.
She said that they all cared most about the children and
that the only important thing to her was that they were
safe. Three came in and tugged at her father's arm. Tristan
kissed her and said ten more minutes and she ran through
the parlor yelling ten minutes to Samuel.

Decker suggested Cuba where Tristan had a small *finca*
he had bought years before and now managed by his two
Cuban crew members who had shipped up two good mares
the previous spring for breeding. Tristan worried aloud
about the children's schooling and Decker said their father's life was more important than schooling. Pet went
rigid, first hearing the car, but Samuel called out that the
police were here and she relaxed. Decker followed Tristan
out onto the porch and paused with his grandchildren as

JIM HARRISON

Tristan approached the two troopers standing by the Ford coupe.

Tristan was easeful and almost bored as he nodded to the troopers but then his heart jumped against his ribs when he saw that one was actually the elegant Irishman from San Francisco, and the other a thug looking ungainly in a uniform. They studied each other for a moment.

"I've lost my two brothers. We best settle this," the man said.

Tristan glanced back at the porch where Decker stood next to Samuel and Three and One Stab. He knew he had come to the end and his heart ached for his children standing in the sunlight on the porch.

"Would you mind if I went with you, I don't want the children to see," Tristan said.

The Irishman nodded yes then was startled at Ludlow tottering across the dry brown grass barefoot in a nightshirt with the big buffalo robe wrapped around him. Tristan said politely that this was his father but Ludlow shook his white head holding his slate upon which he had written "What is the meaning of this?"

The Irishman began a quiet speech with an apology saying that he was sorry but Tristan must pay his debt to society by a long term in prison. Ludlow shook, his body jerking as if he were a hawk hooding its prey. He lifted the Purdey twelve-gauge shotgun along his leg up through the parting in the robe and blew the two Irishmen into eternity.

EPILOGUE

That October morning was the end of Tristan's story for our purposes. In the stunned aftermath Ludlow collapsed but revived by dinner. Tristan embraced his children to whom Pet later explained that the evil men had come to murder their father. Isabel was quietly hysterical. Decker, the Cree and Norwegian buried the bodies and that night the Cree dumped the car in a deep pool in the upper Missouri. But it was One Stab who went mad before the full echo of the shots had faded. He danced and sang around the bodies, his body arched and prancing and his voice crooning, then he stooped and held the fainting Ludlow in his arms. Tristan knew if it were not Ludlow's kill, One Stab in the excitement might have taken scalps.

Tristan took the children then to Cuba on the schooner and left only twenty-three years later during the beginning of the revolution for a ranch owned by Three and her husband up near McLeod in Alberta. If you are up near Choteau and drive down Ramshorn Road by the ranch, now owned by Alfred's son by his second marriage, you won't get permission to enter. It's a modern efficient operation, but back there in the canyon there are graves that mean something to a few people left on earth: Samuel, Two, Susannah and a little apart Ludlow buried between his true friends, One Stab and Isabel; and a small distance away Decker and Pet. Always alone, apart, somehow solitary, Tristan is buried up in Alberta.